Midnight Crystal
Canyons of Night

OBSIDIAN PREY

Titles by Jayne Ann Krentz writing as Jayne Castle

OBSIDIAN PREY
DARK LIGHT
SILVER MASTER
GHOST HUNTER
AFTER GLOW
HARMONY
AFTER DARK
AMARYLLIS
ZINNIA
ORCHID

Titles by Jayne Ann Krentz writing as Amanda Quick

THE PERFECT POISON
THE THIRD CIRCLE
THE RIVER KNOWS
SECOND SIGHT
LIE BY MOONLIGHT
THE PAID COMPANION
WAIT UNTIL MIDNIGHT
LATE FOR THE WEDDING
DON'T LOOK BACK
SLIGHTLY SHADY
WICKED WIDOW
I THEE WED
WITH THIS RING
AFFAIR
MISCHIEF
MYSTIQUE
MISTRESS
DECEPTION
DESIRE
DANGEROUS
RECKLESS
RAVISHED
RENDEZVOUS
SCANDAL
SURRENDER
SEDUCTION

Other titles by Jayne Ann Krentz

RUNNING HOT
SIZZLE AND BURN
WHITE LIES
ALL NIGHT LONG
FALLING AWAKE
TRUTH OR DARE
LIGHT IN SHADOW
SUMMER IN ECLIPSE BAY
TOGETHER IN ECLIPSE BAY
SMOKE IN MIRRORS
LOST & FOUND
DAWN IN ECLIPSE BAY
SOFT FOCUS
ECLIPSE BAY
EYE OF THE BEHOLDER
FLASH
SHARP EDGES
DEEP WATERS
ABSOLUTELY, POSITIVELY
TRUST ME
GRAND PASSION
HIDDEN TALENTS
WILDEST HEARTS
FAMILY MAN
PERFECT PARTNERS
SWEET FORTUNE
SILVER LININGS
THE GOLDEN CHANCE

Anthologies

CHARMED
(with Julie Beard, Lori Foster, and Eileen Wilks)

Titles written by Jayne Ann Krentz and Jayne Castle

NO GOING BACK

OBSIDIAN PREY

JAYNE CASTLE

JOVE BOOKS, NEW YORK

THE BERKLEY PUBLISHING GROUP
Published by the Penguin Group
Penguin Group (USA) Inc.
375 Hudson Street, New York, New York 10014, USA
Penguin Group (Canada), 90 Eglinton Avenue East, Suite 700, Toronto, Ontario M4P 2Y3, Canada
(a division of Pearson Penguin Canada Inc.)
Penguin Books Ltd., 80 Strand, London WC2R 0RL, England
Penguin Group Ireland, 25 St. Stephen's Green, Dublin 2, Ireland (a division of Penguin Books Ltd.)
Penguin Group (Australia), 250 Camberwell Road, Camberwell, Victoria 3124, Australia
(a division of Pearson Australia Group Pty. Ltd.)
Penguin Books India Pvt. Ltd., 11 Community Centre, Panchsheel Park, New Delhi—110 017, India
Penguin Group (NZ), 67 Apollo Drive, Rosedale, North Shore 0632, New Zealand
(a division of Pearson New Zealand Ltd.)
Penguin Books (South Africa) (Pty.) Ltd., 24 Sturdee Avenue, Rosebank, Johannesburg 2196,
South Africa

Penguin Books Ltd., Registered Offices: 80 Strand, London WC2R 0RL, England

OBSIDIAN PREY

A Jove Book / published by arrangement with the author

Cover art by Phil Heffernan.
Cover handlettering by Ron Zinn.
Cover design by George Long.

ISBN: 978-1-61523-339-7

JOVE®
Jove Books are published by The Berkley Publishing Group,
a division of Penguin Group (USA) Inc.,
375 Hudson Street, New York, New York 10014.
JOVE® is a registered trademark of Penguin Group (USA) Inc.
The "J" design is a trademark of Penguin Group (USA) Inc.

PRINTED IN THE UNITED STATES OF AMERICA

Acknowledgments

I want to thank Nancy Halifax, proprietor of the Halifax Gallery (17 Quartz Lane, Old Quarter, Frequency City), for her professional insight and advice. Her bold efforts to expand the accepted critical boundaries of modern art have redefined the meaning and definition of the artistic vision.

And to Chimera, the daring artist who started it all.

Boy, howdy, I couldn't have written this book without you two. Any mistakes are, of course, entirely attributable to Miss Halifax and Chimera.

A Note from Jayne

Welcome to my other world, Harmony.

Late in the twenty-first century, a vast energy Curtain opened in the vicinity of Earth, making interstellar travel practical for the first time. In typical human fashion, thousands of eager colonists packed up their stuff and lost no time heading out to create new homes and new societies on the unexplored worlds. Harmony was one of those worlds.

The colonists brought with them all the comforts of home: sophisticated technology, centuries of art and literature, and the latest fashions. Trade through the Curtain flourished and made it possible to stay in touch with families back on Earth. It also allowed the colonists to keep their computers and high-tech gadgets working. Things went swell for a while.

And then one day, without warning, the Curtain closed, disappearing as mysteriously as it had opened. Cut off from Earth, no longer able to obtain the equipment and supplies needed to keep their high-tech lifestyle going, the colonists were abruptly thrown back to a far more primitive existence. Forget the latest Earth fashions; just staying alive suddenly became a major problem.

But on Harmony, folks did one of the things humans do best: they survived. It wasn't easy, but two hundred years after the closing of the Curtain, the descendants of the First Generation colonists have managed to fight their way back from the brink to a level of civilization roughly equivalent to that of the early twenty-first century on Earth.

Here on Harmony, however, things are a little different, especially after dark. There are the creepy ruins of a long-vanished alien civilization, a mysterious underground rain forest, and a most unusual kind of animal companion. What's more, an increasingly wide variety of psychic powers are showing up in the population. Seems that something in the environment on Harmony is bringing out the latent psychic talents in people.

Of course, there are some folks who don't need any help from the environment. They already possess paranormal abilities. Turns out that several members of the Arcane Society were among the First Generation colonists . . .

If, like me, you sometimes relish your romantic suspense with a paranormal twist, Harmony is the place for you.

Love,
Jayne

Chapter 1

SOME MEN WALKED STRAIGHT OUT OF A WOMAN'S dreams. Some qualified as full-on nightmares. As far as Lyra Dore was concerned, Cruz Sweetwater had a booted foot planted solidly in both realms. When the jolt of awareness shot through her, she almost dropped her glass.

"I can't believe it," she said, sputtering a little on a sip of champagne. "The bastard is here."

But the truth was, she was not all that shocked or surprised. Deep down, she had known that sooner or later he would come back into her life. There had been a relentless, disturbing sense of inevitability about the whole thing. Like watching a slow-motion train wreck, she thought.

A part of her had even dared to hope that when he did come back, it would be on his knees. But with her luck—the infamously unreliable Dore luck—that was highly unlikely to happen.

That was the way with dreams. The good ones had the decency to vanish forever with the dawn. Nightmares, on the other hand, had a nasty tendency to return to haunt you again and again.

"You're kidding." Nancy Halifax looked around the crowded gallery, her attractive face alight with excitement. She did not have to ask who "the bastard" was. "Are you sure?"

"Positive," Lyra muttered into her glass. Another whisper of intense awareness shivered across her senses. She knew Cruz was nearby in the same way she would have known if any other species of top-of-the-food-chain predator was in the vicinity.

"This is just a small gallery affair," Nancy said. "It isn't the sort of high-end auction or museum exhibition a Sweetwater would attend. There's only one reason why your guy would come here tonight. He knows you're here. He wants to talk to you."

"He's definitely not my guy, and if you think he's here to see me, I've got a lovely amber mine I can sell you," Lyra said. But deep inside, hope spiraled through her.

"I'll bet he wants to beg you to forgive him and take him back. I don't see him, though. Are you sure he's here?"

Nancy was a striking woman who stood close to six feet tall in her bare feet. Tonight she was wearing three-inch heels to accent her sleek-fitting black sheath. Her view of the room was no doubt excellent.

"Positive," Lyra said. "If you don't see him, it's because

he doesn't want you to see him. Not yet, at any rate. He's hunting."

"Oh, come on, Lyra. You make him sound like a specter-cat stalking its prey."

"Wrong analogy."

"I should hope so."

"Think professional hit man," Lyra said. "A really, really well-dressed hit man."

"Isn't that just a little over-the-top?"

"Hmmm. No, I don't think so."

Lyra did not bother to search the crowd. There was no point. She was several inches shorter than Nancy, and even in her stiletto heels she would not be able to see over the heads of those around her. Besides, there was no need to look for Cruz. She already knew he was here. She could feel his presence with every fiber of her being.

She tried to fix her attention on the green quartz artifact in a nearby glass display case. The Swan Gallery's collection of alien antiquities was certainly respectable, but Nancy was right, the Swan wasn't a top-tier establishment like the Fairstead Gallery, which catered to the wealthiest and most exclusive collectors.

If the Swan had been such a high-end gallery, Lyra thought, she and Nancy would never have received invitations to the auction that was scheduled to begin in an hour. Neither of them moved in the higher circles of the art world. Neither of them was in a position to bid on any of the relics that would go on the block tonight. They were here only because they were friends of Harriet

Swan, the proprietor. Harriet had been desperate to turn out a crowd.

"I still don't see him," Nancy said.

"That would be because he doesn't want anyone to notice him yet." Lyra downed another hasty swallow of champagne in a desperate effort to soothe her frazzled senses. "That's what all self-respecting predators do. They lie low, staying out of sight until they're ready to make their move. By the time you spot them, it's too late. Their teeth are clamped around your throat."

Nancy grinned. "Sounds interesting."

Lyra looked at her without saying a word.

"Sorry." Nancy had the grace to appear chagrined. "I know you have every reason to be well and truly pissed because of what Sweetwater did to you. But you've got to admit, those of us who didn't have a dust bunny in that fight have a right to be curious about him. I mean, he is a Sweetwater, after all."

"You didn't have a dust bunny in that fight?" Lyra repeated, outraged. "In case you didn't notice, that was your best friend who got mauled by Cruz Sweetwater and a bunch of overpaid Amber Inc. lawyers."

"Just a figure of speech," Nancy said quickly. "Don't worry, I'm one hundred percent behind you here. Best friends forever. You know that."

"Thank you," Lyra said stiffly. The electrifying tingle of energy that was stirring the fine hair at the nape of her neck was not fading. If anything, it was growing stronger. "Try to remember that friends are supposed to stick together in situations like this."

"Absolutely. I am definitely on your side. It's just that, well, Cruz Sweetwater is one of the men of Amber Inc. Everyone pays attention when a Sweetwater shows up. It's like having a Guild boss walk into the room. Actually, a lot of people would say that now that Cruz has taken over his family's private security business, he's got more power here in Frequency than the head of the local Guild."

"That wouldn't be hard," Lyra said dryly, "given the fact that the local Guild is between bosses at the moment."

"You know what I mean."

Lyra sighed. "I know. Sorry. I'm just feeling a little testy."

Harold Taylor, the chief of the Frequency Guild, had died recently, and the Council had yet to select a new boss. But that was, Lyra had to admit, a technicality. Nancy was right. As the new CEO of Amber Inc. Security, Cruz Sweetwater did wield more power than a Guild chief, at least aboveground. When it came to the underground world, the men of Amber Inc. had historically maintained very close working relationships with the Guilds. In Lyra's opinion, the association was not unlike an alliance between two criminal organizations that had agreed to respect each other's territories.

The ability to psychically resonate with amber had begun to appear in the colonists shortly after they had arrived from Earth. Initially it had been considered an odd adaptation to the environment with no practical importance. But when the energy Curtain that had made travel between the home planet and a host of new worlds possible had closed without warning, amber had become the one thing that stood between the colonists and total disaster.

When their high-tech machines inevitably began to fail, the struggling members of the First Generation—united in their determination not to be the last generation on Harmony—had turned to amber as a source of energy. It had served their descendants well in the two hundred years since the closing of the Curtain. Today it powered everything from washing machines to computers.

The immutable laws of economics being what they were, whoever controlled the mining of standard resonating amber—SRA—controlled a lot of things on Harmony. And for the past fifty years, the mysterious, reclusive Sweetwater family had managed to corner a huge chunk of the market. Amber Inc.'s only serious competitor was the RezStone corporation, which controlled an equally large market share. The rivalry between the two firms was legendary.

"You can't blame me for being a little curious about Cruz Sweetwater," Nancy said. "I never even got to meet him three months ago when you were dating him."

"Take it from me: curiosity is a dangerous thing when it comes to Mr. Sweetwater," Lyra said.

He was very close now. The sparkling sensation fluttering across all her senses was making it hard to breathe. The half-empty glass she held trembled ever so slightly in her fingers. She could literally feel Cruz closing in on her. The urge to run was almost overpowering. Unfortunately, what she wanted to do was run *to* him, not *from* him. It was crazy, she thought. If she had any common sense, she would slip out the back door. Whatever Cruz wanted from her, it was a sure bet that it would not be good for her.

But the memory of the purple orchids sitting in the black vase on her coffee table swamped common sense. The latest delivery of the spectacularly gorgeous, outrageously expensive flowers had arrived that afternoon. The card that had accompanied them was identical to all the others: "We were meant for each other." There was no signature. There was never a signature.

She had dared to dream these past few weeks, but she was forced to acknowledge that her lovely little fantasy involving the return of Cruz Sweetwater had a dark side. Part of her was terrified that the romantic scenario she had conjured was nothing more than a seductive new variant of the strange, waking nightmares that had been plaguing her recently. If that was the case, at least it was a far more enjoyable hallucination than the others she had experienced.

The unnerving episodes were getting worse. She had not confided in anyone, including Nancy, half afraid that even talking about the strange visions would somehow make the awful dreams more real.

"There he is," Nancy said in a breathy voice. "He just walked into the room. I recognize him from the pictures in the newspapers. Wow. I see what you mean."

"I told you, the clothes are good."

"The suit is terrific," Nancy said. "Nothing like black on black to bring out the best in the male of the species, I always say. But that wasn't what I was talking about. It's that cool, sophisticated hit man thing he has going. You're right. Wouldn't want to run into him in a dark alley." She managed a slinky, theatrical shudder. "Now a darkened bedroom, on the other hand—"

"Don't go there," Lyra warned.

"You're just saying that because you didn't get there, yourself. I ask you again, as I have so many times these past three months. What were you thinking, woman?"

"Gee, I don't know. Maybe about self-preservation? What was I supposed to do, after I discovered that he was about to screw me out of the amber discovery of the decade, if not the century? Let him screw me literally? I don't think so. Besides, I was reading that marriage manual at the time, and it strongly advised against going to bed with a man too soon."

She had bought *Ten Steps to a Covenant Marriage: Secrets of a Professional Matchmaker* immediately after meeting Cruz. She had been so sure he was the right man. She had not wanted to leave anything to chance. The Dore luck had a way of going sour when you needed it the most.

But in the end, she had never had the opportunity to fall victim to temptation. And it was not *Ten Steps to a Covenant Marriage* that had saved her. The truth that she would never admit to anyone, not even her best friend, was that it was Cruz who had drawn the invisible line in their short-lived relationship.

He had never even tried to lure her into bed. There had been plenty of torrid kisses and a lot of heavy breathing three months ago, but that was as far as matters had gone. How much worse would she have felt after the heavy boot of Amber Inc. had come crashing down on her if she had made the mistake of sleeping with Cruz?

Then again, how much worse *could* she have felt?

"Here's a tip, friend," Nancy said. "Next time you meet a really interesting man, you might want to wait until after you've had a little fun in bed before you file a lawsuit against him and his company. Guys tend to get annoyed when they get sued."

"For all the good it did me." Amber Inc. had swatted her pathetic lawsuit and her even more pathetic lawyer without breaking a sweat.

"How did you do that, anyway?" Nancy asked, her attention still riveted on the scene behind Lyra.

"File a suit?" Lyra shrugged. "It's not that hard. It just takes money. A lot of it. More than I had, as it turns out."

"I wasn't talking about the lawsuit," Nancy said impatiently. "I meant, how did you guess that Cruz Sweetwater was about to walk into this reception a few minutes ago? You knew he was here before he even entered the room. What's up with that?"

"Probably some sort of primitive survival instinct. Too bad it wasn't working three months ago."

But the reality was that her para-senses had been instantly and indelibly tuned to Cruz Sweetwater the first moment they had met. She had never actually concocted a mental image of her personal dream man, but she had recognized Cruz the moment she met him. *This is the one you've been waiting for.*

That bone-deep certainty had intensified with each hour they had spent together and with each scorching kiss. Three months and a futile lawsuit later, the psychic bond had not weakened one bit. She was pretty sure that three years, three decades, or the rest of her life could pass, and still a frisson of knowing recognition would alert her if Cruz suddenly showed up anywhere in her vicinity. *You were supposed to be mine.*

"Don't look now, but I think he's spotted you," Nancy said. "He's coming this way."

A cascade of tangled emotions slammed through Lyra. Anger, frustrated desire, the yearning for revenge, and a fragile sense of hope all snarled together in a chaotic mix.

"Looks like he's expecting you to make a run for the ladies' room," Nancy said. "He's circling around through the crowd, cutting off that route."

That did it. Adrenaline, hot and bracing, surged through Lyra. If there was one thing that was sure to make her stand her ground tonight, it was the knowledge that Cruz thought she might try to bolt. She was a Dore, damn it. The last of her line. She had a family tradition to uphold. Dores did not run from anything. Most definitely they did not run from a Sweetwater.

She did not need Nancy's wide-eyed expression to tell her that Cruz had invaded her personal space. She could feel him directly behind her.

"Hello, Lyra," he said.

His voice was low, dark, infused with power, utterly masculine.

She turned coolly to face him, amazed that she was able to maintain a degree of self-control now that the confrontation was upon her. She even managed an icy bright smile.

Nothing had changed, especially not his hunter's eyes. She had seen those eyes night after night in her dreams. Like the black stone in the heavy ring he wore, they were obsidian dark with green fires burning in the depths.

His hair was just as black as she remembered it, still cut close and short. The roughly sculpted planes and angles of his hard face were just as thrillingly feral. An intimate excitement swept through her.

Down, girl.

"Good evening, Mr. Sweetwater," she said, giving him smooth surprise for all she was worth. "I wasn't aware that you were interested in picking up antiquities at gallery auctions. I was under the impression that you preferred to acquire whatever you wanted with more direct methods."

"Such as?" Cruz raised one black brow, politely quizzical.

"Oh, say, by crushing the competition," Lyra said sweetly.

Nancy gasped and choked on her champagne. "For heaven's sake, Lyra."

Cruz looked at her. "I don't believe we've met. I'm Cruz Sweetwater."

"Yes, of course, Mr. Sweetwater," Nancy said. She

coughed a couple of times but recovered quickly. "I'm Nancy Halifax. Halifax Gallery in the Old Quarter? I'm sure you've never heard of it. I specialize in modern art."

"A pleasure to meet you, Nancy. Lyra mentioned you several times."

"Back when you two were seeing each other, you mean?" Nancy asked.

Cruz looked at Lyra. "Yes."

"Back when I believed that Mr. Sweetwater was a legitimate client who wished to engage my professional services," Lyra said evenly. "Back when he was using a phony name."

Nancy looked vaguely horrified.

True to form, Cruz did not take the bait. That was the thing about Cruz Sweetwater, Lyra thought. He never lost his cool. He was probably just as controlled in bed. Not that she was likely to find out.

Cruz was all about control. She was no para-shrink, but she had a strong suspicion that powerful self-mastery was a direct result of the psychic side of his nature. He had never confided the truth about his psi senses to her—one of the many secrets he had kept three months ago—but she would had to have been incredibly dim not to have realized that he possessed a lot of raw power.

Anyone endowed with a high degree of talent required an equally high degree of control. Those who wound up with the former but not the latter generally spent most of their lives in nice, quiet parapsych wards knitting scarves and taking little pills.

"I was out of town at the time," Nancy said, trying to paper over the awkward moment. "I always close the gallery for a couple of weeks in early summer. Mandatory family gathering at the lake house." She made a face. "You know how it is with family."

"Yes," Cruz said. He looked amused. "I do know how it is with family."

The two of them exchanged a smile of mutual understanding. If there was one thing most people could bond over, it was the subject of family. After the Curtain had closed, stranding the colonists, the First Generation settlers had understood that their very survival depended on the strength of the family unit, the basic building block of any society. They had set out to shore up family ties with every legal, social, and moral tool at their command.

The Founders had achieved their goal. Family was all on Harmony—except when you did not have one of your own.

Lyra took another sip of champagne and made no comment, her customary response whenever the subject of family ties arose. Her grandfather, who had raised her after her parents had been killed in a mining accident, had died four years earlier, leaving her alone in the world.

"And then I decided to tack on a buying trip to Resonance and Cadence," Nancy continued, evidently feeling pressured to carry the conversation. "That took another week. By the time I got back . . . uh . . ." She broke off, reddening, and she darted an uneasy glance at Lyra.

"By the time you got back it was all over," Lyra said,

amazed by her own calm. She flashed another polite smile for Cruz and swept out a hand to indicate the artifacts on display. "Which of these lovely things brings you here tonight, Mr. Sweetwater?"

"You," he said.

She felt as though the floor of the gallery had fallen away beneath her feet. He really *had* come back to apologize and make amends. The weeks of amethyst orchids had been an effort to pave the way, just as she had hoped.

But she had to be strong, she told herself sternly. There was a lot of groveling left to be done. If she let him back into her life too quickly, it would set a very bad precedent. She had the edge in this relationship now. She had to maintain it. Cruz Sweetwater had a bad habit of getting whatever he wanted. That had to stop. Boundaries had to be established.

"I'm confused," she said with just the right amount of bewilderment. "Did you want to hire me to tune some amber or consult on an amethyst artifact?"

"No," he said. "I'd like to talk to you."

"Certainly." She assumed an expectant look.

"In private," Cruz added.

"Oh, look," Nancy said before Lyra could respond. "There's Mr. Fitzburn." She smiled at Cruz. "You'll have to excuse me. I need to have a chat with him. Fitzburn is a potential client. He missed out on the first three Chimera paintings that I had in my gallery, and he's afraid I won't give him a chance at the next one."

"I understand," Cruz said.

"Are you interested in modern art, Mr. Sweetwater?" Nancy asked.

"It's not really my thing," Cruz said. "I take it this Chimera is popular?"

"He's a hot new talent. Just on the brink of being discovered by the art world, according to the critic at the *Frequency Herald*. But he's very reclusive. Won't do interviews or promotion of any kind. He'll only display in my gallery."

"I see."

"You're welcome to visit my gallery," Nancy said. She whipped a card out of her little black bag. "It would be an honor."

"Thank you," Cruz said. He took the card and dropped it into the pocket of his black jacket.

Lyra frowned at Nancy. "I think Mr. Fitzburn is waiting for you."

"Right," Nancy said. "Bye."

She hurried off, pausing briefly behind Cruz to wink at Lyra over his shoulder and make encouraging motions with her hands. Lyra pretended not to notice.

"What was it you wanted to speak to me about, Cruz?" she said.

"I'd rather not talk here. Your apartment is nearby. Would you mind if we went there to have this conversation?"

Alarm zapped through her. Her first thought was that going back to her place alone with him was probably not a good idea. Not yet, at any rate. Following hard on the heels of that bit of common sense was the memory of the breakfast dishes she had left sitting in the kitchen sink. And then there was the silky, chocolate brown bra she had washed by hand before leaving the house that morning. The bra was spread out on a towel on the window bench.

Her apartment was a small, open, loft design. Both the kitchen and the window bench were clearly visible from the entrance and sitting area. There was no way she could keep Cruz from seeing either the dishes or the bra.

This was so typical of the Dore luck, she thought. The man of her dreams walked back into her life, showing every indication that he wanted to make amends for his betrayal, and she had to worry about dirty dishes and a little hand washing.

She cleared her throat. "Well, the thing is—"

"If the idea of being alone with me makes you nervous," Cruz said, "we could probably find a quiet restaurant somewhere nearby."

"No." The word was out before she could stop herself. She drew a deep breath. She could do this. Cruz had his pride, too. She could allow him a little privacy for his groveling, and if one thing led to another, as seemed increasingly possible, there would be a lot of kissing and making up to be done. That required privacy, too. "No, that's okay. We can go back to my place."

"Thanks." He took her arm and started toward the door. "Sorry to catch you by surprise. I thought about calling, but I figured it would be better to talk about this in person. Some things can't be said over the phone."

"Especially in view of the fact that all of our recent

communications have been conducted through lawyers," she said.

His mouth edged up slightly at the corner. "That does tend to limit the conversation."

"Actually, it turned out to be a pretty one-sided conversation."

"That was because you had a pretty bad lawyer."

Heads turned as Cruz steered her through the room toward the glass doors. Like most members of the notoriously reclusive Sweetwater clan, he tried to keep a very low profile. Until recently, he had spent his career working as an agent in the various field offices of AI Security. It was that anonymity that had allowed him to deceive her three months ago. But his recent appointment to the CEO slot had brought with it a lot of media attention. Her lawsuit had only added fuel to the fire. These days, in a gathering like this one, he was bound to be recognized.

An eerie silence descended on the crowd. It was followed almost immediately by a buzz of conversation that sounded a little too forced. The unmistakable rhythms of hot gossip, Lyra thought. Tomorrow there would be talk on the streets of the Quarter where the galleries and antiquities shops were located and possibly a mention in the art section of the *Frequency Herald.* Harriet Swan was no doubt giddy. Nothing could have elevated the status of her modest gallery more than having word go out that Cruz Sweetwater had been present tonight.

Three months ago this kind of attention had not been an issue. In his guise as a secretive underground collector, Cruz had favored secluded, dimly lit restaurants and romantic meals in her loft. But tonight things were different. Tension twisted her insides. She did not like this feeling. It was like being onstage.

"Ignore it," Cruz said.

As if he read my mind. She did not like that notion any better. The experts were certain that telepathy was impossible, but they had never met Cruz Sweetwater. He might not be able to actually read minds, but there was no one better when it came to predicting an opponent's next move. He was always one step ahead. She must not forget that.

Nancy caught her eye from across the gallery and waggled her fingers in a subtle high-rez sign: closed hand, thumb and pinky extended in the air.

Lyra took a deep breath. One thing, at least, was clear. This was not another one of the horrible waking nightmares. Cruz was no illusion. She could feel the power in him, sense the energy resonating between them. Whatever happened this evening, at least it would be real.

She went with him out into the glowing night.

Chapter 2

NIGHT WAS NEVER TRULY DARK IN THE OLD QUARTER of Frequency City. The gentle emerald light that illuminated the streets and rooftops emanated from the massive green quartz walls that surrounded the ruins of the Dead City.

The four major city-state capitals, Frequency, Resonance, Cadence, and Crystal, had been founded in the shadows of the largest of the walled cities that had been abandoned by the long-vanished aliens. But the free street lighting wasn't the only reason that the First Generation colonists had built their initial settlements directly adjacent to the aboveground ruins. In those early years there had been no way to know what dangers lurked in the vast wilderness of the new home world. The four Dead Cities—their towering quartz barricades impervious to even the most sophisticated machines and weapons of Earth—had offered the promise of protection.

As it happened, there had never been any need for the colonists or their descendants to seek refuge in the ruins. Harmony had a wide assortment of wild animals, but it had soon become apparent that there were no local inhabitants to object to the newcomers from Earth.

In the two hundred years that had passed since the Curtain had closed, stranding the colonists, Frequency, like the other major cities, had grown far beyond its humble beginnings. Its gleaming office towers were clustered downtown, not in the Quarter. Neighborhoods and suburbs sprawled far and wide. The most expensive properties were now found on the hillsides and along the river, far from the colonial heart of the city.

But it wasn't just the cheaper rents in the Quarter that had attracted Lyra, although that was certainly a huge factor. It was the subtle effect of the paranormal energy that leaked from the ruins and the strange catacombs underground that made the neighborhood attractive to her. Walking through the glowing streets at night was always something of a rush. Walking through them with Cruz at her side was even better.

"My car is over there," Cruz said.

She looked at the sleek black Slider parked at the curb. It was the same vehicle he had been driving three months ago.

"I see you didn't change your car when you changed your name," she said.

"I didn't use a fake name. Marlowe is my middle

name." He opened the passenger door of the Slider. "Came from my mother's side of the family. Are you going to snap at me all evening, or can we have a reasonable discussion?"

"That probably depends on your definition of reasonable."

"What I have to say is important, Lyra."

She hesitated, her grandfather's words echoing down through the years with a warning she had heard since childhood: "Never trust a Sweetwater."

But the ridiculously hopeful side of her nature was in control.

"Okay," she said. She slipped into the embrace of the leather seat and looked up at him. "I'll play nice. At least until I know what this is all about."

"Thanks. I appreciate it. This conversation is going to be hard enough as it is."

That did it. She suddenly felt sorry for him. An apology of this magnitude would not be easy for anyone, let alone a man like Cruz. He was always so sure of himself, so certain that he was doing the right thing, so determined to carry out what he felt was his responsibility. As far as he was concerned, he had been doing his job three months ago. She had to remember that the situation between them had placed him, along with his rigid code of honor, in an untenable position.

Great. She was not just feeling sorry for him, she was actually making excuses. She had to get a grip.

Cruz closed the door before she could ask him any more questions. A few seconds later, he got in beside her and rezzed the engine. Flash-rock melted, and the Slider eased away from the curb. Cruz turned at the corner, driving deeper into the Quarter. Navigating the maze of twisting streets in the Colonial neighborhoods was not for the faint of heart or those who depended on maps. But Cruz piloted the Slider with unerring precision. She did not have to prompt him even a single time. She was not surprised. Cruz always knew exactly where he was going.

He did not speak until he parked the Slider in front of her apartment building. For a moment he sat quietly, his hands resting on the steering wheel. The black stone in his heavy gold ring glinted a little in the green-tinged shadows.

"Did you get the new sofa?" he asked.

Startled, she looked at him. "What?"

"Three months ago you were planning to buy a new sofa. I've been wondering if you got it."

"Right, the sofa. No. I didn't get it."

"Why not?"

"Turns out suing Amber Inc. is sort of an expensive hobby. I've had to economize lately."

"You had a really bad lawyer," Cruz said grimly.

"You've already mentioned that." She unbuckled her seat belt. "Turns out really good lawyers are even more expensive than sofas. I thought we weren't going to snipe at each other."

"Sorry. Just wondered about the sofa."

It struck her that his curiosity about the sofa was another positive indicator. Evidently he had been thinking about her a lot, and in a personal way, if he had been musing about homey things such as her plans to purchase new furniture.

He got out from behind the wheel. She opened her own door before he could get around the front of the Slider to do it for her. At the lobby entrance of the apartment building, she took the key out of her small green clutch and rezzed the lock.

They got into the rickety elevator and stood, a little distance between them, until the door opened on the fourth floor. Without a word they went down the hall. She opened her door, stepped into the apartment, and turned on the light switch.

A large ball of dryer lint with bright blue eyes tumbled toward her, chortling a cheerful welcome. Its six paws skittered on the hardwood floors. A small, jaunty red beret was clipped to the tatty fur in the vicinity of the top of its head.

Lyra scooped up the dust bunny and plopped him on her shoulder.

"I'm home, Vincent," she said.

The greeting ritual satisfied, Vincent burbled happily and hopped onto Cruz's much broader shoulder.

"At least the bunny is glad to see me," Cruz said. "Hey, there, pal. How's it rezzing?"

Vincent chortled again.

Dust bunnies were not overly concerned with petty things like the legal ownership of spectacular amber discoveries in the jungle, Lyra thought. Nor did they fret about having fallen in love with the wrong man. But she rose above the impulse to make that observation out loud. She had to stay focused. The window bench was at the far end of the room, still in shadow, but she could make out the curves of the bra cups

"While you two reminisce, I'll get out of these heels," she said.

She hurried toward the window bench.

The plan was simple. She would keep her body between Cruz and the bra.

She reached her goal, grabbed the end of the towel, and rolled the bra inside with a few quick twists. Still moving fast, she darted behind the sliding screens that concealed the bedroom area and dropped the towel and its contents onto the dresser.

In the outer room, Cruz rezzed another light switch. The resulting glow permeated the bedroom through the translucent screens.

"I see Vincent is still painting," Cruz said from the other side of the screen.

Oh, damn, the painting. She had been so focused on the bra that she had forgotten about the artwork. Well, there was nothing for it but to brave it out. The odds were seriously against Cruz ever discovering the truth.

She went back out into the main room, deftly sliding the screen closed behind her to conceal the bed. There was something about having a bed clearly visible when you were alone with a man who could heat your blood and excite all your senses with just a look; something dangerous.

Cruz was standing over Vincent's latest work of art.

The canvas lay flat on the floor atop a protective layer of newspapers. The one attempt at setting up an easel had ended in disaster when Vincent had tried to climb it to get to the top of the painting. He'd had a blue rez-brush in one paw at the time. The easel had toppled over. Vincent had landed with his usual adroitness, but the rez-brush had shattered when it hit the floor. The little tube of paint attached to the brush had broken off, splattering blue paint on everything within range, including the artist. It had required a great deal of paint remover and repeated baths to restore Vincent's fur to its customary shade of nondescript gray.

"Painting is just a game to him," she said. "I keep thinking he'll grow tired of it. But so far he hasn't. I still have to lock up the rez-brushes whenever I'm not around to supervise, though. Three weeks ago, I went downstairs to take out the trash while he was playing with his paints. I was gone for only five minutes, but by the time I got back, the lower portion of the refrigerator was green."

Cruz studied the bright, chaotic swipes and blobs of color that covered a third of the canvas. "Looks like he's heavily into magenta. When I left he was still in his blue period."

She thought about what had happened to the three blue paintings and cleared her throat. "He's gone through several colors since we last saw you," she said.

Cruz looked at her across the room. He had removed his jacket and tossed it over the reading chair, just as he had done so often during the time they had dated. His black tie was unknotted, and he had opened the top three or four buttons of his shirt. Making himself at home, she thought wistfully. Just as if nothing had happened.

The coffee table, with its vase of amethyst orchids and the little stack of cards, stood between them. He must know that she had gotten the message of the unsigned cards. A woman would not keep flowers from a man unless she was prepared to forgive him. The anticipation was almost unbearable.

"Things got very complicated three months ago," he said.

"Yes, they did." She went around behind the kitchen counter. "Would you like a drink? I still have the Amber Dew you bought before the complications set in."

"Sounds good." He lowered himself onto one of the counter stools and hooked a foot over the bottom rung. "I'm surprised you didn't throw out the bottle."

"I considered it a few times, but it seemed like a waste of good liqueur."

"Smart thinking." He watched her take the two-thirds-empty bottle down from the cupboard. "Looks like you've been enjoying it. We only had one drink each out of that bottle."

"Well, it has been three months, and I must admit it is rather nice to be able to serve a fancy liqueur like Amber Dew when I have guests."

"Guests?" he repeated very deliberately.

"Mmm. They're always very impressed."

She gave him a warm smile and set one of the filled glasses on the counter within reach of his hand. Let him think that she'd been dating madly since he had shattered her world. She was not about to tell him that the only person she had invited to dinner in the past three months had been Nancy, and that every time they had shared a glass of the fabulously expensive Amber Dew they had chanted, "To the bastard, may he rot."

He picked up the glass. "Thanks for trusting me enough to let me come back here with you tonight. I know that must have been hard for you."

She took a small sip of the potent Amber Dew, lowered the glass, and went for sultry. "I've had a lot of time to think in the past three months, Cruz."

"And you finally realized that I had no choice but to do what I did?"

"Don't be ridiculous," she said. "I still think Amber Inc. had no right whatsoever to confiscate my find. But I understand that you sincerely *believe* that you did what you had to do. I can respect that."

"The ruin you discovered down there in the jungle was potentially dangerous, Lyra. By law you should have reported it immediately to the authorities."

"Oh, wow. A lecture."

His mouth tightened at the corners. "You know as well as I do that under the Alien Antiquities Act, any find that poses a potential hazard or generates unknown power of any kind must be analyzed and classified by the appropriate authorities."

"Who will then confiscate it. If said antiquity happens to be made of amber, especially an extremely rare form, the appropriate authorities will naturally hand it over to Amber Inc., which has a contract with the federal government." She widened her eyes with mock astonishment. "Gosh, I wonder why so many small, independent prospectors like me don't routinely tell the *appropriate authorities* about their little finds."

"The amethyst ruin was no small find. You knew that better than anyone. And it wasn't stolen from you. Amber Inc. offered generous compensation."

"Hah. There was no way your company could possibly compensate me for what you snatched from me. That ruin was priceless."

"This isn't about the legalities, is it?" he said quietly. "It's about us. You and me."

That was another thing about Cruz Sweetwater. He always went straight to the bottom line. She exhaled slowly, leaned against the counter, glass in hand, and looked at the coffee table with its vase of exotic flowers.

"Yes," she said. "It's about us and the fact that you lied to me."

"I had no choice."

"I understand that now. I don't have to like it, but I'm okay with it. I've moved on with my life."

"That's why you dropped the lawsuit?"

"Well, that and the fact that I finally came to my senses and realized that I could not afford to go up against Amber Inc. for even another week."

There was a silence while they drank the quartz-green liqueur. The champagne had not done diddly-squat, but the Dew was succeeding where the lightweight stuff had failed. Her nerves were settling down nicely.

"I got the orchids," she said after a while.

He regarded the flowers, eyes narrowing faintly. "I noticed them when we came in."

"They're very beautiful."

He did not take his attention off the orchids. "Expensive."

"Mmm." She ran the tip of her finger around the rim of her glass. "Amethyst orchids are very pricey. Especially when you send that many of them twice a week for six weeks."

"Someone has been sending you orchids twice a week for six weeks?"

She froze. Okay, this was not another waking nightmare episode, but in some ways it was a whole lot worse than one of the hallucinations.

Dread in her heart, she made herself look at Cruz. His hard face was set in implacable lines. She did not say a word, but words were unnecessary. She saw sudden comprehension burn in his eyes.

"You thought I was the one who was sending the flowers," he said softly. It was not a question.

She could feel herself turning as bright as the magenta paint on Vincent's latest canvas. She set the half-finished Amber Dew on the counter with great care and cleared her throat.

"Well," she said. "This is certainly embarrassing. Now that we've cleared up that little misunderstanding, why don't you tell me exactly why you decided to walk back into my life tonight?"

Chapter 3

HE KNEW AT ONCE THAT HE'D MADE A MISCALCULATION of monumental proportions. But the damned orchids had annoyed him more than he wanted to admit. *Should have kept my mouth shut,* Cruz thought. Then again, it wasn't as if he'd had a lot of options. It would have been a little awkward to take credit for the flowers when the guy who'd actually sent them eventually showed up. The SOB would be able to produce receipts.

Vincent, evidently sensing the change in the atmosphere, popped up onto a stool and then onto the counter. He fluttered across the surface toward Lyra. When he reached her, he hopped up onto her shoulder and made small, soothing noises in her ear. She patted him gently, clearly taking comfort from his presence.

She looked even better tonight than she had in the very private, very hot fantasies that had been keeping him awake for the past three months, Cruz thought. The little black number she was wearing was no couture gown, but the flirty neckline, tiny sleeves, and narrow skirt discreetly emphasized her gentle curves. Her dark brown hair was pulled back into a sleek knot that emphasized her incredible hazel eyes.

Simple amber hoops decorated her ears. She had worn them on several occasions three months ago. There was a charm bracelet on her wrist. He remembered it, too. He'd heard its light, musical clash in his dreams. It was composed of interlocking gold-toned links. Myriad small charms dangled from the links. Each was set with a tiny chip of amethyst amber. She had told him that her grandfather had given the bracelet to her.

Like the dress, the earrings and the bracelet were attractive but not expensive. Lyra made her living as an amber tuner and did a little independent prospecting on the side. Amber tuning was a notoriously low-paying business, due to the competition. The ability to tune standard resonating amber was a common talent. There was a tuning shop on every street corner and in every mall in the city.

As for independent prospecting, that was a fool's endeavor. Very few indies ever struck good amber or discovered truly valuable ruins. When they did, the big companies were always poised to move in and take over the claim, just as Amber Inc. had moved in on Lyra three months ago. The best an indie could do in a situation like that was make a deal. Lyra had refused to bargain.

Typical Dore, Cruz thought. His grandfather was right; they were too proud and too stubborn for their own good.

He briefly contemplated the sizzling midnight fantasies that had haunted him since his house-of-cards relationship with Lyra had come tumbling down. The dreams had all begun the same way, with Lyra rushing into his arms the moment she saw him across a crowded room. Said fantasies had progressed from there to a variety of interesting and very hot scenarios.

But when he had walked into the Swan Gallery tonight, he was the one who had wanted to run to her, sweep her up in his arms, and carry her off into the night.

He could see that there was no point trying to explain any of that to her now. She wouldn't believe him if he tried. He forced himself to stay focused. His responsibilities came first.

"We've got a problem with the ruin," he said, keeping his tone as businesslike and nonconfrontational as possible.

"Would that be the royal we?" she asked politely.

"That would be the research team from the lab."

"Oh," she said. "You mean the cretins from Amber Inc. Research and Development."

"I'm told that the members of the research team prefer to describe themselves as scientists, archaeologists, and technicians."

She nodded. "Job titles like that probably pay more than cretin. Okay, so what went wrong at the ruin?"

"The doorway to the chamber closed."

She blinked, obviously startled. An instant later a slow, wicked smile curved her mouth. Laughter gleamed in her eyes. For a heartbeat he allowed himself a few more memories from three months back. He saw Lyra smiling as she demonstrated the full potential of the incredible artifact of amethyst amber that she had tuned especially for him. He had kept the relic close all these months. He'd lost track of how many times he had taken it out of its leather case and held it, savoring the strange beauty of the alien artwork.

"Define *closed*," Lyra said.

"There's a small energy storm filling the opening. No one can get in or out."

"Interesting," she said.

"Any idea how it was closed?" he asked.

She raised one shoulder in a tiny shrug. "There are a couple of possibilities. There may have been some stray currents from a ghost river or even a storm in the vicinity."

"None were detected."

"Then it was probably triggered accidentally by someone who can work one of the exotic ambers like silver or diamond."

"Or amethyst?" he asked quietly.

She stilled.

"Or someone who can work amethyst," she agreed without inflection.

"The ruin was open when the AI lab team began work at the site," he said.

She raised a finger. "Point of semantics here. The ruin was open when it was stolen from me in the course of a hostile takeover, the legality of which is highly questionable."

"I think we'll leave semantics out of this for now."

She looked at him with wide-eyed innocence. "Why would we want to do that?"

"Because there's too much at stake," he said.

"Not for me." She smiled. "To quote Nancy, I don't have a dust bunny in this fight."

He ignored that. "The ruin was closed when you discovered the amethyst chamber, wasn't it?"

She grinned. "Yep."

"You opened it."

"Sure did. I take it none of your cretins can get the job done now that it's closed again?"

"No," he said. "The lab guys have tried everything. So have I, for that matter, and I'm pretty good when it comes to tuned amber. The energy in that amethyst is unlike anything anyone in the lab has ever dealt with before. We haven't even been able to rez or activate any of the artifacts that have been recovered so far. All the pieces are just sitting in the lab vault like so much purple rock."

"I did get that impression," she said lightly. "I've had a number of phone calls from your head cretin demanding my help. Someone named Webber."

"Dr. Felix Webber. He's in charge of the lab."

"I haven't returned any of his calls, naturally."

"He mentioned that you had been less than cooperative," Cruz said dryly.

"Call me petty, but it gives me so much pleasure to decline to assist Amber Inc. in every possible way, shape, and form." She tilted her head slightly. "So that's why you're here. You want me to open up the ruin for you."

This was not going well, he thought.

"Yes," he said.

"I assume you intend to offer me lots and lots of money?"

"Name your price."

"Forget it," she said softly. She put down the glass and folded her arms on the counter. "You can't afford me, Sweetwater."

"Something else you should know."

"Mmm?"

"When the ruin closed, there were five people inside the chamber: two lab techs and the head of the lab's security team. There were also two Guild men in there. We can't make contact. We don't even know if they're alive."

She sighed, closed her eyes, and dropped her forehead onto her folded arms. "I'm going to have to have a chat with my Harmonic Meditation instructor. There must be something really screwed up with my karma. I don't even get to enjoy a little innocent revenge. Instead, I have to go rescue three cretins who work for Amber Inc. and a couple of Guild thugs."

He had known that she would agree to help. Their time together had been brief, but it had been long enough to be sure of a few things about her. His Sweetwater intuition had not failed him. For all her hostility toward him, personally, and the company in general, she would never leave five trapped and helpless people to their fate.

"Lyra," he said gently. He started to reach across the counter to touch her bare arm.

She straightened abruptly, stepped back out of reach,

and came briskly around the end of the counter. "No one got caught in the doorway itself, when it closed?"

"No."

"Good. Give me a few minutes to change my clothes. I don't intend to ruin this dress in the jungle for the sake of Amber Inc."

He watched her walk toward the sliding screens that concealed the bedroom area.

"About the orchids," he said.

She disappeared behind the screens. "What about them?"

The screens were opaque but translucent. He could make out tantalizing glimpses of her shadow as she unzipped the little black dress and stepped out of it. Everything inside him got tighter.

"Just wondered who sent them," he said. "Given the fact that it wasn't me."

"Haven't a clue. There's never a signature."

He looked at the stack of cards. "Must be someone you know well, if he figured he didn't need to sign the cards."

"Mmm."

He contemplated the graceful shadow of her leg and the curve of her hip as she stepped into a pair of pants. She had a very fine rear, he thought. Truly excellent. The presence of the flowers indicated that some other man admired the same assets.

"What do the cards say?" he asked, unable to stop himself.

She appeared at the opening in the screens dressed in

jeans, a faded denim shirt, and a pair of low leather boots. She had a jungle pack slung over one shoulder.

"See for yourself," she said.

He could tell from her smile that he was not going to like whatever was written on the cards. But he had to know. He rose from the stool, crossed to the coffee table, and picked up the top card. A strange, icy feeling twisted through him.

" 'We belong together,' " he read aloud.

"Romantic, don't you think?"

It took some major willpower, but he managed to suppress the urge to rip the card into little pieces. "That's a damn personal message from someone you can't identify."

"Yes, it is," she agreed. "Guess I've got myself a secret admirer. Never had one of those. You know, my life has suddenly become a heck of a lot more interesting." She looked at Vincent. "Ready to go on a trip to the jungle, buddy?"

Vincent chortled enthusiastically and scampered across the room. Lyra scooped him up and headed for the door.

"Let's go," she said to Cruz. "The sooner I get your cretins out of the chamber, the sooner I can go to bed. It's been a very long day."

Chapter 4

THEY ENTERED THE CATACOMBS THROUGH ONE OF THE official gates located inside the Dead City. That alone told Lyra just how seriously everyone was taking the situation.

"Oh, wow," she said when Cruz brought her to a halt at the doorway of one of the ethereal green quartz towers. "I get to go in through an actual authorized gate? I thought the only people allowed to use the Guild gates were corporate- and academic-sponsored R&D teams that paid top dollar for the privilege. I'm just a small-time independent, remember? Are you sure the Guild honchos know about this?"

"I'm aware that you don't like the Guild any better than you do Amber Inc.," Cruz said.

"Mostly because they have always worked hand in hand with AI to monopolize exploration underground and in the jungle, not to mention crush small indies like Dore Tuning & Consulting. Aside from that, I have absolutely nothing against either AI or the Guild."

"Do you think you could hold back on the sarcasm until we get those five people out of that chamber?"

"Sorry. Sometimes I just can't help myself."

"I noticed."

She gave him another glowing smile, aware that she was feeling downright reckless. Okay, so he hadn't come crawling back on his hands and knees to beg her forgiveness. He was back, and like it or not, he needed her, at least for a short time. As vengeance went, it was pitiful, but it was something.

They made an odd-looking pair, she thought. She was dressed for the jungle in the jeans and work shirt that she usually wore when she went underground. Cruz had removed his black jacket and tie, but he still had on the black trousers and black shirt he'd worn to the gallery reception. He had not wanted to waste time returning to his town house in a gentrified section of the Quarter to change clothes. But he had replaced his dress shoes with a pair of black leather boots, and he had a pack on his back. Both items had come out of the trunk of the Slider, where they were evidently kept for emergencies. *Assassin informal,* Lyra thought.

There were no windows inside the tower room, but the interior green quartz floor, walls, and ceiling glowed gently, just as the outside walls did at night. As far as anyone knew, the aliens had never used any openings other than strictly necessary gates and doors in their aboveground structures. It was as if they had done everything possible to avoid letting sunlight and fresh air into their strangely graceful buildings. As far as the experts could determine, the lush, thriving surface of Harmony, with its fertile valleys, thickly forested mountains, broad rivers, and vibrant oceans, had been toxic to the long-vanished civilization. For the most part, the aliens had lived their lives underground.

Two ghost hunters guarded the tunnel entrance. They were dressed in the traditional khakis and leather that rank-and-file Guild men favored. The macho attire went with the swagger. They had been lounging against a green wall when Lyra and Cruz walked into the chamber, but they straightened quickly.

"Mr. Sweetwater," one of the two said, nodding respectfully. "We were told to expect you. The sled is standing by down below. There's an extra locator on board. Anything else you need, sir?"

"Not at the moment," Cruz said. "This is Miss Dore. She'll be accompanying me to the site."

"Yes, sir," the second man said. He gave Lyra an appraising survey. "They said you'd be bringing someone who could open that damned ruin."

"That would be me," Lyra said coolly.

"Yes, ma'am." The first man eyed Vincent. "That a dust bunny?"

"Yes," Lyra said. "His name is Vincent."

The second ghost hunter frowned. "Not sure we're authorized to allow a varmint into the tunnels."

Lyra narrowed her eyes. "The bunny is with me. He goes where I go."

Cruz took a locator out of his pocket and checked his amber as he walked past the men. "They're both with me."

"Yes, sir," both hunters said simultaneously.

They stepped quickly out of Lyra's path. She made to follow Cruz, Vincent tucked firmly under one arm.

One of the men spoke behind her.

"Miss Dore?"

She paused. "Yes?"

"Do you really think you can open that amethyst ruin?" he asked. "We've got two good men trapped in there with the research team."

"Morgan and Estrada," the second man said. "Morgan is a friend. Estrada is my brother-in-law. My sister is in a real panic."

Their anxiety was genuine, Lyra thought. She gave them an equally genuine smile. "Don't worry; I'll get it open."

"You think they'll be okay?" the first man said. "There's talk about some weird energy inside that ruin."

"I've been informed that no one was caught in the entrance when it closed, so unless they've done something really dumb like try to get through the energy field, they should be fine," she said. "I spent a lot of time in that chamber before Amber Inc. and the Guild forced me out. There's nothing inside the ruin that would harm your friends."

Both men looked relieved.

"Thanks," the first one said. "Don't mind telling you we've all been damn worried."

The second one exhaled heavily. "We appreciate what you're doing for us, ma'am."

"Right," Lyra said. She turned away before either of the two men could remind her of the old Guild saying, "The Guild always repays a favor."

"The Guild always repays a favor, Miss Dore," the first hunter called after her.

She winced. "Thanks, but I'll pass on any Guild favors."

She hurried toward the staircase. Cruz was waiting for her at the top of the glowing green steps. He looked amused.

"Amber Inc. has the same policy," he said.

"Excellent. If you want to repay me, you can return the ruin to me." She started down the staircase.

He ignored the comment and started down the stairs behind her. "You were nice to those two guards," he said. "Thought you said all Guild men were thugs. Sort of like all Amber Inc. people."

"Amber Inc. is a closely held family business. They don't actively recruit. But the Guilds do. What's more, they focus their efforts on vulnerable young males, seducing them with notions of an adventurous life in the underworld. But the reality is that most ghost hunters are nothing more than bodyguards for the research and excavation teams that go down into the tunnels and the jungle."

"And Amber Inc.?"

"The power behind the throne," she said. "For the past fifty years, ever since your grandfather cheated mine out of the Radiance Springs claim, your family has controlled half the SRA production in the four city-states."

"My grandfather tells the story a little differently."

"I'm sure he does. But the truth is, AI tolerates wildcatters and independents only so long as we don't get in your way or come up with any really spectacular finds. If we do get lucky, you step in and take over. What's more, you have all the connections with the Guilds, the archaeologists, and the government to make it happen legally. On top of that, you keep things in the family. You've never gone public with your stock, so you don't have to explain things to shareholders or follow the usual corporate rules."

"We don't like the idea of outsiders trying to tell us what to do," Cruz said mildly.

"Trust me, I know the feeling," she said. "Let's move. It's late, and I've got to be up early in the morning."

"Appointment with a client?"

"No, my Harmonic Meditation class."

"When did you start taking classes in meditation?"

"Shortly after you told me your real name and walked out the door. I thought the classes would help me deal with the stress and my hostility issues."

"Any luck?"

"Let's just say that if you had come looking for my assistance two months ago, I would have told you that your research team and those two Guild men could stay in that chamber until green hell freezes over."

"No," he said. "You wouldn't have let five people suffer because of what I did."

He sounded far too certain of his conclusion. What could she say? It was the truth. She pretended she hadn't heard him and concentrated on keeping her balance on the dizzying staircase.

The steps were fairly wide, but they twisted down into the green world in a convoluted pattern that made no sense architecturally. Like everything else constructed by the aliens, the proportions were slightly off to human eyes. But the heavy dose of psi flowing up from the tunnels gave her a familiar little rush. She knew that Cruz felt the buzz, too.

Vincent wriggled out from under her arm. She set him on a step. He scampered ahead of her down the staircase, his little red beret flopping in a jaunty fashion.

"Looks like he knows where he's going," Cruz observed.

"As far as I can tell, dust bunnies are right at home down here. They don't seem to have any trouble navigating the tunnels or the jungle."

"Unlike us humans."

No one knew why the aliens had constructed the vast network of catacombs that crisscrossed the planet. In two hundred years of excavation and exploration, the descendants of the colonists had succeeded in charting only a small percentage of the seemingly endless maze of tunnels.

Recently the discovery of an even greater mystery, the massive underground rain forest, had attracted so much attention from explorers and archaeologists and treasure hunters that mapping the tunnels had dropped to a low priority for most corporations engaged in underworld business. The strange jungle held out the promise of far more scientifically and financially rewarding discoveries.

As the Guild men had promised, the little utility sled was waiting at the foot of the staircase. Cruz got in behind the wheel. Lyra slid onto the bench seat beside him. Vincent bounded up onto the dashboard, where he had a clear view. He looked like a fluffy hood ornament.

Cruz ran a check of the sled's navigation instruments. Lyra automatically pulsed a little psi through her bracelet as well as the standard resonating amber she always carried with her. Getting lost in the catacombs was all too easy, and the results were deadly if you didn't have tuned amber. Independent prospectors became downright obsessive about amber. In addition, loners like her were always at risk of falling prey to thieves and the antiquities gangs underground. Both had a nasty habit of getting rid of people by stranding them in the jungle or the catacombs without amber. She always carried plenty of backup, and a lot of that backup was concealed.

"The jungle gate we'll be using is about ten minutes from here," Cruz said.

He rezzed the sled's simple little motor. More sophisticated engines and high-tech tools and equipment in general did not function well, if at all, in the heavy psi environment. The small vehicle raced along the corridor at top speed, which was just a little faster than the average person could run. Vincent leaned into the light breeze and made happy little noises.

"He likes to go fast," Lyra said.

"I remember."

They passed a dizzying array of vaulted chambers and rooms, all fashioned of glowing green quartz, all empty. In a rotunda intersection that served seven branching passageways, Cruz paused to check the instruments again. Then he swung the sled to the left. They made a few more disorienting turns before Lyra spotted the gate that opened into the rain forest.

Several people were milling around the opening. In addition to a number of Guild men, there were a lot of worried-looking tech types dressed in jungle uniforms bearing the Amber Inc. logo. There were also some folks holding cameras and notebooks. They looked bored, but that changed fast when they spotted the sled.

"Damn," Cruz muttered. "I was afraid that the press would get wind of this situation."

Once again Lyra found herself feeling a tiny drop of unwilling sympathy for him.

"Face it," she said. "There are some things even Amber Inc. can't control."

"Yeah, I discovered that the hard way three months ago when you started bashing the company in the media."

"Give me a break. I couldn't even put a dent in Amber Inc."

"I wouldn't say that. The public relations department had to work overtime for weeks to deal with the inquiries they got from every reporter in town. Even the tabloids were calling, wanting to know if Amber Inc. was participating in another Guild cover-up like the one that took place in Crystal City a couple months back."

She smiled, pleased. "Well, you were conspiring with the Guild to keep the discovery of the amethyst ruin under wraps."

"Only because we were concerned with security issues. We didn't want to have to deal with every tunnel rat, souvenir hunter, and low-rent antiquities thief in the four city-states. But that's pretty much what happened after you took your story public."

"Nice to know your PR people at least learned my name."

He brought the sled to a halt and looked at her. Laughter glinted briefly in his dark eyes. "Believe me when I tell you that at company headquarters, you are legendary."

"I'll try to take some comfort from that."

The reporters reached the sled before the Guild men could stop them. Lyra recognized several familiar faces in the crowd. Cruz was right; she had given a lot of interviews three months ago when she had filed the lawsuit.

Tina Tazewell from the *Frequency Herald* rezzed one of the low-tech cameras designed to work in the underworld and snapped off several shots. "Miss Dore, is it true Amber Inc. had to call you in to rescue a team trapped inside the ruin?" she asked.

"That's my understanding, Tina." Lyra scooped Vincent off the dashboard and climbed out of the sled.

"Evidently they don't have anyone on staff who can handle the job."

Excited by the commotion, Vincent fluttered up onto her shoulder. She heard more cameras rez.

"Can we assume that you agreed to assist in the rescue effort because you and Cruz Sweetwater have a personal relationship?" Tina asked.

"Heavens no," Lyra said airily. "This is strictly business."

Out of the corner of her eye she saw Brett Bolton from the *Current* step in front of Cruz. He had a notebook in hand.

"Does this mean that the Amber Inc.–Dore feud is concluded, Mr. Sweetwater?"

"What feud?" Cruz asked.

He went past Bolton and sharked through the gaggle of reporters until he got to Lyra.

"If you'll excuse us," he said, "Miss Dore is a little busy at the moment. She's got a team to rescue. For the record, Amber Inc. is very grateful to her for assisting us in this crisis."

"How grateful?" Tina Tazewell demanded.

Cruz ignored her. He took Lyra's arm and steered her toward the jungle gate where the hunters and the people in AI uniforms waited.

The entrance to the rain forest was a large, rectangular opening in the green quartz wall. Humid heat flowed out into the corridor, but it evaporated almost instantly, nullified by the always steady temperature of the catacombs. Lyra saw a little dirt and one or two dead leaves on the floor of the tunnel and knew that they had been carried out on the bottom of someone's boots. The debris would soon disintegrate and disappear altogether, thanks to some as yet unidentified mechanism that kept the tunnels clean.

Nothing escaped the jungle unless it was carried out. A number of gates had been opened during the past few months, and at each of them a mysterious and—to human senses undetectable—force field kept the flora and fauna securely confined within the rain forest the aliens had created. The researchers and scientists had quickly discovered that living specimens did not last long aboveground. The plants and animals in the artificially constructed jungle required the heavy psi atmosphere inside their bioengineered world to survive. Like the aliens themselves, they found the surface of Harmony an inhospitable and deadly place.

The green glow of artificial sunlight was clearly visible. It was night on the surface, but the jungle ran on its own schedule.

Lyra moved through the gate, Cruz at her side. At once the rich, living energy of the jungle enveloped her. The Guild maintained a clearing directly in front of the tunnel entrance, but she knew it required daily maintenance. The jungle reclaimed territory with startling speed. Paths established one day usually vanished by the following afternoon.

Beyond the perimeter of the clearing the massed greenery pressed close. It was impossible to see more than a few feet because of the dense foliage, all of it shimmering in various hues of luminous green. The trees towered upward, forming a leafy canopy that concealed most of the quartz sky. Small things skittered in the undergrowth. Birds screeched in the distance.

"Thanks for coming down here, Miss Dore," one of the Guild men said.

She gave him her most vivacious smile. "Well, it wasn't like I was doing anything else more entertaining this evening."

Relieved laughter greeted that remark. The small crowd of ghost hunters and Amber Inc. people seemed to relax.

"How far to the ruin from here?" she asked. "When I discovered it, I used a different gate. You know how it is; distances are deceptive underground."

Her not-so-subtle claim to the ruin did not go unnoticed. Cruz smiled slightly. The AI people exchanged glances. The Guild men, however, were a lot more focused. There was a team trapped in the jungle. It was their responsibility to rescue it.

"The amethyst chamber is only a thirty-minute hike from here," the lead hunter said. He hesitated. "That's if you're accustomed to jungle travel. If you're not used to it—"

"I've done this before," Lyra assured him.

"She's a pro," Cruz added.

She glanced back over her shoulder and saw the reporters crowded around the entrance, still snapping photos. "Are they coming with us?"

"No," Cruz said. "They are not. Those of us in charge

of this project are trying to pretend that the ruin is still a secure site and that only authorized personnel are allowed anywhere near it."

Lyra thought about all the unwanted free press she had given him and the discovery of the amethyst chamber in the past three months with her lawsuit. She laughed.

"Good luck with that," she said.

"Tell me about it. We're having to pay the Guild overtime for twenty-four-seven security in the field, not to mention covering the costs of several search-and-rescue operations. Amazing how many treasure hunters and curiosity seekers have managed to sneak into the rain forest in search of the ruin and gotten themselves lost in the process."

"See, we independents don't face those logistical problems," she said smoothly. "Because we keep our mouths shut when we make significant discoveries."

"And then you screw up by trying to sell your finds on the underground collectors market."

"Well, yes, that, too," she admitted.

He looked at her. "Thought we agreed to save the snappy comments until some other more convenient occasion."

"Right. Let's get going. I'd still like to get some sleep tonight."

They plunged into the jungle, the two hunters in the lead using machetes to cut a path through the thickest sections. Taking Lyra at her word, they set a difficult pace.

Mostly it was a matter of pushing through masses of vibrantly green plants and flowers and scrambling over vines and downed trees. Since there was no way to maintain a road or even a rough trail suitable for sleds, the only way into the rain forest was on foot.

As far as the researchers and explorers had been able to discern, there was little to fear from the flora and fauna. The aliens hadn't been so dumb as to fill their artificially constructed jungle with a lot of dangerous wildlife and poisonous vegetation. But the Others had been gone a long time, and everyone knew that life had a way of evolving on its own, even in a controlled, bioengineered environment. The experts continued to issue warnings, and no one took unnecessary chances.

There was, however, no doubt at all about the other two major concerns in the underground world. Getting lost was a serious hazard. In addition, powerful currents of dangerous psi energy flowed in rivers and occasionally manifested in full-blown storms. Blundering into the heavy stuff could be lethal. Those who survived the experience usually ended up with their para-senses permanently shattered.

But in its own way, the rain forest was incredibly beautiful. Lyra savored the experience as she always did. Green sunlight filtered through the canopy. Magnificent peridot green flowers bloomed everywhere. Vast curtains of vines studded with green orchids of every size and description hung from the trees. Here and there small green lizards and other creatures scurried into the undergrowth to avoid the tread of human feet. Emerald green butterflies with impossibly large iridescent wings flitted from blossom to blossom.

"You like it down here, don't you?" Cruz asked.

"Who wouldn't?" she said. "It's an astonishing experience. I'm so glad the Guild has begun to allow some tourism. Everyone should have the opportunity to see this place. It's one of the wonders of our world, like the mountains and the oceans and the forests on the surface. No one has a right to monopolize the rain forest."

"In principle I agree with you," Cruz said. "The problems, as usual, are in the details. People get killed down here. The jungle is dangerous."

"So are mountains and oceans and forests. But people go hiking, swimming, and camping all the time on the surface. And sometimes they get killed."

"Okay, I'll concede there are a few parallels," he said.

"The only real difference down here is that access is limited to those who possess the kind of psychic talent it takes to open a gate. Since most people don't have the ability to do that, the Guilds have been able to maintain some control. But they are fighting a rear guard action."

"I know," Cruz said. "At the rate talents are appearing in the population, it probably won't be long before the majority of people will be able to open a jungle gate. Another couple of generations, maybe."

"Don't worry about it," she said cheerfully. "I'm sure Amber Inc. won't have any difficulty hanging on to its mining monopoly down here, just as it hasn't had a problem hanging on to it aboveground."

"We'll certainly do our best," Cruz said.

She knew that if she glanced back over her shoulder, she would see the unmistakable spark of dark humor in his eyes, so she concentrated instead on pushing through a veil of hanging orchids.

Something small and green darted along a tree limb. Vincent's little paws tightened slightly around Lyra's shoulder. His second set of eyes, the ones he used for hunting, popped open. He studied the small rodent with great interest.

"Uh-oh," she said.

"Hey, you hang out with predators, you're going to see some blood once in a while," Cruz observed.

She recalled her words to Nancy earlier that evening. *He looks like a really well-dressed hit man.*

"Yes," she said. "I have noticed the blood."

There was a short silence behind her.

"I was talking about dust bunnies," Cruz said finally.

"Oh, were you?"

Thankfully, the small creature on the tree limb disappeared into a tangle of leaves, and Vincent lost interest.

Twenty minutes later, she sensed the faint aura of energy that emanated from the chamber before it came into view. Vincent picked up on her anticipation and made enthusiastic noises. She was breathing hard, and her shirt was soaked with perspiration, but her spirits lifted immediately.

She had always had an affinity for amber of any kind, but the purple variety called amethyst was her specialty. It sang to her senses in a way that no other version of the stone did.

Amethyst amber was one of the extremely rare forms of the stone. But until the discovery of the ruin, it had not been viewed as valuable except to collectors of rare ambers and to those who liked amethyst jewelry.

The relics that she had found inside the ruin had caused the experts to reconsider that analysis, however. It was evident that there was a lot of latent energy in the artifacts. The problem for the Amber Inc. lab experts was accessing that energy. They badly needed someone who could work amethyst amber to aid them with their testing and experiments. Such individuals had proven to be scarce. To date, the only person they had found who could resonate with the energy in the relics was a stubborn, low-rent tuner who had steadfastly refused to cooperate.

"Almost there," one of the Guild men called back to the sweating trekkers behind him.

A few minutes later they walked into the small clearing that the hunters had established around the amethyst chamber. A half dozen men and women in AI gear were arrayed around the scene. Most sat glumly on bedrolls or other convenient pieces of camping equipment, drinking bottled water and munching on energy bars. They surged to their feet in unison when they saw the rescue team.

"You got her," someone said. "Thank God."

"I didn't think she'd come," a woman said. She gave Lyra a grateful smile. "Thanks, Miss Dore."

"Always happy to be of service to Amber Inc.," Lyra said lightly.

The bald-faced lie produced a wave of nervous laughter.

The amethyst chamber stood in the center of the clearing, a windowless structure carved out of what appeared to be a single massive block of purple amber. The ruin was circular in design, nearly thirty feet high, and a little over half that in width. Lyra knew the numbers because one of the first things she had done after finding the chamber was measure the interior. A colonnade of amber columns surrounded the outer wall, giving the structure an oddly graceful appearance. The columns supported a dome-shaped roof.

The door of the chamber was an imposing, vaulted entrance that was a little more than half the height of the structure. At the moment, it was sealed with a roaring, pulsing cascade of intense, flaring energy. It was impossible to look directly at the hot, flashing bolts of raging purple psi for more than a second or two at a time. Lyra noticed that no one was sitting close to the entrance of the chamber. So much throbbing, churning energy had a disturbing effect on human senses.

One of the men came forward. He was in his late forties or possibly early fifties, a tall, thin, sharp-featured individual in thick, dark-rimmed glasses. A goatee framed his narrow, unsmiling lips. Lyra decided he probably did not have much of a sense of humor.

"Dr. Felix Webber," Cruz said. "The head of the lab. Felix, this is Lyra Dore. She very kindly agreed to help us."

Webber nodded brusquely and managed to look even more irritated.

"Miss Dore," he said. "I've tried several times to get in touch with you during the past few weeks."

"I've been busy," she said. She started toward the door filled with purple lightning. "Let's get this done, shall we?"

"Are you sure you can handle this, Miss Dore?" Webber demanded.

"With one hand tied behind my back." She stopped in front of the door, her eyes slightly averted from the veil of searing energy that filled the entrance from top to bottom. "What did you guys do to close this thing?"

Webber's expression tightened with outrage. "What makes you think it was something that one of the team members did?"

"Let's just say I'm a tad suspicious, because I know how this door works. Someone must have triggered it. You know, you people really should be careful when you fool around with alien ruins like this one. Someone could get hurt."

"Who are you to lecture me on how to deal with alien technology?" Webber snarled. "You're just an opportunistic little tuner who happened to get lucky when you found this ruin. But you didn't have the training, the talent, or the education to appreciate its real value. To you this place was just a source of expensive relics you could sell on the underground antiquities market."

Cruz moved forward. "That's enough, Dr. Webber. If it hadn't been for Miss Dore, we might never have found this chamber."

Webber's jaw clenched. "I don't trust her, Mr. Sweetwater. She has made her hostility toward the company and the lab abundantly clear."

"I trust her," Cruz said simply. "She says she can get our people out. Let her do her job."

Webber swung around to face him. "How do we know she isn't going to make the whole thing explode? Or maybe she'll booby-trap it so that the next time it will close on one of us?"

Lyra wrinkled her nose. "No offense, Dr. W, but you've got some serious paranoia issues. You might want to try a few sessions of Harmonic Meditation exercises. I'll be happy to give you the name of my instructor."

There was some smothered laughter from the others.

Rage flashed in Webber's eyes, but he managed to keep his expression stone-faced.

"I think that's enough, Lyra," Cruz said. "Would you mind opening the chamber?"

"Sure," she said.

She slid the pack off her back and took a pair of dark glasses out of a side pocket. Slipping the glasses onto her nose, she walked directly up to the lightning-filled entrance. The shades dimmed the bright energy to the point where she could look at it directly.

She put her hand on the amethyst wall close to the opening and heightened her senses. The stone warmed under her hand. Vincent chortled in excitement and bounced up and down, delighting in the game.

Energy surged through Lyra, thrilling her all the way to her toes. Her hair stood straight out on end, forming a wild halo around her face. Her shirt lifted a little away from her skin as though caught by a storm wind. She suddenly wanted to fly. She was on fire with power, intoxicated with it. For a tuner, there was nothing like the rush of really hot amber.

But she was also a professional. A lot of people had a low opinion of tuners, but she took pride in being an expert. And when it came to amethyst, nobody worked stone better.

She forced herself to concentrate and began to search for the pattern of the wildly oscillating currents. She found it almost at once. Vincent vibrated with excitement. He was always up for a little psychic thrill. His hunting eyes opened again.

She identified the frequencies needed to control the forces of the lightning that locked the door and sent out counteracting wavelengths, pushing her own energy through the amber charms on her bracelet. The purple lightning flashed even hotter for a moment and then quickly faded. With a few final sparks and crackles and hisses, it subsided altogether.

Her hair tumbled back down around her face, and her clothes settled on her body. The heady sensation of power evaporated.

For few seconds there was stunned silence behind her. Everyone crowded closer, trying to peer through the entrance of the chamber. Purple light glowed from the interior of the ruin.

Five people appeared in the de-rezzed opening, all wearing varying expressions of amazement and relief.

A cheer went up from the group gathered around Lyra.

"They're okay," someone shouted.

One of the ghost hunters walked out first, probably testing to be certain that there would be no surprises for the others. He looked at Lyra.

"Appreciate it, ma'am," he said. "The Guild owes you."

"No," Cruz said. "Amber Inc. owes this favor."

Another man emerged from the chamber. He was in his midthirties, tall and powerfully built, with the sort of rugged features, macho attitude, and short haircut that just screamed cop or private security. He looked first at Cruz.

"Mr. Sweetwater," he said. "Sorry about this."

"It's not your fault, Garrett," Cruz said. "Hell, it's an alien ruin. There's always a surprise of some kind. Miss Dore, here, is the one who opened the chamber. Lyra, this is Garrett Flagg, head of lab security."

"Mr. Flagg." Lyra inclined her head politely.

"Miss Dore." Flagg nodded once, serious and intent. "Sure didn't expect you to come to the rescue tonight, not after what went down between you and the company. But I'm damn grateful. I owe you. If there's ever anything you need from me, just pick up the phone."

"Thank you," Lyra said. She looked at Cruz. "There is one thing I'd like to do before I leave tonight."

"Name it," Cruz said.

"I want to take one more look around inside the chamber," she said.

Flagg frowned uneasily. "Sorry, Miss Dore, but no

unauthorized personnel are allowed inside. Access to the interior of the chamber is strictly controlled."

"By Amber Inc.," Cruz said. "As the CEO of the security division, I'm in charge of operations down here. Miss Dore can enter the chamber. I will escort her inside, myself."

"Don't worry," Lyra said, rezzing up another dazzling smile for both men. She was feeling the aftereffects of the highly charged amethyst energy that had been rushing through her moments ago, still feeling reckless. "I'm not going to steal anything."

Cruz gave her a patient look. "I know that."

They waited until the last member of the trapped team had emerged from the chamber and thanked Lyra. Then Cruz waved her inside. He followed, watching her with an unreadable expression.

Another buzz of energy, much lower in volume this time, whispered through her when she walked to the center of the chamber. The interior walls, floor, and ceiling glowed with a muted purple light, just as she remembered. But all of the small relics of carved amethyst amber that had been stacked around the edges of the room were gone.

She turned slowly on her heel, surveying the scene. "What did you do with the stones?"

"They've all been removed and taken to the lab," Cruz said. "Where, as I'm sure you know, we haven't been able to rez a single damn one of them."

"Hence all the nasty phone calls I've been getting from Webber."

"I knew he had tried to contact you," Cruz said. "I wasn't aware that he had been rude. I'll make sure that doesn't happen again."

"Well, it wasn't like I was being polite to him, either," she allowed. "I told you, I never returned any of his calls."

Cruz studied her with an unreadable expression.

"The ability to work unusual forms of amber is rare," he said finally. "We could really use your talent at the lab. You would be well-paid."

"Sorry, no."

He shook his head, amused. "You are one stubborn woman."

"It's the principle of the thing."

"I think it's got more to do with the fact that you're a Dore and I'm a Sweetwater."

"That, too," she admitted.

"You know, we don't have to keep fighting our grandfathers' feud."

"We're not fighting it." She went toward the door. "Your grandfather won, remember?"

"Damn it, Lyra—"

"I'd like to go home now, if you don't mind. It has been a very long night."

"One more thing."

She stopped, turning. "Yes?"

"It isn't just old-fashioned Dore stubbornness that is making you refuse to assist my research staff with the experiments, is it?" Cruz walked toward her. "You know or suspect something very important about this ruin and the artifacts we took out of it. I need to know whatever it is you're keeping secret, Lyra."

"I have no idea what you're talking about."

"Yes," he said, "you do. And eventually you're going to tell me. But it can wait."

She managed another sparkling smile. "You're right. It can wait. Forever."

Chapter 5

THE FIRST LIGHT OF DAWN HAD BARELY BEGUN TO REplace the green glow of the Dead City walls by the time Cruz brought the Slider to a halt in front of the apartment building. He could feel Lyra's exhaustion. Her head was resting against the back of the seat. Her eyes were closed. The psychic lift that came from being underground had faded. So had the exhilaration created by the bio-cocktail that had exploded through her bloodstream when she had worked the exotic amber. He knew the sensation well. Energy was energy, whether it took a normal or paranormal form. Using a lot of it gave you a rush, but later you paid a price.

"You need sleep," he said.

"I know." She opened her eyes and glanced at her watch. "If I go straight to bed, I can get in a couple of hours before my Harmonic Meditation class."

Vincent was perched on the seat above her shoulder. His floppy painter's beret was still on his head. Of the three of them, he was the only one who showed no indications of having been through a long night. Cruz patted the top of the red beret.

"Perky as ever, buddy, aren't you?" he said.

Vincent mumbled cheerfully.

Cruz opened the driver's side door and climbed out. Lyra had her own door open, Vincent tucked under one arm, and was heading for the lobby entrance by the time he got around the front of the car. Stubborn Dore.

She dug out her key. "It's okay," she said, yawning a little. "You don't have to see me upstairs."

"Yes," Cruz said, "I do."

She shrugged. "Whatever. Believe it or not, I'm too tired to argue with you."

"I'll treasure the moment."

They got into the elevator. When the doors slid open on the fourth floor, he followed her down the hall to her apartment. There he waited again while she let herself inside and turned on a light.

Vincent muttered happily and tumbled down to the floor. He headed immediately toward the kitchen. Lyra turned toward Cruz. She gave him a wan smile.

"Thanks for an interesting evening," she said.

She started to step back. He put the toe of his boot just over the threshold, making it impossible to shut the door. From where he stood, he could see the vase of purple orchids.

"I want another chance, Lyra," he said.

She shook her head wearily. "I'll admit I've had a few revenge fantasies over the past three months, but tonight was a reality check. I understand that you need someone who can rez those amethyst stones, but I won't let you seduce me into doing it. Don't worry; I'm sure there are other people out there who can work purple amber. Try placing an ad in the newspapers."

"I'm not talking about the damn rocks in the lab. I'm talking about us. You and me."

She folded her arms and lounged against the doorjamb. "If you'd been serious about a relationship, you wouldn't have waited this long to ask for another chance. To be more specific, you wouldn't have waited until you found out you needed me to reopen that chamber."

"You're the one who threw me out of your life, and then you filed a lawsuit against me. What the hell was I supposed to do?" He paused, searching for the right words. "I figured you needed time."

"Is that so?" She raised her brows. "Tell me, if you hadn't had a crisis down there at the ruin tonight, when, exactly, would you have come back?"

"You probably won't believe this, but I've been planning to call you."

"You're right. I don't believe you."

"Do you really think I'm lying to you?"

"How would I know? You fooled me last time."

"I was conducting a security investigation three months ago. It's called working undercover. You were in danger because you were trying to conceal that ruin. If one of the antiquities gangs had discovered the location of the chamber first, you would have ended up as jungle compost, and you know it."

She exhaled deeply. "I've already said that I understand that, as far as you were concerned, you were just doing your job, fulfilling your responsibilities to your company and your family. But please don't tell me that you were doing it for my own good, okay? When I hear that, I see red."

"It's the truth. Look, we were both keeping secrets from each other back then. We both had our own agendas. You were skirting the law, trying to protect your find. Believe it or not, I was trying to protect you."

"Well, the end result is that we got off on the wrong foot, and now it's too late."

He braced one hand against the wall beside the door. "It doesn't have to be too late. You know, you're overlooking one very critical detail here."

"What's that?"

"We've got something important going on between us, some good energy. You can't deny it."

"It's called physical attraction. I'm told it happens between men and women once in a while. Don't worry, it'll pass."

"No," he said, very sure of his ground now. "It's more than physical attraction, at least on my side."

"Well, I do realize there are all those attractive amethyst artifacts sitting in your lab that you'd like rezzed."

"Forget the rocks. I don't care if you never activate

a single one of them. This is about you and me. What the hell do I have to do to prove that I'm interested only in you, not your talent?"

Something in his voice seemed to catch her off guard. She frowned.

"Good question," she said finally. "Darned if I know. See, that's the thing about getting off on the wrong foot in a relationship the way we did. I'm not sure there's any way to get back on track."

"Let's find out."

He leaned into the doorway a little. She did not step back. He took that as a good sign. She waited for the kiss, brows slightly crinkled, as though awaiting the outcome of a scientific experiment. Dubious of the results but not resisting. She was willing to allow the test, but if he failed, he was doomed.

He wouldn't fail. That option wasn't even on the table. Not for a Sweetwater; not when it came to something this important.

He kissed her slowly, deliberately; a real first date kind of kiss.

She responded cautiously, but she *did* respond. Relief followed by a flash of exultation heated his blood and his senses.

Her mouth softened under his. She put her hands on his shoulders. For a few worrisome seconds he thought she was going to push him away. But he could sense the rising heat of her arousal. Knowing that she still responded to him physically gave him an advantage that he fully intended to exploit. He came from a long line of hunters, after all, although his talents were quite different from those of the para-resonators called ghost hunters who joined the Guilds.

He slid one hand around the exquisitely sensitive, incredibly soft skin at the nape of Lyra's neck and drew his thumb along the delicate line of her jaw. She trembled.

Unlike most people on Harmony whose latent psychic talents were evolving rapidly, thanks to something in the environment, the men of the Sweetwater family traced their abilities back to their ancestors on Earth. He had been born to hunt human prey, not alien energy ghosts. But that was not all his talent allowed him to hunt. Sweetwater men recognized their true mates with the same certainty they recognized their true prey. He had known Lyra for who she was the moment he met her—the woman he had been waiting for all of his life. He was a Sweetwater. He would do whatever he had to do in order to make her his own.

For the moment, his senses told him more clearly than words that she still wanted him, at least physically. He could work with that. The trick was to remain in full control of himself and his passions.

Her fingers sank into the fabric of his shirt, tightening. Without warning, a shuddering thrill whipped through him. Memories of all the long nights he had spent working late or restlessly prowling the empty streets of the Old Quarter in an effort to distract himself from thoughts of Lyra slammed through him.

She was in his arms again. That was all that mattered now.

He had been semi-aroused all night, and now he was consumed with a sense of rising urgency. The kiss was unleashing the full force of his own need. It was all he could do not to push through the door and drag Lyra into the bedroom.

The only thing holding him back was the hunter in him. Strategy was everything.

He felt the hot little shivery chills going through her and took another chance. He deepened the kiss, silently willing her to remember how it had been between them. Energy flashed and spiked in the atmosphere. Their auras sparked invisibly around them, testing, teasing, enticing, challenging. He and Lyra were dancing through a warm, iridescent shower of psychic rain.

He heard a low, urgent groan and realized somewhat vaguely that it had come from his own throat. Probably time to stop. He could not afford to lose it, not at this juncture.

Releasing her was the hardest thing he had ever done. All of his instincts were urging him to seize the opportunity to imprint himself on her forever.

But he managed, somehow, to let her go. He took a step back out into the hall. For a moment she just looked at him, her eyes sultry and a little unfocused with desire. Her lips were full and slightly parted. She blinked a couple of times, and then she was back in command of herself and the situation.

"You always were a really good kisser," she said softly.

He was not sure how to take that, but he could not

afford to be choosy. Any kind of wanting on her part was better than total rejection.

"Will you let me take you out to dinner tonight?" he said. "We'll make it an early evening, since you're not going to get much sleep this morning."

"I'll think about it. I'm too tired to make a decision now. Call me this afternoon."

She closed the door very gently but firmly in his face.

He stood looking at the closed door for a while, wondering if she was setting him up for a refusal later. When he realized he could not decide, he went back downstairs and headed home.

Chapter 6

FOUR HOURS LATER SHE DRESSED FOR HER HARMONIC Meditation class in the uniform that signified her beginner's status: baggy gray trousers and a loose-fitting, wide-sleeved gray shirt secured with a plain gray sash. She was still a little groggy in spite of two large mugs of strong coffee.

When she opened the door of her apartment, she woke up fast. Her own face stared back at her from the front page of the *Herald*. She was not alone in the photo. Vincent was on her shoulder, looking like an adorable ball of badly wrapped yarn in a red beret. Cruz was also in the picture. He looked like he always did, the chief hit man in charge.

"Looks like we're famous, again, Vincent. Just like the old days when we sued Amber Inc."

Vincent made chirpy sounds and peered out of the

partially unzipped gym bag that she used to carry her meditation gear. He showed no interest in the newspaper.

She scanned the headline and read the story with a rising sense of unease.

CRISIS DRAWS NEW AI SECURITY CEO

> An emergency at a recently discovered alien ruin in the underground rain forest brought the new CEO of Amber Inc.'s security division to the scene. Cruz Sweetwater was accompanied by Lyra Dore, who recently dropped a lawsuit she had brought against Amber Inc.
>
> A spokesperson for AI indicated that Miss Dore was an antiquities consultant who catered to an exclusive clientele. He stated that she possessed the unique skills required to rescue five members of a research team who were trapped in the ruin known as the Amethyst Chamber. The precise nature of the problem was described as a "technical malfunction." The team emerged, unharmed.
>
> Mr. Sweetwater and Miss Dore left the scene together, leading observers to question whether Dore's lawsuit had been dropped because the pair was involved in a personal relationship.

"Well, I suppose the speculation was inevitable," Lyra said to Vincent. "There will be a lot more of the same if I'm seen having dinner with Cruz tonight. But, hey, they called me an *antiquities consultant who caters to an exclusive clientele.* That's a step up from three months ago when the press implied that I was a low-end tuner who dabbled in the shady side of the relics trade."

She tossed the newspaper onto the hall table and continued downstairs. A glance at her watch informed her that she was going to have to hurry to get to the morning class on time. Fortunately, Master Quinn's studio was only a few blocks away.

The waking nightmare struck half a block later. Between one step and the next she suddenly found herself in a twisted, horribly distorted version of reality. The familiar street coiled like an infinitely long snake ahead of her, the head vanishing into dark infinity. The old Colonial-era buildings on either side of her loomed, impossibly high and strangely narrowed, over her head. Windows glittered like the eyes of great insects.

"Oh, damn," she whispered. "Not again."

She stopped, afraid to take another step because her sense of balance was almost gone. The world veered and teetered around her. Nausea stirred in her stomach.

And then the monsters began to emerge from the alleys.

She heard Vincent making anxious noises. She looked down and discovered that the gym bag had become the mouth of a strange beast. There was blood in the creature's mouth.

No, not blood. She was looking at Vincent's red beret.

Vincent rumbled again. He wasn't growling at her, she realized. He was trying to get her attention. But at that instant, one of the alley monsters started toward her. It was a strange, shambling, vaguely human thing that looked as though it had just arisen from a grave. Its eye sockets were empty. The skin was gone in several places, exposing bare bone.

I'm hallucinating again, she thought. She knew from experience that she had to stay focused on that one single bit of hard information. *There's nothing real here.*

Vincent made more urgent noises. The red beret bobbed up and down and side to side, making her even more dizzy than she already was. She tightened her grip on the gym bag, but Vincent was no longer inside. Panic slashed across her senses.

"Vincent. Where are you?"

When she realized that he was scuttling up her sleeve, she cried out with relief. He arrived on her shoulder, murmuring anxiously and huddled close. The physical contact steadied her. She dropped the bag and reached up to touch him.

The nightmare dissolved as swiftly as it had coalesced. Just like that, she was out of the dark Alice in Amberland world and back on a normal-looking street. Her pulse was racing, and her palms tingled. She was breathing much too quickly, and she still felt nauseous, but she was no longer hallucinating.

A retired hunter she saw frequently in the neighborhood peered at her with concern. Harvey Wilkens always took a morning walk at this time of day. He no longer looked as if had just arisen from a grave.

"You okay, Miss Dore?" he asked.

"Yes. Yes, I am. Thanks, Harvey. I didn't get much sleep last night. Guess I'm a little jumpy this morning."

Harvey nodded. "Heard how you went down to the jungle to rescue that AI team."

"You saw the morning papers?"

"Nah. I never read the papers. Papers lie. I heard the rumors on the streets."

"Already?"

"There were a couple of hunters trapped in that ruin," Harvey said "Word travels fast in the Guild. Also heard that you and the new CEO of Amber Inc. Security have patched things up. Glad to hear it. Sweetwater is Guild, you know."

She went cold. "No, I didn't know that. I knew that the Sweetwaters maintained close relationships with the Guilds, but I was not aware they were a Guild family."

"Sort of depends on how you define Guild."

"I define it by whether or not some or all of the men in a family are ghost hunters," she said very carefully.

"Yeah, well, it gets complicated when it comes to the Sweetwaters," Harvey said. "But I can tell you this much. There were Sweetwaters fighting side by side with the Guilds back during the Era of Discord."

"Have you ever noticed, Harvey, that the farther away we get from the Era of Discord, the more people claim they had family members present at the various battles?"

"This ain't no made-up family legend, I can tell you that much. Sweetwaters was there."

"So were Dores," she said with a flash of pride.

"Right. I'm just trying to tell you that the Sweetwaters' connection to the Guilds goes back all the way to the founding of the organizations. But that family likes to keep a real low profile. Word is, they've got some unusual talents in that line."

Now, that was interesting, she thought. The Sweetwaters made no secret of the fact that there were a lot of powerful talents in the family. But they were supposedly all amber talents, like hers. Being an amber talent was not considered weird or threatening. It simply meant that you had a highly developed affinity for amber. That ability was useful for discovering and tuning amber but not much else. But if Cruz and his relatives possessed other kinds of paranormal abilities—especially if those abilities were powerful—it would explain why the family had a reputation for secrecy.

It was true that a variety of talents were appearing more and more frequently in the population, but social attitudes toward the paranormal changed more slowly. It was one thing to have a common, socially accepted talent such as the ability to work ghost energy or illusion traps or tune standard amber. It was another thing altogether to possess a rare or dangerous ability. Such talents made others nervous.

Her grandfather had explained the facts of life to her as they applied to those who possessed nonstandard talents. He'd followed the brief lecture with an even briefer piece of advice: "You're one of them, girl. Keep your head down. Let 'em think the only thing you can do is tune amber."

As it turned out, the advice had been of little use. She might be a very strong talent, but tuning amber and prospecting had proved to be the only practical application of that ability. At least, it had been the only application until she had found the amethyst chamber.

"Is that so?" she said politely.

"Yes, ma'am, lot of stories about Sweetwaters," Harvey said with a knowing air.

"Really? I was under the impression that the only talent the Sweetwaters possessed was an affinity for amber. That's not so unusual."

Harvey gave her a conspiratorial wink. "Right you are, Miss Dore. Just an affinity for amber. Nothing unusual about Cruz Sweetwater or anyone else in that family. No, siree. Absolutely not. Don't you worry, I know how to keep a secret. I'm a Guild man, after all."

"I think we've got something of a misunderstanding here," she said.

"Don't worry, I can take a hint. I won't say a word about the Sweetwaters to anyone else. The only reason I mentioned their talents is because I figure you already know all about 'em, what with you and Cruz Sweetwater being so close and all." Harvey chuckled and gave Vincent a friendly pat. "You and the little varmint have a good day now. See you later."

"Bye, Harvey."

Harvey moved off briskly. She watched him until he turned the corner at the end of the block. When he was gone, she went warily on her way, every muscle and nerve tensed in case the sidewalk started to twist and heave beneath her feet again.

To date, she had never had more than one of the hallucinatory nightmares in a twenty-four-hour period, but there was no way to know when that pattern might change. The lawsuit had taken her bank account so low that she could no longer afford flash-rock tune-ups and routine maintenance for her car. But even if she had been able to drive, she would not have dared to get behind the wheel for fear that one of the dreams would strike.

"They're affecting my quality of life, Vincent," she said. "I think that's when you're supposed to get help. But how can I explain the dreams to a para-shrink? Any decent doctor will assume I'm suffering psychotic episodes and blame it on some kind of psi trauma. Then I'd have to explain that my senses aren't entirely normal to begin with, and it will be all downhill from there."

Vincent mumbled encouragingly.

"Thanks, pal. I knew you'd understand."

Two blocks later she halted in front of the Hole in the Wall, a small restaurant that occupied the ground floor of the building that housed the Harmonic Meditation Institute. She pushed open the door and was greeted with the fragrance of warm muffins and strong coffee.

"Good morning, everyone," she said.

There was a round of "Hey, there, you made the morning papers," and "What's up with you and Sweetwater?" and "You two back together?" from the regulars.

The early crowd in the Hole was a mix of small-time,

independent tunnel and jungle treasure hunters and local shopkeepers who catered to the low end of the alien relics trade. They had welcomed Lyra into their midst three years earlier right after she had moved into the neighborhood and fired up Dore Tuning & Consulting.

"For the record, there is nothing between Cruz Sweetwater and me except a little business," Lyra said firmly. "One of his teams got into trouble at my ruin last night, and he had to come to me to get them out of the trap."

Someone snorted. "Hope you made Amber Inc. pay big-time."

"I intend to," Lyra said.

"The papers implied that you and Cruz Sweetwater are an item again," Josie Taylor, the proprietor of Taylor's Relics, said.

"Don't believe everything you read in the papers." Lyra glanced at her watch and then smiled at the grizzled cook. "I'm on my way upstairs to class. Okay if I leave Vincent down here with you as usual, Adele?"

"You bet." Adele waved her spatula. "I've got a muffin with his name on it."

Vincent chortled with his customary enthusiasm. After three years, he knew the routine. He fluttered down from Lyra's shoulder, drifted across the floor, and tumbled up onto one of the vacant stools. Ben Symmington, owner of Symmington's Colonial Collectibles, was seated on the neighboring stool. He grinned.

"Howdy, little guy," he said. He patted the top of Vincent's beret and then looked at Lyra. "You two are running late this morning."

"We didn't get back from underground until nearly four," Lyra explained. She patted away a yawn. "Adele, just put Vincent's muffin on my tab. See you in an hour."

"I'll have your coffee ready," Adele promised.

Lyra smiled. "Now, Addy, you know I'm not supposed to drink coffee after my meditation class. Master Quinn says that caffeine is bad for the senses."

Adele made a face. "It's what keeps mine working."

"Mine, too," Lyra admitted. "Later, all."

She went out the front door, turned right, and entered the main lobby of the building. A flight of stairs led to the floor where the Institute's headquarters was located. When she walked through the door of the studio a short time later, she saw immediately that she was the last one to arrive. The other fourteen students, already seated cross-legged on their mats, turned to look at her with reproachful gazes.

"Sorry I'm late," she said, embarrassed. Students were expected to be on time. Coming into class late was a sign of a lack of harmonic balance.

Master Quinn, seated on a mat at the front of the room, nodded solemnly. His head was shaved, a style that emphasized his ascetic features and deep, insightful eyes. He wore long, flowing amber robes and several strands of amber beads. Lyra thought that he was probably in his late thirties or early forties.

"Welcome, Lyra," he said in his calm, serene tones.

"Good morning, Master Quinn," she said.

She gave him a formal, if somewhat perfunctory, bow

and then quickly pulled her mat out of the gym bag and sat down.

"Let us begin," Quinn said. "Breathe deeply. Open your inner window and listen to your senses. Find the harmonic balance within."

Lyra closed her eyes and concentrated intently on following the instructions. Unfortunately, she had been unable to get the knack of meditating. Sadly, the harder she tried to sink into the tranquil mental state that the other students achieved so easily, the more difficult the process became.

An unpleasant restlessness descended on her in class, making her edgy instead of calm. She found herself consciously trying to suppress the sensation. Master Quinn had urged her to stop fighting the agitation, explaining that the key to harmonic balance was to let go of the illusion of control. But that, she had learned, was easier said than done.

"Pay attention to the whispers of your senses," Master Quinn intoned. "All the answers are there, within you . . ."

Chapter 7

CRUZ CAME AWAKE WITH A JOLT OF ENERGY THAT HAD become all too familiar in recent weeks. His senses slammed into full throttle, leaving him feeling unpleasantly overstimulated; a hunter ready to go for the throat but no target in view.

The sudden blasts of urgency had become more frequent, occurring unpredictably. They were accompanied by fragments of images that he could not make out clearly. He got only a vague impression of towering canyons formed by strangely warped structures and buildings. Along with the glimpses of the nightmarish cityscape came a sense that Lyra was in danger. But the shards of the vision always disappeared as inexplicably as they had come.

The first couple of times he'd had the experience, he'd sent his young cousin Jeff, an agent from AI Security, to check up, very discreetly, on Lyra. He knew she would be furious if she thought he had spied on her during the past three months. But he'd had to be sure that she was all right. Jeff had reported that she was fine and going about her usual routine. He had found no evidence that she was in any danger. She was not even dating. She had appeared fully preoccupied with her work as a tuner and her lawsuit against Amber Inc.

Cruz had taken a few crumbs of comfort from the knowledge that she wasn't seeing another man.

After a few more of the disturbing episodes, he had, for a time, questioned his own psychic mental health. He'd done some research. He and his two brothers were the latest in a long line of unusual talents. For generations, those abilities had brought the family considerable wealth.

But the inheritance had a very dark side. The family talents were strong, but his very pragmatic ancestors had concluded that there was only one truly profitable application for those unique abilities. The result was that for several hundred years his ancestors had made their livings in ways that did not always look good in the light of day. There was no getting around the fact that the family tree was populated with a lot of professional assassins, hit men, contract killers, and mercenaries.

True, Sweetwaters had always taken pride in taking contracts from what they believed to be the right side. They considered themselves the good guys. But when you hunted and killed for money, what did that make you? And what did it do to the individual psyches of the members of a family that had engaged in such a business for a few hundred years, ever since the late 1880s, Old Earth time?

But those days were over, he reminded himself. Mostly. Fifty years ago his grandfather had put an end to what had been the family business for generations. Big Jake Sweetwater had set the clan on a new course. More or less.

Of course, some things never changed.

In the end, however, he had concluded that the disturbing dreams were simply a result of the psychic bond he shared with Lyra. The hunter in him was prowling his unconscious mind, frustrated because he had not been able to claim his mate.

Soon, he thought. *Not much longer.*

The phone rezzed. He sat up on the edge of the bed and looked at the number on the tiny screen. Speak of the devil. A call from his grandfather was never a great way to start a day. He picked up the phone.

"Good morning, sir."

"Did you have to use Lyra Dore to get that team out last night?" Jake Sweetwater growled.

The lack of a "Good morning" or "Did I wake you?" was classic Big Jake Sweetwater style. He had little patience for the routine pleasantries unless it suited him to use them for some reason of his own. On those occasions when he did resort to politeness or diplomacy, smart people headed for the door. Affability was a sure indication that Jake was up to no good. The only person who could exercise some measure of control over him was his wife, Madeline.

"No one we've got on staff could de-rez that chamber entrance," Cruz said patiently.

"Yeah, the papers made that damn clear. The press is having a field day with this. For the past three months Lyra Dore has tried to make the company look bad in the media. She portrayed AI as a big, bad specter-cat that likes to gobble up innocent little independent prospectors for lunch. Now she shows us up as complete idiots because we had to call her in to open the ruin."

"That is one possible interpretation."

"It's sure as hell the interpretation that's all over the news. And what's this about the two of you being involved in a romantic relationship? Where did the reporters get that idea?"

"You know the press," Cruz said. "Always looking for an angle."

"How much did you pay Lyra Dore for de-rezzing the chamber, anyway?"

"We haven't discussed the matter of her fee yet. There wasn't time last night. She agreed to help as soon as I told her that there were five people trapped inside the chamber. After that, things got busy."

"Hah. She's a Dore. She'll find some way to turn this to her advantage. Probably hold us up for a fortune, and we'll have to pay, because if we don't, AI will look like the evil corporate empire she wants everyone to believe it is."

"I'll let you know the price tag. By the way, there's something you might want to consider here, sir."

"What's that?" Jake demanded.

"We still need her expertise in the lab. Nothing has changed since last night. Webber hasn't been able to find anyone else who can tune amethyst, let alone rez those relics."

"Damn." Jake was silent for a moment. "Well, hell, maybe those stones are just pretty little alien sculptures after all, like Lyra Dore claimed."

"Got a hunch that the ones that we found in the ruin may be nothing more than attractive works of art," Cruz agreed.

There was a short silence while Jake digested that. "You think she held out on us? Stashed some of the stones?"

"What would you have done if you had been in her situation with a big company moving in to take over your discovery?"

Jake snorted. "Hell, I'd have picked out some of the most important pieces and tucked them away someplace safe where I was sure no one would ever find them. Then I'd bide my time until the heat died down and move them on the underground collectors' market."

"That same thought crossed my mind, too."

"Green hell. Should have figured she'd try something like that. She's a Dore. Chip of amber straight off the old block. If she'd had a lick of common sense, she would have taken the cash we offered. That's what any reasonable person would have done."

"I don't think Lyra was feeling reasonable three months ago when we moved in on the ruin."

"What caused the chamber entrance to close?" Jake asked.

"We don't know. Lyra said it was probably some stray currents from a nearby psi river or storm. The only other possibility, according to her, is that someone deliberately closed the entrance by working silver, diamond, or amethyst amber."

"You said there was no indication of any rivers or storms in the area."

"Right."

"Well, we know we don't have anyone on staff who can work amethyst. If we did, you wouldn't have had to pull in Lyra Dore." Jake paused. "Anyone on that team who could work silver or diamond?"

"No. After I got back to the surface I checked the para-psych profiles of everyone involved last night. I looked at the files of the two Guild men, as well. None of them could rez any of those three varieties of rock. And even if it did turn out that one of them had kept his or her talent a secret, there's no obvious motive for trying to murder five people."

"We sure as hell know one person who could have closed that entrance, don't we? And she had a motive. Revenge. Where was Lyra Dore when the chamber locked up?"

"I don't know," Cruz admitted. "But it doesn't matter. She didn't sabotage the ruin."

"Maybe she figured out how to set some kind of time-delayed trap before she turned over control of the chamber," Jake mused.

"No," Cruz said. "Lyra is pissed at AI, but she would

never have put lives at risk for the sake of a little vengeance."

"What makes you so sure of that?"

"You know why I'm sure."

Jake exhaled heavily. "Face it, you were wrong about her. She's not the right woman for you."

"Yes," Cruz said quietly, "she is."

"Damn it, if she were the right woman, you wouldn't be in this situation. She's playing you."

"Things got complicated three months ago. My fault. She doesn't trust me now. I need to change that."

"What you need to do is your job. Find out what she's hiding from us."

Jake ended the connection.

Cruz looked at the dead phone in his hand. "Hate to tell you this, Big Jake, but I've got other priorities."

Chapter 8

"FORGIVE ME FOR SPEAKING OF PERSONAL MATTERS, Lyra." Master Quinn smiled his gentle smile. "I cannot help but notice that you seem increasingly uncentered lately. I sense that something is making it difficult for you to find the harmonic balance within."

The last of the meditation students was leaving the studio. Lyra finished rolling up her mat and stuffed it into her gym bag.

"I know I haven't been a great student," she said. "I can't seem to concentrate properly. Things have been somewhat hectic lately."

Quinn nodded somberly. "I saw the morning papers. The head of Amber Inc. Security asked you to assist in a rescue mission at the ruin that you discovered a few months ago. I'm surprised you agreed to help."

"Not like I had much choice." She crouched to zip up

the bag. "There were several people trapped inside. Amber Inc. didn't have anyone else available who could derez the entrance."

"I understand. It was a generous and charitable action on your part. But I suspect that now that AI knows that you are the only one they can call on to work that amethyst amber, they will request more and more assistance from you."

"They can ask, but my answer will be no."

"I hope for your sake that you will find the strength to refuse."

The concern in his quiet voice startled her. She rose slowly to her feet.

"Why do you say that?"

He did not respond immediately. Instead, he watched her for a long moment. She wondered uneasily what he saw.

"I hesitate to say anything more," he said finally. "It is not my place. My job is to provide guidance to you as you seek balance and harmony in your life. But you are my student, and I have a responsibility toward you. I feel I must warn you."

A chill swept through her not unlike the sensation she got when one of the nightmares struck. She gripped the handle of the gym bag tightly.

"If you intend to warn me not to get any more involved with Amber Inc., don't worry," she said. "I realize that would be asking for trouble."

"It is not just your renewed association with Cruz Sweetwater and his family firm that makes me uneasy."

Quinn walked to the high windows on one wall of the studio. He clasped his hands behind his back and contemplated the view of the Dead City wall. "It is the escalating energy of disharmony I perceive in your aura that worries me. Once again I apologize for intruding, but are you feeling well, Lyra?"

She was afraid to breathe. If Quinn could sense that something was happening to her, something that affected her mind and her perception of reality, maybe she had an even bigger problem than she thought. But damned if she would admit it to anyone, including Quinn. At least, not yet. There was still a possibility that she was just suffering from stress. *Also an excellent possibility that I'm in complete denial,* she thought.

But she could not get past the fact that, except for those harrowing moments when the nightmares enveloped her, she felt normal. Well, as normal as she ever had. Of course, crazy people usually thought they were normal, too. *Take Grandpa, for instance,* she thought sadly.

Arthur Dore had spent his last years obsessed with finding various and assorted legendary lost amber claims. He had spent all of his money on phony treasure maps and fake journals purporting to contain the secret locations of fabled mines of rare and exotic amber. In the end he had died penniless. She had been the only one at his bedside. She'd had to dig into her own small savings account to pay for the funeral.

Her grandfather had been a gruff, disappointed, unhappy man, but in his own way, he had loved her. And he had taught her a few things, one of which was the importance of keeping her secrets.

"I'm all right, Master Quinn," she said politely. "I appreciate your concern, but I'm in excellent health. Really."

"I was not referring to your physical health." Quinn did not take his eyes off the emerald towers. "It is the state of your psychic well-being that worries me. I can see that you do not wish to discuss it, and that is most certainly your prerogative. But I sense that whatever is going on within you is linked to your talent. The harmonic imbalance in your aura this morning is worse than usual."

"Please don't worry about me, sir."

"Have you considered the possibility that working that amethyst amber last night might have exacerbated the problem?"

"I don't have a problem," she said briskly. "I'm just a little tired and stressed out. Got home late. Didn't get enough sleep. Didn't have time for breakfast. What with one thing and another, I probably am out of whack this morning, harmonically speaking. Nothing another cup of strong coffee can't fix."

He turned back to her, his expression serene, as always. He smiled his wise smile again. "You owe me no explanations or apologies. I have said enough. You are entitled to your privacy. I will merely add that if you ever decide that you need some guidance of a more private nature than what I can offer in a group class, I hope you will feel that you can come to me."

The hair lifted on the nape of her neck.

"Uh, thank you," she said.

Good grief. Was Master Quinn suggesting what she thought he was suggesting? Was he coming on to her?

No, of course not. It was just her imagination. He was a Harmonic Meditation guru, for goodness' sake.

That was the problem with having once been burned by a Sweetwater. You started seeing every man as a potential fire hazard.

Clutching the gym bag, she hurried out the door and down the stairs.

Chapter 9

AN HOUR LATER, DRESSED FOR WORK, VINCENT PERCHED on her shoulder, Lyra kicked the back door of the Halifax Gallery three times with the toe of her black business pump. Knocking was out of the question, because it took both hands to hold on to the package she was carrying.

Nancy opened the door immediately and leaned out to look both ways, checking to see that the alley was empty. Satisfied, she smiled at the sight of Lyra clutching the blanket-wrapped object.

"Oh, good," she said. "It's a big one this time."

"You told me you wanted them larger."

"Size matters to my clients."

"Give me a hand," Lyra said. "This thing is heavy."

"Right. I'll take this end." Nancy moved out onto the bottom step and grasped one side of the package. "Ugh.

You're right, it weighs a ton. I can't believe you carried it six blocks."

"Through back alleys, no less."

"Why didn't you just put it into your car and drive it over here?"

"You know I'm trying to walk more these days."

"Yes, but this is ridiculous." Nancy angled the package through the door. "By the way, I assume you know you're on the front page of both the *Herald* and the *Current* today? Also on the morning rez-screen news?"

"Just like old times. At least Vincent looked adorable."

They got the package inside the back room. Vincent hopped down from Lyra's shoulder and scurried to the top of the small refrigerator, where Nancy kept a plate of cookies for him.

"So that was the real reason Cruz Sweetwater showed up at the reception last night?" Nancy studied Lyra closely. "He needed you to rescue that team?"

"Yes, but he claimed that was just unfortunate timing. He said he was planning to call me, anyway, because he wants another chance." Lyra winced. "What are the odds?"

"I knew it." Nancy lit up with excitement. "I told you he'd be back one of these days. You said yourself that from his point of view he was just doing his job three months ago. You have to admit you were in danger. Those antiquities gangs are utterly ruthless. If one of them had found out about that ruin, you would have been jungle plant food by now."

"Thanks for that visual."

"I gotta tell you, I was scared to death that whole time you were trying to move those relics on the underground market. It was sort of a relief when your first client turned out to be an undercover agent from Amber Inc. Security. So where do things stand now?"

"He asked me out to dinner tonight."

"You said yes, I hope?"

"I'm thinking about it," Lyra said.

"Oh, that's real decisive. Don't be an idiot. Where's the harm in a dinner date? If nothing else, you'll get a free meal out of the deal, and it will probably be a very, very expensive meal. It's not much in the way of payback, but it's better than nothing."

"There is that. But it turns out the AI lab still hasn't been able to locate anyone who can rez amethyst amber."

Nancy's enthusiasm faded. "In other words, you think Cruz Sweetwater may have ulterior motives for asking you out to dinner?"

"I'd say that's a distinct possibility, yes."

"Damn." Nancy wrinkled her nose. "And here I was thinking that we were going to be looking at a happy ending after all."

"Don't hold your breath."

They lowered the package onto the wooden surface of a wide workbench.

"I still say you should have dinner with the guy," Nancy said. "Give him a chance. At the very least, being seen with him will be good for your career."

"Hmm. Hadn't considered that angle."

"Are you kidding?" Nancy grinned. "You're already famous again this morning, thanks to Cruz. Didn't you read any of the stories in the papers?" She nodded toward the copy of the *Herald* lying on a nearby table. "They called you a private antiquities consultant who caters to an exclusive clientele."

"I noticed. Twelve weeks ago I was just a shady amber tuner, as far as the press was concerned."

"You've been upgraded," Nancy said. "Of course, they also implied that the reason you dropped the lawsuit was because you're having a secret affair with Sweetwater."

"Those rumors will only get worse if I go out to dinner with him."

"So what? Beats sitting at home every night the way you've been doing."

"Maybe."

Lyra undid the ties that secured the wrappings and pulled the old blanket aside. Nancy studied the painting, hands on her hips. She smiled slowly.

"What do you think?" Lyra asked.

"I think it's another Chimera original, and it will sell in a minute. Mr. Anonymous will snatch it up instantly, just like he did the others, if I give him the opportunity. But you know, I'm starting to think it might be time to go for an auction."

"I'm not so sure," Lyra said. "An auction will attract the press."

"There are already rumors about the mysterious Chimera circulating in the art world. It's great PR."

"Yes, but too much attention could ruin us. You told me that critic at the *Herald* has been pestering you recently for details on the new artist in your gallery. What if he decides to do some investigating?"

"I can handle him," Nancy said confidently.

"Hmm."

Vincent bounced up onto the end of the workbench, a cookie in one paw. He munched enthusiastically, showing no interest in the painting.

They both looked at him. Lyra noticed that the jaunty red beret was sitting at a precarious angle. She leaned forward to adjust the clip that kept the little red cap in place.

"Come on," Nancy coaxed. "What's one more little art auction at a small gallery? It won't even cause a ripple."

"You know as well as I do that if word gets out that Chimera is actually a dust bunny, the bottom would drop out of his market overnight," Lyra said. "Mr. Anonymous would want all of his money refunded. Worse yet, he'd probably sue both of us. Not only would we both be ruined financially, our reputations would be shot."

"Okay, okay, we'll make it a very *private* auction. Only the most exclusive and discerning connoisseurs of modern art will be invited. And Mr. Anonymous, of course. We'll keep it very hush-hush. The collectors will love it. The bidding will go crazy. We'll get rich."

"Well—"

"This is our chance to make some really big money, Lyra. Time to go for the amber ring, my friend. Why the hesitation? This isn't like you. Where's that gutsy Dore spirit? Is this the woman who tried to sue Amber Inc.?"

"This is the woman who is knee-deep in debt because she tried to sue Amber Inc.," Lyra said dryly. "But when you're right, you're right. This is a golden opportunity. Let's do it." She paused, glancing at the copy of the *Herald*. "I can't believe they called me an antiquities consultant instead of a tuner."

"An antiquities consultant with an exclusive clientele. They made it sound as though Cruz Sweetwater, himself, was one of your clients."

"Wonder where the press got that idea?"

"Something tells me it came straight from the Amber Inc. publicity department," Nancy said. "And that means they got it from Cruz Sweetwater. His way of trying to make amends, I'll bet. In the art and antiquities world, you can't buy publicity like that. He did you a huge favor. It was a very romantic thing to do, if you ask me."

Lyra exhaled slowly, thinking about it. "You know, you're right. Dinner with Cruz Sweetwater might be good for my career."

"That's it. Tell yourself you're dating him because the publicity will be good for business."

Chapter 10

HER PHONE RANG JUST AS SHE OPENED THE BACK ROOM of her shop.

"Dore Tuning and Consulting," she said, hitting the lights. She watched Vincent scamper across the room to where she kept a locked box of rez-brush paints and a canvas to entertain him during the long workdays.

"Miss Dore, please."

The voice was male, smooth, authoritative, with just the right amount of upper-class power vibe. Not one of her regulars.

"Speaking," she said.

"This is Wilson Revere. I understand you're something of an expert on rare ambers."

She froze, excitement pulsing through her. It was, of course, entirely possible that there was more than one Wilson Revere in Frequency City. But how many of them would be interested in a tuner who could handle rare ambers?

She cleared her throat and tried to assume an assured tone. "Would this be Wilson Revere of the RezStone corporation?"

He laughed. "One and the same. Sorry, I should have done a better job of introducing myself. Call me Wilson."

"What can I do for you, uh, Wilson?"

"There's an auction at the Fairstead Gallery tomorrow afternoon. I understand that there will be some interesting raw stones of rare amber up for sale. One of the specimens is amethyst. The consultant I usually employ for this sort of thing has no experience with that particular variety. I'd like you to attend the preview with me and give me your opinion before I bid. Are you free?"

She gripped the phone tighter. It was all she could do to maintain her cool, professional voice. "Let me check my appointment book."

"Certainly."

She forced herself to let a few seconds pass before she spoke to him again.

"Yes, Mr. Revere, it appears I'm free tomorrow afternoon. I'll meet you at the Fairstead Gallery."

"That will be fine. And, remember, it's Wilson."

"Right. Wilson."

"Thank you, Miss Dore. I'll look forward to meeting you in person tomorrow."

He ended the connection.

Lyra looked at Vincent, who was perched on top of the rez-brush paint box, waiting for her to open it.

"I don't think we'll mention the name of my new client to Cruz," she said. "I get the feeling there's some bad blood between the Reveres and the Sweetwaters. Remember the tuner's motto: 'What happens in a tuner's shop stays in a tuner's shop.' "

Chapter 11

"I'M HAVING DINNER WITH YOU TONIGHT BECAUSE Nancy and I decided that being seen with you may be good for the antiquities consulting side of my business," Lyra said. "Especially given the articles in today's papers."

Cruz looked at her across the width of the small, intimate booth. "I appreciate the honesty."

"Sure. Anytime. I take it that informing the media that I'm an exclusive antiquities consultant with an exclusive clientele was your idea?"

"Figured it was the least I could do."

"Well, thanks for that."

Cruz's eyes gleamed with amusement. "Does that mean we're even?"

"No."

The small restaurant was not only one of the most

expensive in the city, it was considered to be among the best by people who cared a lot about fine dining. Lyra tried not to appear impressed, but it was hard to fake a blasé attitude when you were sitting in one of the most exclusive restaurants in town, and your dinner partner was one of the most powerful men in the city.

The Emerald Bistro was located in the heart of a recently gentrified section of the Quarter. It was an elegant, discreetly lit enclave where the wealthy and the powerful could dine in a relaxed atmosphere among their own kind. The service was exquisite, the exotic cuisine was served in itty-bitty portions, and the wines on the leather-clad list started at a price that was well above her entire weekly food budget.

She and Cruz had been the subject of a number of veiled glances when they had arrived. But the staff and the other diners were giving the impression that her presence here tonight with one of the men of Amber Inc. was no big deal.

Cruz picked up his wineglass. "You look incredible this evening."

"Thank you."

She had gone with her standard gallery reception look, a sleek little black dress, high-heeled evening sandals, a pair of amber earrings, and her charm bracelet.

Cruz was once again in hit man black, but tonight he wore a more casual version of the look, a slouchy linen jacket, snug black trousers, and a black crewneck pullover.

"What are we going to talk about?" she asked.

"My second chance?"

"I haven't made a decision yet. At the moment, I'm not looking beyond dinner."

Cruz smiled. "Guess I'd better hope dinner goes well."

Little thrills chased down her spine. The edgy, reckless awareness was back again tonight. She knew the sensation had nothing to do with the ambient psi in the neighborhood. This was all about Cruz, she thought.

"I think we need to find a neutral subject," she said.

"You and I don't do neutral. Tell me about your grandfather."

Startled, she narrowed her eyes. "Why do you want to know about him?"

"I've got the other side of the story from my grandfather. I'm curious about the Dore version of events."

"The Dore version is the correct one, of course."

He looked amused. "Is that so?"

"Your grandfather stole my grandfather's amber claim in a crooked game of poker."

"My grandfather swears that he did not cheat. He won the deed to the Radiance Springs mine fair and square."

"Hah. Well, he would say that, wouldn't he? Not many people would admit that they came by something as valuable as that amber claim dishonestly."

"My grandfather also says that there was a woman involved," Cruz added.

She sat back in the booth. "I never heard that. Who was she?"

"My grandmother. According to the Sweetwater edition of the story, our grandfathers both pursued her. She chose Jake Sweetwater. Arthur Dore did not take that well. That's when he got drunk and challenged my grandfather to the poker game. It's hard enough to play a decent game of poker when you're sober, let alone when you're three sheets to the wind."

"But knowing that his opponent was drunk didn't stop Big Jake Sweetwater from accepting the challenge, did it?"

"I'm not going to make excuses for him. Big Jake can look after himself. But I do know that things were rough out on the frontier fifty years ago. There was no room for screwing up, and that's what your grandfather did."

She winced. "I seem to be following in his footsteps."

"What the hell does that mean?"

"First, I lost what will probably be the most important discovery of my career to a Sweetwater, and then I spent way too much money trying to sue your company in an obviously futile attempt to get some revenge."

Cruz drank a little wine and lowered the glass. "Sometimes you have to know when to walk away from the table."

"Clearly you Sweetwaters are lucky when it comes to gambling."

"Something else you should remember," Cruz said.

"What's that?"

"We're lucky in love, as well."

She went cold. "How nice for you."

"Actually, it's not an issue of luck for us Sweetwaters. More like an instinct."

She widened her eyes. "Wow. An instinct for sex.

Imagine Mother Nature coming up with something that clever. Who knew?"

"I didn't say the instinct was for sex. Sex is different."

"Oh, really? The members of your family aren't interested in sex?"

Laughter lit his eyes. "You're enjoying this, aren't you?"

"Well, I suppose it does explain why we never made it into the bedroom."

Heat replaced the amusement in his eyes. "That worried you?"

She shrugged. "I'll admit it made me a little curious at the time. But afterward I realized that what was going on between us was just a job as far as you were concerned."

"Think so?"

"You got what you wanted with a few kisses and some sweet talk. There was no need to take advantage of the situation. In your own way, you're an ethical man, Cruz Sweetwater. You live by a code. I can respect that." She gave him a cool smile. "Just doesn't happen to be my code."

"It started out as a job, but that's not how it went down. In the end, I figured you would forgive a few kisses. I wasn't so sure that you would be able to forgive me if I took you to bed and then took control of the ruin."

She swirled the wine in her glass. "It mattered to you whether or not I forgave you?"

"Sure."

"Why?"

"I told you, the men in my family have an instinct for knowing the right woman when she comes along," he said. "You're the one for me."

She raised her brows. "Do you get lucky with that line a lot?"

He did not return her smile. "Thought I explained; it's not really luck. It's an aspect of our talent."

"You've got a talent for seduction, too? That must come in handy."

"You know I'm not talking about seduction. I'm talking about the ability to sense a bond like the one that exists between you and me."

"You're telling me you're psychic in that way? Gee, that's a new one."

He exhaled slowly. "Maybe we should talk about something else."

"Why? This is an interesting topic. We're just getting into it."

"True, but I can see that the subject has certain pitfalls."

He was getting impatient, she realized. Maybe even a little irritated. She could tell it bothered him to know that he was not in complete control of the situation tonight. The poor man was probably not accustomed to having someone bait him the way she was doing.

A lot of people would no doubt say that poking a Sweetwater with a sharp stick was unwise. But it gave her some satisfaction to know that she was rezzing a few of Cruz's hot buttons tonight. Besides, Dores had never been known for their common sense, just as they had never been known for their good luck. She had a family tradition to uphold.

"As far as everyone knows, the men of Amber Inc. are all amber talents of one kind or another," she said. "Are you telling me this psychic power that runs in your family is connected to your affinity for amber? Because let's get real here. I'm an amber talent, too, remember? So was my grandfather. And I'm here to tell you we didn't get the good luck thing."

"It has nothing to do with the ability to rez amber. The family records show that our ancestors on earth possessed similar abilities."

"And just what kind of talent do you have, Mr. Sweetwater?"

"I think we should change the subject again."

She shrugged. "Go for it. What would you like to talk about? The weather?"

"You're going to make this as difficult as possible, aren't you?"

She gave him her most dazzling smile. "I'm certainly going to try."

Chapter 12

IT HAD RAINED WHILE THEY WERE IN THE RESTAURANT. By the time Lyra walked out into the night with Cruz, the Quarter was more luminous than usual. The sheen of moisture on the streets reflected the psi green glow of the Dead City. A light fog infused with the deep peridot light of the great wall was coalescing quickly. All around them the senses-stirring, intoxicating currents of energy pulsed and resonated. Lyra knew that a lot of the hot psi was being generated between herself and Cruz.

Careful, she thought. *This is how it was when we were seeing each other, and it did not end well.*

Cruz got her into the front seat of the Slider. There was something both protective and proprietary about the way he did it, as if she were an extremely valuable possession. She was a long way from trusting him, but she had to admit that, deep down, she was responding to the careful, attentive way he was treating her.

He opened the driver's side door of the vehicle and got in beside her. Just sitting this close to him within the dark, intimate confines of the car's front seat was an exhilarating experience.

He rezzed the engine. The car glided away from the curb. He drove into the maze of twisted streets near the wall, as usual, never hesitating at any of the intersections.

"How do you do that?" she asked impulsively.

"Do what?"

"Find your way around this part of town without ever making a wrong turn?"

"Never thought about it. Comes naturally."

She smiled. "So now you've got a psychic sense of direction, too?"

"It's not a separate ability," he said seriously. "It's all part of the Sweetwater talent."

"Just what is this strange ability the Sweetwaters possess?"

"Someday I'll tell you all about it."

"But not tonight."

"No. Not tonight."

"Deep, dark family secret?" she asked, amused.

"Yes."

The seriousness in his tone stopped her cold. It also heightened her curiosity.

"So when will you tell me about this weird talent?"

"When you know for sure that you and I are meant to be together."

"What if that never happens?"

"It will happen." He turned another corner. "But enough about me. Let's talk about you."

"What do you want to know?"

"One thing you never told me," he said.

"There are a lot of things I never told you."

"I don't doubt that. But the one that interests me tonight is how you found that amethyst ruin in the first place."

"Ah, yes. The ruin. I thought we'd get back to that sooner or later."

She could not be certain in the darkness, but she was pretty sure she saw his powerful hands tighten a little on the wheel. Green psi light glinted ominously on the black stone in his ring. She could have sworn she felt energy spike in the atmosphere. When he spoke, however, Cruz's voice was perfectly controlled.

"My family has been in the amber business for fifty years. We've got the best collection of raw specimen stones and amber antiquities in the four city-states housed in our private vault. Our research is cutting-edge. But until you discovered that ruin and the stones inside, everyone figured amethyst was just so much pretty purple rock with no practical use other than in jewelry making."

"Obviously the aliens considered it valuable," she said lightly.

"Yes," he said. "And that fact changes everything. It means that the potential of latent energy in amethyst has to be reevaluated. So, how did you find the ruin?"

"You can't expect a Dore to spill all of her secrets to a Sweetwater."

"The underground jungle has been open to exploration and prospecting for barely a year. Most of it hasn't even been mapped. Yet you walked in one day all by yourself and made an incredible discovery."

"Sometimes even a Dore gets lucky."

"My gut tells me that luck was not all that was involved."

She drummed her fingers on the car seat. "You really want to know how I found that ruin? I'll tell you. Vincent led me to it."

He shot her a quick, searching glance. "Are you serious?"

"Dead serious. I think he somehow sensed that I could work amethyst amber. In his little bunny brain, he probably figured that the ruin and the stones would make pretty toys for me. Dust bunnies are big on toys and games."

"You opened your own gate. How did you manage that?"

She moved one hand slightly. "Turns out those of us who can work amethyst are good at opening jungle gates." She paused a beat before adding, "Guess you could say it's an aspect of our talent. Not quite as interesting as the Sweetwater instinct for sex, of course, nevertheless—"

"When did you find out that you could resonate with amethyst?" he asked.

"When I was fourteen. My grandfather had a small sample of it. He thought it was just a pretty specimen. But one day he let me hold it, and we both realized that I could work it the way other people work standard amber.

Trouble was, there didn't seem to be any practical application."

"Until you found the chamber and the relics inside."

"Yes."

"What's your theory about the artifacts that you found in the ruin?"

"Believe it or not, I already told you the truth. I really do think that those stones are nothing more than some kind of alien psi art. When I tune them to an individual, the way I did that one for you, the person can experience the art with his or her paranormal senses. But that's it. There's no big secret to discover in your lab."

He was silent for a while.

"Okay," he said. This time his voice was a little too neutral.

She stilled. "Okay?"

"You're not ready to trust me. I can handle that. For now."

Oh, damn. He knows. No, more likely he had made a calculated guess. Either way, he suspected her of holding out on him.

"Look, Cruz, I'm telling you—"

"Time to change the subject again."

"We seem to be doing that a lot tonight."

"Yes," he said. "We do."

He brought the car to a halt in front of her apartment building. This time she waited in her seat until he came around to the passenger side to open the door. She needed the few seconds alone to think about what had just gone down between them. There could no longer be any doubt.

Cruz not only wanted her cooperation at the lab, he was certain that she had concealed some of the artifacts that she had found in the ruin. So much for Nancy's romantic imaginings and all that talk about the Sweetwater instinct for true love.

Now what?

Before she could come up with an answer, Cruz opened the door. She got out and walked with him toward the entrance.

She was digging into her little handbag for her key when two balls of violent green ghost fire exploded on the sidewalk, trapping both her and Cruz against the wall of the building.

There was nothing supernatural about ghost energy. Technically, energy ghosts were known as UDEMs—unstable dissonance energy manifestations. They were essentially small storms of chaotic alien psi.

Even a brush with the flaring green fires could fry the victim's para-senses, sometimes beyond recovery. A sustained encounter could kill.

Wild energy ghosts were a common problem in the catacombs, but they did not exist aboveground unless generated by someone who could work ghost energy: a ghost hunter. Two ghosts meant two Guild men were in the vicinity. Rogue hunters were known to use their talents to commit street crimes. Having a ghost shoved in your face was as intimidating as having a mag-rez gun pointed at you.

"Oh, geez, we're going to get mugged," Lyra said. "Talk about the perfect ending to the evening."

Cruz did not respond. He was watching two men move out of the fog-bound shadows of an alley. The fierce glow of the raging green energy ghosts gleamed on the highly illegal mag-rez guns in their hands. The weapons were aimed at Cruz.

"Get him," one of the men said. "But don't hurt the woman."

Lyra had only an instant to comprehend the fact that this was no routine street robbery, that the thugs intended to murder Cruz.

And then all the light went out of the night.

Between one panicky heartbeat and the next, she was plunged into a nightmare of absolute darkness and terrifying silence.

There should be gunshots, she thought. *Why don't I hear the gunshots?*

They say you never hear the shot that gets you.

Maybe this state of utter oblivion was death.

Chapter 13

CRUZ SAW LYRA COLLAPSE TO THE PAVEMENT BESIDE him, but there was nothing he could do for her now. There would be time for explanations later, he thought. First things first. Priorities.

He continued to focus energy through the obsidian amber in his ring, trapping his prey in a disorienting no-man's-land of featureless psi fog.

He could not shield Lyra. The talent did not work that way. It was linked to his aura. When he was generating this much power, everyone in a radius of twelve to fifteen feet around him was enveloped in the mist. Except for him.

In this eerie state he was the ultimate predator, because only he could use his senses. The others had gone night blind in the most extreme manner imaginable, all of their normal senses shut down.

The nasty energy ghosts the two thugs had generated guttered and went out like candles extinguished in the rain as the attackers lost their ability to hold a focus. The men yelled in panic and floundered. Their guns clattered on the pavement.

The dark thrill of impending violence swept through Cruz. He went swiftly toward the first man.

NOTHING MADE SENSE. THE DISORIENTATION WAS COMplete. The world as she knew it had vanished. It was as if she had been plucked from the street and dropped into the deepest ocean abyss. Even the eternal glow cast by the Dead City wall disappeared. The balls of ghost fire vanished. There were no headlights in the street. Nothing.

All of her normal senses were affected. In addition to not being able to see or hear, she could no longer orient herself physically. Up and down had no meaning. The only reason she knew she had fallen to the sidewalk was because of the pain that jolted through her.

The shock of the fall was oddly reassuring. If she could feel normal pain, she probably wasn't dead.

Her first coherent thought was that two men were intending to gun down Cruz, and she was unable to do anything to help him because she had been struck by one of her waking nightmares. Panic and rage surged through her. *Not now, damn it.* He couldn't die. He had just come back to her. She would not let him go again, even if he was trying to manipulate her.

Her physical senses were deadened, but perhaps her para-senses were not as badly affected. Desperately she concentrated on pushing energy through her amethyst charms, willing the world to snap back into focus around her.

The street scene rushed back, but because she was viewing it with only her other senses, it had a strange, surreal quality. The colors of objects were all in the paranormal range. The street sign glowed ultraviolet. The wet pavement gleamed ultragreen. The lights of an upstairs window across the street appeared as an aurora of ultra-yellow.

She had never before been forced to rely only on her para-senses. They usually worked naturally with a person's normal senses. But in this strange state, all of the stimuli came to her from only the paranormal end of the spectrum.

She heard sound, but she perceived it differently. There was, however, no mistaking the thuds, grunts and—most unnerving of all—the shriek of a man crying out in shock and pain.

She turned her head and saw two shadowy figures. It was impossible to see their physical features, because each was surrounded by a spiking aura. One man staggered around in a circle, arms flailing. The other moved in on him, gliding forward in a frighteningly graceful dance that promised to end in violence. A third man was motionless on the ground.

She had no doubt as to the identity of the man who

was closing in for what looked like the kill. She would know him anywhere.

"Cruz," she whispered.

In this para-dimension, her voice echoed weirdly. She could not hear herself the way she did when she was using her regular senses. The lack of familiar auditory feedback added to the hallucinatory atmosphere.

A small creature, its aura glowing brightly, dashed out of the darkness and charged for the man Cruz was about to take down.

"Vincent," Lyra said. "No, wait. Come here."

Vincent, fur sleeked back, ignored her. He dashed in to nip at his target's heels.

The thug screeched. "Get away from me. *Get away.*"

But Cruz was also moving in, lightning fast. He made a quick, chopping motion with one hand. The ghost hunter went down, crumpling on the pavement beside his partner.

The world jolted back. Lyra's normal senses kicked in with jarring suddenness. Vincent leaped up into her arms, rumbling with concern. She gathered him close and watched Cruz scoop up the mag-rez guns.

"Are you all right?" she whispered. Her voice sounded tense but normal once again.

He came toward her, still moving with that disturbingly lethal grace. She sensed that he was startled to see her on her feet.

"I'm fine," he said. "What about you?"

"I'm okay. I'm . . . a little shaken up, I guess."

"Sorry about that."

"Yeah, well, it's not exactly your fault."

"We'll talk about it later. Right now we have to deal with this pair."

"Okay."

Vincent was once again fully fluffed, hunting eyes closed. He chortled his customary cheerful greeting to Lyra, as though nothing out of the ordinary had just occurred.

Cruz took a phone from his pocket. "I'll have someone pick up these guys."

"Someone?" She frowned. "You mean the police, right? Please tell me you're calling the cops."

"Sort of."

"Sort of?"

"I'm calling the Guild's security people."

"Damn it, Cruz, the police are supposed to handle this sort of thing."

"Those two are ghost hunters and, like they say, the Guild polices its own. Besides, I need answers, and I'm a lot more likely to get them faster out of my friends at Guild security than I am from the Frequency PD."

There was no point arguing with him. She subsided, fuming. It was just one more example of the arrogance of both Amber Inc. and the local Guild. But she also knew that Cruz was right. When it came to rogue ghost hunters, the Frequency cops took the old-fashioned view. They, too, preferred to let the Guild take care of its own problems.

Cruz spoke briefly to someone on the phone and then cut the connection. He looked at Lyra again.

"Take Vincent upstairs," he said. "I'll wait here until Guild security collects these two, and then I'll be up. We need to talk."

"About what?" she asked.

"About what just happened here."

She searched his face. "It was an attempted mugging. A street robbery."

"Maybe." He dropped the phone into his pocket and crossed to the nearest of the two unconscious men.

A fresh wave of alarm shot through her. "What do you mean?"

Crouching, he went swiftly, methodically, through the hunter's pockets. "I don't think that these two were just a pair of opportunists. They were waiting for us."

"How do you know that?"

"Got a talent for this kind of thing."

Chapter 14

FIFTEEN MINUTES LATER HE GOT INTO THE ELEVATOR and rode it to the fourth floor. The gunmen had been taken away in the back of a black-windowed Guild car, but he was still feeling the intense aftereffects that always followed the use of a lot of psi.

He was in control—he was *always* in control. With a talent like his, it was a necessity. But he knew from previous experience that willpower alone did not protect him from the afterburn. In some primitive part of his brain, he was the hunter returning from a successful kill. And tonight the sensation was a thousand times more charged, because his mate was waiting for him.

Except that Lyra did not yet get that part of things, he thought.

She must have heard him coming down the hall, because the door of the apartment opened just as he reached it. Lyra stood in the little entryway, her eyes dark with anxiety. A white robe and a pair of slippers had replaced the black dinner dress and sexy heels. Her hair was down and a little tousled. Vincent was on her shoulder, looking cheerful as usual. Of the three of them, he was the only one who was unconcerned, Cruz thought. Dust bunnies lived in the moment.

"Are they gone?" Lyra asked, peering out into the hall as though fearful that the thugs had followed him.

"They're gone." He just stood there on the threshold, looking at her, aware that everything inside him had just tightened up another notch. He should not go inside the apartment, not in his present condition. But he had to talk to her. He needed to take the edge off first, though.

"I could use a drink," he said.

"You aren't the only one." She stepped back. "I got out the bottle of Amber Dew."

"Works for me."

When she turned away to walk toward the kitchen, it was all he could do not to reach out and catch hold of her. Everything in him was clamoring to pull her into his arms. He managed to keep his hands off her, but it was one of the hardest things he had ever done. He really should not have come up here. This was a mistake, a really big one.

He closed the door with a sense of doomed finality and followed Lyra. Halfway across the living room area, he dropped his jacket over the back of the reading chair.

Seemingly oblivious of his mood, Lyra went behind the counter and poured a stiff measure into each of the two glasses she had set out. Losing interest, Vincent hopped down from her shoulder and went to investigate the cookie jar.

Lyra lifted the lid off the jar. "Take your choice, pal. You deserve it."

Vincent vibrated with anticipation. He jumped up onto the rim of the jar and surveyed the offerings with the air of a pirate savoring his loot. After a moment of dithering, he seized a cookie and hopped back down onto the counter.

Lyra replaced the lid and picked up her drink. She gulped some down and promptly started to cough.

"Are you sure you're okay?" Cruz asked.

"Oh, yeah, swell." Gasping, she set the glass down with a crack. "Never better. You?"

He loved this about her. She was a real fighter, endowed with enough spirit, guts, and determination to power an army. Nothing got her down for long. No matter what you did to her—lie to her; steal her amber claim; crush her sleazy, ambulance-chasing lawyer with high-powered attorneys; terrify her by plunging her into psychic limbo—she always bounced back. His true mate, for sure.

"Never better," he agreed. He drank some of the Amber Dew.

She leaned forward and braced her elbows on the counter. "Well? Did you learn anything about that pair?"

"The security guys who picked them up ID'd them for me." He lowered himself onto one of the stools. "A couple of rank-and-file ghost hunters who were kicked out of the Guild a while back. They were caught stealing artifacts from an archaeological team they were hired to protect."

Lyra made a face, unimpressed. "That's all you know?"

"They're both still unconscious. When they wake up, they'll be questioned, but I doubt that we'll learn much more. Whoever hired them wouldn't have told them anything other than what was absolutely necessary."

She tipped her head to one side, pondering that. "You're still assuming someone hired them and that they weren't just a couple of street thieves?"

"I'm sure of it."

"What makes you so certain of that?"

"They didn't just wander past your door tonight and happen to notice us getting out of the car. They were waiting for us, Lyra."

"How can you know that?"

He took a breath and exhaled it slowly. "Because any other scenario would be just too much of a coincidence."

"What? Where's the coincidence? Random street crimes happen all the time in the Quarter."

He met her eyes. "Not to me. Not a couple of weeks after I've discovered that one of the amethyst relics we removed from the ruin was stolen from the lab."

"What?"

"And not two weeks after a lab technician was found murdered. And not less than twenty-four hours after three of my people and two Guild men were trapped in that amethyst ruin."

"Hold on here." She held up a hand to stop him. "You're going way too fast for me. There's been a murder? Someone stole one of the amethyst relics? Why didn't you bother to mention any of this before?"

"It's complicated."

"You keep saying that."

He took another sip and lowered the glass. "Probably because it's the truth."

"I didn't hear anything about a murder in the AI lab and, trust me, I've been paying extremely close attention to any and all news of Amber Inc."

"I managed to keep it quiet. Hoped it would buy me a little time."

She shook her head and clicked her tongue against her teeth, making a tut-tutting sound. "So you lost one of the stones already? Nice going, Sweetwater. So much for all that sophisticated security AI was supposed to provide for those *priceless* archaeological relics."

"Doesn't make us look good, does it? We think the killer escaped into the jungle. Opened his own gate. You know how it is down there. You can't track anyone in the rain forest unless you have his locator frequency."

"I will give you credit for being able to keep the murder and the theft out of the media. Very impressive."

"Thanks."

She frowned. "And now you're telling me that you don't think those five people got caught in that ruin by accident last night?"

"No."

"But what was the point? Why would someone deliberately close that chamber on five people? For heaven's sake, they could have died in there."

"This is where the complications set in," he said.

"I'm listening."

"The really complicated part is that whoever is behind this is doing his or her best to make it look like there's only one obvious suspect in the murder, the theft, and the accident at the ruin."

"Who?"

He waited.

Comprehension finally struck. She straightened abruptly behind the counter, eyes huge with shock.

"Me?" she squeaked.

"Look at it from the point of view of the killer. Everyone knows there's been no luck rezzing those stones in the lab. Everyone thinks that you are the only talent around who can access the energy of those rocks, and everyone is aware that you have refused to cooperate in the research we've tried to conduct on them. Last but not least, everyone knows that you've been waging a one-woman vendetta against me and Amber Inc. That adds up to a lot of motive."

She looked as if she had just been kicked in the stomach.

"*That's* why you came back," she whispered. "You think I stole that artifact and murdered the technician."

"You know damn well that's not true." Fury and outrage twisted through him. He got up off the stool and circled the counter.

The sudden elevation of tension in the room must have

alarmed Vincent. His fur sleeked back. His second set of eyes opened.

"Great," Cruz said. "Now I'm going to have to deal with an irate dust bunny. So much for the Sweetwater luck."

"Do you think I hired those two goons to kill you to-night, as well?" Lyra demanded.

"No." He closed the distance between them. "I came back to protect you."

"Right. You're from Amber Inc., and you're here to help me. And if I believe that, you've got a really nice amber mine treasure map you can sell me."

"I tried to avoid dragging you into this thing, but yes-terday when that crew got trapped in the ruin, I knew that was no longer an option. Whoever is trying to set you up to take the fall is going to keep pushing in that direction until I get the point. The only thing I can do now is to make it look as if I've come to the conclusion that you're the most likely suspect."

"So you take me out for dinner?" Her voice rose with outrage. "Try to seduce me? That's supposed to convince the killer that you think I'm guilty?"

"Why not?" he said through his teeth. "It's what I did the first time around when I wanted to get the location of that ruin out of you. Remember?"

"How could I possibly forget? You are a deceitful, ruth-less, cold-blooded son of a bitch, Cruz Sweetwater."

"Sometimes. But not tonight. Everything I'm telling you tonight is the truth. Including this."

He pulled her close and kissed her hard, willing her to sense the full force of the hot storm ripping through him, willing her to acknowledge the psychic bond between them, willing her to trust him. She had to trust him now, because her life depended on it.

For the first time in their relationship he held nothing back. There was no longer any reason to bank the fires of his need. He set free the prowling hunger and the aching, haunting, all-consuming desire that he had kept on a mag-steel leash for the past three months.

Heat and energy flared in the atmosphere around them as passion infused their auras. She planted her hands on his shoulders and wrenched her mouth away from his.

"Damn it," she gasped. "I do trust you. I'm pissed as hell, but I trust you. I must be an idiot."

"No," he said. "You feel it, too."

"Feel what?"

"The psychic link between us. It's not going to go away, Lyra. Take my word for it. *I'm* not going to go away. Not this time."

He trapped her against the counter and kissed her again. She shivered, and then, in the next instant, she came alive in his arms, hotter than ghost light. She kissed him back with a feminine ferocity that took his breath. They fought each other for the embrace. He finally managed to pin her against the counter. Breathing hard, he yanked open the robe. She was wearing a pair of black silk panties and a black silk bra but nothing else. The scent of her body was intoxicating.

He grasped her thighs and wrapped them around his waist. She clung to him, kissing his throat wildly. The delicate charms of her bracelet clashed sweetly, seductively, just as they had in his dreams.

"It's because of what happened earlier," she gasped.

"What are you talking about?" he growled against her breast.

"I've read about it. The aftereffects of adrenaline and violence and using a lot of psi energy. It makes people want to have sex. Something to do with hormones and stuff. Survival instinct."

"Do me a favor and shut up," he said very softly.

"Okay."

He picked her up and carried her around the kitchen counter, heading for the bedroom. He spared a single glance for Vincent. The dust bunny was fully fluffed once more, munching contentedly on his cookie.

Satisfied that he was not going to have to fend off Vincent, he paused just long enough to de-rez the lights. The loft was plunged into shadows drenched with the luminous emerald glow of the ancient quartz wall.

He angled Lyra through the opening in the sliding screens that veiled the bedroom and dropped her lightly on the bed. She lay there, swathed in the pristine white robe, her dark hair tangled around her face, and looked up at him with half-closed eyes. Her cheeks were flushed. Her mouth was soft and full from his kisses.

He got his shirt off with a few quick, impatient motions and sat down on the edge of the bed to remove his shoes. He got rid of the ankle sheath and the knife at the same time and kicked them out of sight under the bed before Lyra could see the weapon. She'd already had enough violence for one night. The last thing he wanted to do now was spoil the mood.

A moment later he was where he had been in his dreams every night since he'd met her: on the bed and on top of Lyra. She twisted sleekly beneath him, warm and vital. Her arms went around his neck. He opened his senses, drugging himself on her scent and her energy.

"You can't know how many times I've thought about how it would be to be here like this with you," he said against her throat.

She speared her fingers through his hair. "You really missed me, Sweetwater?"

"No." He framed her face with his hands. "I was obsessed with you."

She smiled. "I can see where a lawsuit might have that effect on a man."

"I pay lawyers to deal with lawsuits. Believe me, the legal garbage had nothing to do with it. This was all about you."

He kissed her heavily, silencing the possibility of any more teasing.

She raised one knee. The robe fell back, exposing the inside of her thigh. He stripped off the silk panties and slid his palm upward along bare skin until he could feel the dampness of her arousal. Three months ago he had never dared touch her so intimately. He had known that if he went this far, he would not be able to resist the temptation to make her his completely. He had told her the truth earlier. He'd sensed that she might forgive a few kisses, but if he had made love to her under false pretenses there would have been hell to pay.

She drew a sharp, unsteady breath when she felt his hand on her. She was already wet and full. He was damp, too, sweating with the effort required to hold himself in check until she had come for him at least once.

He found the tight little bud of nerve endings above her cleft and worked it gently with his thumb, pushing under and then up until she started to lift herself off the bed.

"Cruz." She clutched at his shoulders.

He hooked two fingers into her and pressed upward again, searching for the sensitive, slightly swollen place just inside.

"You are so hot, so tight," he whispered. "Incredible."

She dug her nails into him. "Now. Do it right now."

He used his thigh to force her legs wider apart.

"Come for me first," he said.

"Damn it, Cruz. *Cruz.*"

Her climax blossomed through her. She shuddered in his arms, one leg wrapped around his hips. She cried out, sounding half-astonished and half-euphoric. The energy of her release soared across his senses, nearly shattering his control. But he held on. This was too important. He had to get this right.

When she had just begun to go limp beneath him, he settled more intimately between her legs. Bracing himself on his elbows, he eased carefully inside her. She shivered, and he knew it was because she was very sensitive now.

"Wait," she whispered. Her hands flattened on his chest. "I think I need a little time here."

"Don't worry," he vowed. "We'll take it slow. We've got all night."

"You don't understand," she gasped. "That has never happened before. Not unless I used a small personal care appliance. But, oh, my, this was different. Really, really different."

He smiled. "In a good way?"

"A very good way." She took a few recovering breaths. "But it was a little over-the-top."

"I'm a Sweetwater. I do over-the-top."

She was laughing when he pushed gently into her, an inch, no more. She stopped laughing. He withdrew just as slowly. He could tell that she was tensed for possible discomfort. He was determined to give her only pleasure.

Gradually she relaxed, trusting him not to hurt her. After a while she began to tighten around him again.

"Cruz?"

She did not cry out his name in passion this time. She sounded startled. Unnerved.

"Don't worry," he said. "I've got you."

When she went taut and desperate beneath him a second time and started to tremble through another climax, he finally released the chains of control that had bound him for what seemed like forever.

He poured himself into her, hard and fast and exultant.

His senses were still flung wide, and he knew hers were, too. She bound him tightly to her, her arms and legs snug and possessive around him.

He heard the amethyst charms clashing melodically in the night. A thousand shades of psychic fire burned in the shadows.

Chapter 15

THE FEATURELESS, SOUNDLESS VOID OF THE DREAMSCAPE *was terrifying. She had to escape. Instinctively she pushed energy through the charms on her bracelet . . .*

The nightmare broke up into fragments.

She came awake on a surge of adrenaline that left her damp and shivering. She sat up quickly, breathless, pulse racing.

The first thing that struck her was that she was alone in the bed. Cruz was gone. Everything inside her went cold.

Vincent drifted across the quilt toward her. He huddled close, making anxious little chittering noises. She picked him up and cuddled him, taking comfort from his furry little frame.

"I'm not alone, am I?" she whispered. "I've got you, pal."

"Are you okay?" Cruz asked from somewhere near the window.

Shocked, she turned her head and saw him silhouetted against the pale green night light spilling through the window. The lines of his sleek, powerful shoulders and back were sharply etched, but his face was hidden in the shadows. Suddenly she was warm again.

Of course he was here, she thought. She would have known if he had left in the middle of the night. She had been so disoriented—so panicked—by the nightmare that she had not been paying attention to her senses.

"Bad dream," she explained. "I've been having them a lot lately." She hesitated. "But not usually at night. This one was different."

"You have dreams while you're awake?" he asked.

She drew a breath and let it out slowly. "More like hallucinations, I'm afraid. I know, I should probably see a para-shrink. I've been thinking about it. The thing is, most of the time I feel so damn *normal.* I can't bring myself to believe I'm going crazy."

"You're not crazy, Lyra."

"Something's going on, that's for sure. I've been telling myself that it's just stress. But after what happened tonight, I have to face the fact that the waking nightmares are getting worse."

"Tell me about them."

"Don't be ridiculous." She swung her legs over the side of the bed and got to her feet. "There's nothing more boring than listening to someone else's dreams."

He came around the foot of the bed, reaching her just

as she was pulling on her robe. She saw that he was back in his trousers.

"Getting ready to leave?" she asked, managing somehow to keep the pain out of her voice. "There's no need to sneak out. I won't be filing any lawsuits this time."

"I wasn't leaving. I was thinking." He tipped her chin up with one finger. "I've discovered that when I'm around you, I think better with my pants on."

From the beginning he'd had a way of making her feel like the sexiest woman alive. She allowed herself to relax a little.

"That's an interesting observation," she said.

"Tell me about the dreams."

She tried to see his expression more clearly, but in the shadowy room his face was all hard planes and angles.

"You're serious?" she asked. "You really want to hear about my weird dreams?"

He stroked his thumb along her bottom lip. His eyes were pools of fathomless darkness.

"Yes," he said. "Start with the one that just woke you up."

She swallowed uneasily. "That's the one that was different. Actually, it was more or less a repeat of the hallucination that hit me earlier tonight when those two men attacked us. It was as if my senses had been muffled. I couldn't see or hear anything. There was no up or down, just this endless thick fog."

He cupped her face in his hands. "That was me, Lyra. I did that to you."

"What?"

"You asked me about my talent earlier. Well, that's part of it. Makes it easier to hunt."

"I don't understand."

"Various kinds of psychic talents have run through the Sweetwater family for generations, most of them related to the senses that happen to be very useful when it comes to hunting."

"Good grief."

"Things have taken a few twists for us here on Harmony. We've discovered we can use various kinds of amber to enhance our natural talents. I happen to have an affinity for obsidian amber."

She glanced at his ring. Green fire danced in the depths of the obsidian.

"Black amber," she whispered. "Most tuners believe that it is only a legend."

"It's rare, but it exists. Others in my family work different varieties of amber, but obsidian is the one I resonate with the best. What I'm trying to tell you is that when those two men attacked us tonight, I used my talent to deaden their normal senses: vision, sound, smell, touch, balance. I knocked out everything. Unfortunately, you got caught in the net because you were so close."

"Okay, that's weird."

"There's no way I can direct the effect toward a specific target. The energy is generated by my aura, and it sweeps out in a field all around me for a radius of about fifteen feet."

"You're saying it wasn't one of my waking nightmares?"

"I'm not sure what you mean by a waking nightmare, but I can guarantee you that you weren't hallucinating tonight."

Relief crashed through her, leaving her a little jittery. She sank slowly back down onto the bed, hugging Vincent close.

"That's it?" she asked, incredulous. "That's your family's secret talent?"

"Well, it's my version of it. Like I said, the men in my family are all hunters of one kind or another, but no two talents are ever identical."

"But you still need amber to focus your psi, right?"

"No. Our talent has been in the family for generations. There were Sweetwater hunters on the Old World long before the Curtain opened. But here on Harmony, it turns out that certain forms of nonstandard amber can be used to enhance our natural abilities."

"You say you're hunters but not ghost hunters?" she asked.

"In the old days they called us para-hunters. We don't use the term anymore. We think of ourselves as amber talents. Sounds a little more modern, you know?"

She looked at him. "A little less scary, you mean? A tad more politically correct?"

"Yeah, that, too." He sat down beside her.

"Who called you para-hunters back on Earth?"

He shrugged. "It's the label that was used to describe

people like me in the historical records of the Arcane Society."

"What in the world is the Arcane Society?"

"An organization that was founded by an alchemist several centuries ago, Old Earth time. Its members were all psychically talented people. The group was devoted to the study of the paranormal. The Society maintained a very low profile back on the home world."

"Why?"

"The paranormal was never really accepted as normal back on Earth."

She gripped the lapels of her robe with one hand. "In some ways, it still isn't. People get nervous around those who have strong or unusual kinds of talents."

He threaded his fingers through hers. "And that's why the Society still exists in the shadows."

"You're saying this Arcane Society exists here on Harmony?"

"A lot of registered members came through the Curtain, just like everyone else. When it became obvious that something in the environment here on Harmony was encouraging the development of latent psychic talents of all kinds, those in the Society thought things would be better here. But it turns out that being different is still not a good thing."

"The definition of what is normal may shift but not the pressure to fit the definition."

His smile held no trace of humor. "That's even truer when your brand of talent just happens to be really useful for pursuing and taking down a certain kind of prey."

"What kind would that be?" she asked warily.

"Human."

She swallowed hard. "I see. Had a feeling you were going to say that. I saw the way you handled those two men tonight."

"For generations on Earth, my family made a good living working for the Arcane Society and occasionally certain clandestine government agencies."

"Tracking criminals?"

"Not just any kind of criminals. On Earth, the Sweetwaters hunted down psychic sociopaths, the kind of bad guys regular law enforcement couldn't handle."

She cleared her throat. "So you were the good guys?"

"We like to think so. But not everyone saw it that way. The thing is, we did it for the money. A lot of money."

"I see."

"When someone called in a Sweetwater, it meant that all other alternatives had been exhausted. You didn't resort to hiring one of us unless you were convinced that the only option left was to terminate."

Her mouth went dry. "Your ancestors were *assassins for hire*?"

"I know. Talk about politically incorrect. We tried to be selective when it came to employers, but, yes, the Sweetwaters did the dirty work for those who couldn't or wouldn't get their own hands dirty." He paused. "We were good at it, too."

She cleared her throat. "Please tell me that your family is no longer in that profession."

There was a short pause.

"Mostly we're in amber today," he said finally.

"Excuse me, but your job title is CEO of Amber Inc. *Security.* You, personally, are not exactly in amber, Cruz."

"AI Security is a legitimate private security firm," he said flatly. "A division of Amber Inc. We are no longer Murder Inc. My grandfather saw to that fifty years ago. He changed everything for us. That's what it was all about, you see."

"What do you mean?"

"The Radiance Springs mine claim that he won in that poker game he played with Arthur Dore. Big Jake's new mining company was in a life-and-death struggle for survival against Erasmus Revere's RezStone. Big Jake needed the Radiance Springs mine in order to keep from going under."

"So he stole it from my grandfather."

"He won it in a card game."

"Yeah, right." She took a breath. "So you're telling me that up until that point your family was still in the old business?"

He exhaled deeply and with a lot of control. "I think we've talked about this enough tonight."

"Conversation closed?"

"For now."

"Somehow I get the feeling that you don't tell every woman you date about your family history."

"No." He tightened his grip on her hand. "You're the first one I've ever told."

"Boy, howdy, why does that make me nervous?"

"Relax. You're going to be family soon."

Chapter 16

HE COULD FEEL THE PANIC FLARE IN HER AURA. "RELAX, you're going to be family soon" had probably not been the smartest thing he could have said under the circumstances.

"Sorry," he said. "Didn't mean to scare you. I'm moving too fast here, aren't I?"

"It's not the speed that worries me, it's the direction in which you're traveling," Lyra said tightly. "What in the world are you talking about?"

"Sorry," he repeated. "I just thought that, after what happened between us last night, it would be okay to talk about our future."

"We had *sex* last night." She freed her hand and leaped to her feet, sending Vincent tumbling down to the floor. "It was great sex. Best I've ever had. But it was just sex."

She sounded almost frantic. He rose slowly, watching her.

"You still don't trust me, do you?" he said quietly. "In spite of how it was between us last night."

"Or maybe because of it," she shot back. "Everyone knows it's easy to confuse passion with . . . with, uh, the other thing."

"It's called love," he said. "In my family we don't have a problem with the word."

"Well, in mine, we do. Dores have never been lucky in love."

"Maybe because you marry the wrong people."

"Yeah, that's probably it," she said grimly. "Look. Not that long ago I fooled myself into thinking that maybe I could break the jinx with you. I am not going to make that mistake again. You've still got an agenda where I'm concerned. We both know that."

"You call trying to protect you from whoever is attempting to frame you for killing a man and stealing a valuable antiquity 'an agenda'?"

She drew herself up to her full height, which, given that she was barefoot, meant she still had to look up to meet his eyes. "Some might view it that way. I'm thrilled that you don't believe I'm the killer, but the bottom line here is that you are still looking for one, right?"

"Yes."

"It strikes me that one way for you to draw the bad guy out into the open is to hang around me. If he thinks that you are looking at me as a suspect, he's more likely to make a mistake."

"You are a very cynical woman, Lyra Dore. Smart as hell and sexy as hell, but also cynical."

"I prefer the term *realistic*," she said, raising her chin. "And you have to admit, I'm right."

"You're right. But I swear on my honor as a Sweetwater that my goal is to protect you, not use you as bait. Hell, if I'd wanted to stake you out like a tethered goat, I would have come looking for you two weeks ago after the lab tech died. That's when I first began to suspect that someone was trying to set you up to take the fall. Believe it or not, at that point I was doing my level best to divert attention from you."

"I believe you when you say that you didn't intend for me to get caught in the middle of this thing. But you are trying to catch a killer, and I happen to be conveniently in the middle. It's possible I could be useful. We both know that."

He looked out the window at the rising light of dawn, trying to keep his temper in check, trying to think of a way out of the trap. When nothing came to mind, he headed for the bathroom.

"This conversation isn't going anywhere good, so I'm going to take a shower instead," he said.

She leaped into the bathroom doorway, showing an impressive turn of speed, and blocked his path, hands braced against the doorframe on either side.

"One more thing, Sweetwater."

He stopped in front of her. "What now?"

"You said you induced that psi fog that overwhelmed my senses last night."

"I told you, I can't aim my talent like a gun. I apologize again, but if you will recall, there were a couple of guys with mag-rezzes in the vicinity."

"I know. I've got no problem with you saving us from that pair."

"Gosh, thanks. Nothing gets a man hot like having his woman believe that he's a knight in shining armor."

"What I want to know," she said, watching him very closely, "is if you're responsible for the other hallucinations I've been experiencing for the last six weeks."

Anger and a terrible sense of helplessness roared through him. It took everything he had to clamp a lid on the churning emotions. He leaned in very close, gripping the doorframe on either side of her. His knuckles were white

"Let me get this straight," he said. "Do you really believe that I've been stalking you for the past six weeks, inflicting nightmares on you?"

Something in his very soft, very neutral voice must have gotten through to her. She seemed to crumple in on herself.

"No," she said, her tone abruptly dull. "No, of course not."

"So why are you acting as if you would have been happier if the answer had been yes?"

"Because then I would at least have had a reasonable explanation for the waking nightmares." She moved out of the doorway, slipping under his extended arm. "Go take your shower, Cruz."

The last of his frustration and anger evaporated. She

was scared to death and fighting the fear with typical Dore guts and determination. He caught her around the waist.

"Hold it right there," he said. "These waking nightmares you're talking about. What do you think is going on?"

She looked at him. "Well, one explanation is that they are a result of the stress I've been under lately."

"Have you ever suffered hallucinations when you've been under stress in the past?"

"No."

"Damn. You're really worried that you might be going crazy, aren't you?"

"Well, I guess it is a possibility that should be considered."

Her flippant tone belied her haunted eyes.

"Forget it," he said, putting all of his conviction into the words. "You're not going crazy."

"And just how would you know that, Dr. Sweetwater?"

"Believe me, after last night, I would know."

"Sex as a diagnostic tool in the field of parapsychology. Hey, I'll bet you could get a bestseller out of that."

"I don't need a degree in parapsychology to know you're as sane as I am," he said calmly. "There's been a bond between us from the moment we met. Last night strengthened it in ways you haven't even begun to comprehend. If there was a streak of madness in you, I would have sensed it."

Her eyes lit with cautious hope. "You're sure?"

"Positive. Now, I'm going to take that shower. When I'm finished, you can take yours while I make breakfast."

He kissed her lightly and walked past her into the bathroom.

Chapter 17

THE SMELL OF COFFEE, TOAST, AND SCRAMBLED EGGS greeted her when she emerged from the shower. The knowledge that Cruz did not believe that she was crazy was such an overwhelming relief she actually felt a little giddy.

She dried her hair and pulled it back into a ponytail. Grabbing a pair of jeans and a crisp white shirt out of the closet, she dressed quickly and went out into the main room, barefoot.

Vincent was at his favorite observation post on top of the refrigerator, supervising. The red beret was tilted at a rakish angle. He had a piece of toast slathered with peanut butter in one paw. There was more peanut butter on his fur. He chortled a greeting and bounced a little when he saw her.

She winced at the sight of the peanut butter. "Looks like I'm going to be doing a little hand laundry after breakfast. Do you know how hard it is to get peanut butter out of dust bunny fur? It's almost as bad as paint."

"Sorry, didn't think about that problem," Cruz said. He scraped eggs onto the two plates he had set on the counter. "I'll run him under the faucet when I do the dishes."

"He loves that. I'll warn you right now you're going to have water all over the floor before you're finished."

Cruz set the pan down and added several slices of toast to the plates. "Maybe I'll stick him in the shower, instead."

"That works."

He put a plate down in front of her. "We need to talk."

"About what?"

"Your schedule."

She sat down at the counter. "What about it?"

"Given events last night, you're going to have to put your usual routine on hold until I find out who is trying to set you up," he said. He sat down beside her.

"You mean close my shop? I can't do that. I've got a business to run. It isn't Amber Inc., but it pays the bills. Barely. Besides, today I have a real VIP client. The biggest one I've had since, well, since I thought you were a real client."

"Don't worry about the financial side of things. AI will take care of any lost income."

"Thanks, I appreciate that, but this isn't about lost

income. This is about trying to get the antiquities consulting side of my business off the ground. I absolutely cannot cancel on this new client. This is my chance at the big time."

"I'm trying to keep you safe, Lyra."

"I understand. But let's think this thing through. Whoever is behind this doesn't want me dead or disappeared. It would ruin his plan to frame me, right? Last night, those two men were after you, not me. One of them shouted something about not hurting the woman. It was you they were trying to kill. You're the one who needs protection."

"I can take care of myself."

"Yes, I noticed that last night."

"I've got work to do," Cruz said. "I can't stay with you at all times."

"Of course you can't," she said encouragingly. "And it's not necessary. Like I said, I can take care of myself."

"If you're going to be stubborn about this, I'll assign someone to keep an eye on you."

She exhaled, resigned. "I knew you would be difficult. What am I supposed to do with a bodyguard? It will look strange to my clients."

"Call him your assistant." He ate some eggs. "About your afternoon appointment."

She slanted him a wary glance. "What about it?"

"You said the client was important. Anyone I know?"

This was going to be awkward. "I'm sure you've met him," she said coolly. "You and Wilson Revere both grew up in the amber business."

A dangerous stillness came over Cruz. "Wilson Revere as in the head of RezStone?"

"Uh-huh." She ate some eggs in an attempt to pretend that she did not sense the new, dangerous tension simmering in his aura. "He contacted me yesterday. He was looking for someone to evaluate a piece of amethyst amber that he plans to bid on at an auction at the Fairstead Gallery today. He hired me to attend the auction with him."

"You do realize that Revere's company is AI's biggest competitor."

"Of course." She kept her tone even. "Common knowledge."

"Given that fact and the timing, it has probably occurred to you that he may have heard some rumors about the missing relic and wants to know what the hell is going on. He plans to pump you for information."

"That did occur to me," she admitted. "It is also possible that he really does need me to help him evaluate a specimen of amethyst. As you may have heard recently, there aren't a lot of tuners around who can work purple amber. The Fairstead Gallery is known for the quality of its raw amber specimens, and I've heard Wilson is an extremely passionate collector."

"Wilson?" Cruz repeated in ominous tones.

"He insisted I use his first name. He's very casual, very laid-back for such a wealthy, powerful man."

"Wilson Revere would do anything to take down Amber Inc."

"Yes, I'm aware of that," she said lightly. "But I'm not

particularly interested in the corporate infighting between the two major amber monopolies. I'm just trying to fire up my career as a consultant. Besides, it's probably your fault that he called me."

"*My* fault?"

"You're the one who had the Amber Inc. PR department identify me to the media as an antiquities consultant with an exclusive clientele."

"Pay attention, Lyra. You can't trust Revere any farther than you can walk in the catacombs or the jungle without good amber. He's using you."

"He sure is," she agreed. "He's using me to assess a chunk of amethyst for his collection."

"I know this guy. Believe me when I tell you that he has an agenda."

"No offense, Cruz, but you're starting to sound just the teensiest bit paranoid."

"You know the old saying: even paranoids have enemies."

"What is with RezStone and AI, anyway? I know you're business competitors, but the executives of most rival firms are usually capable of a modicum of civilized behavior. At least in public."

Cruz smiled his hit man smile. "We're polite in public. But we Sweetwaters have a saying: never turn your back on anyone from RezStone."

"Is that so?"

"It's a tough outfit," Cruz said. "You don't get into the top echelons unless you're willing to cross a few lines. The Revere family has had a reputation for being ruthless for the past fifty years. People who stand in the company's path have a habit of disappearing."

It took her a few seconds to get her mouth closed. "Are you seriously telling me that RezStone actually kills off people who get in its way?"

"Like I said, there are rumors."

She smiled. "Possibly propagated by Amber Inc.?"

He ignored that. "Revere doesn't hesitate to dabble in Guild politics, either. At the moment, it's no secret that he has a keen interest in getting one of his pals on the Frequency council elected as the new boss of the local Guild."

"Gosh. And the Sweetwaters have no interest whatsoever in making sure that the new Guild boss is a good friend of Amber Inc.?"

"Your cynical side is showing again. Trust me when I tell you that you do not want to get involved with Wilson Revere."

She lowered her fork and twisted on the stool to face him. "Cruz, there's something you need to understand here. I already am involved with Wilson Revere."

She knew at once she had chosen her words badly. Cruz made no overt move, but his eyes went obsidian dark and hard. Green fire sparked in the depths. She felt energy pulse in the atmosphere. The hair lifted on the nape of her neck.

"Professionally speaking," she tacked on hurriedly.

Cruz nodded once, relaxing fractionally. "That's far enough."

It infuriated her that she felt the need to explain her

relationship with Wilson Revere. She could not let Cruz Sweetwater ride roughshod over her life again. This time they would do things on her terms or not at all.

"Furthermore," she said, trying to sound cool and confident; a woman who lived by her own rules, "I intend to remain professionally involved with Wilson Revere as long as he is willing to hire me to consult for him."

"Damn it, Lyra—"

"Give me a little credit here. I'm not an idiot. I know what I'm doing. Revere may have come to me originally to see if he could use me against you. But he and I are doing business together today, and I am going to do my best to impress him with my knowledge and affinity for amber. Not to put too fine a point on it, but I need the business. I went broke trying to sue Amber Inc. Consulting for Wilson Revere is going to go a long way toward getting me back on my feet."

"You should have taken the compensation AI offered you for the ruin, and you know it."

"I couldn't do that."

"Why not?" Cruz demanded.

"Because it would have meant acknowledging that AI had a right to do what it did. I won't do that. Not ever."

"You are one stubborn woman, Lyra."

"I'm a Dore. We do stubborn."

"Yeah, I've heard that."

"Who told you?"

"My grandfather."

Chapter 18

VINCENT WAS SWIPING BROAD, EMPHATIC STROKES OF bright, cheerful magenta onto a canvas when Gloria Ray walked into the little shop. At the sight of her he abandoned his rez-brush and bounced up onto the counter to greet her.

"Hello, handsome," Gloria said. She leaned over the counter to give the canvas an admiring glance. "Nice picture. Red is my favorite color."

Vincent chortled hopefully and batted at the shiny bits of bling that decorated Gloria's handbag.

"Don't worry," Gloria said. "I didn't forget you. I never forget a good-looking guy."

She took a small white sack out of the designer handbag, removed a cookie, and gave it to Vincent. He thanked her in his dust bunny fashion and fell to munching with polite greed.

Gloria smiled radiantly at the young man lounging on the end of the counter.

"You're new," she purred. "And you're cute. Want a cookie?"

There was nothing personal about the purring or the smile. Gloria always purred and glowed when she was speaking to a member of the male gender. Lyra was pretty sure it was some kind of psychic talent. Men certainly responded.

"Temporary help," Lyra said briskly. "Been a little busy lately. This is Jeff. Jeff, this is Miss Ray. She's one of my best customers."

"Hello, Jeff," Gloria said in her sultry tones.

Jeff reddened. "How do you do, Miss Ray."

He *was* cute, Lyra thought, tall and lean and endowed with the predatory grace that seemed to be a hallmark of the men on Cruz's family tree. He was also young, no more than twenty-two or twenty-three. He reminded her of the younger brother she'd never had.

"Do you have a talent for tuning?" Gloria asked Jeff, looking him up and down in a blatantly appraising manner.

Jeff turned a darker shade of red. "No, ma'am. Miss Dore hired me to take care of paperwork and the packing and shipping of the mail-order stuff."

Gloria smiled. "I'm glad to see she has such excellent taste in employees."

Jeff might have been a tough, highly trained bodyguard, but no one had prepared him for Gloria Ray. He looked as if he wanted to sink down through the floor of the shop into the tunnels below.

Lyra took pity on him.

"What can I do for you, Gloria?" she said.

Gloria studied Lyra with a knowing expression. "I have a new piece that I want tuned. By the way, I saw your picture in the papers. You were with Cruz Sweetwater. Is that good news or bad news, honey?"

"It wasn't news at all," Lyra said firmly. "It was business."

"Of course it was." Gloria smiled, her heavily made-up eyes gleaming with cool speculation. A lot of people—including, no doubt, her current lover, a powerful member of the Frequency Guild Council—took her at face value. They assumed that she was nothing more than the fluff-brained, big-bosomed, big-haired blonde bimbo she appeared to be.

The bosom and the hair might be seriously enhanced, but Lyra had dealt with Gloria often enough to know that her IQ was a lot higher than most people gave her credit for, certainly higher than that of her Councilman lover. She was also a woman of talent, although she went to great lengths to pretend otherwise.

There was a saying among professional amber tuners: "Only your tuner knows for sure." Tuned amber—like a finely tuned musical instrument—did not remain clear indefinitely. Over time and with use it gradually blurred and lost its focusing power. It eventually required retuning to restore maximum efficiency. Generally speaking, a properly tuned stone lasted the average user for several months, sometimes as long as a year.

But those who generated a lot of energy burned through their amber much more rapidly. Gloria was a frequent customer of Lyra's, bringing one or more pieces of tuned amber in for retuning every few weeks. That meant that she was a lot stronger than most people were aware.

As was common with a lot of above-average talents, Gloria preferred to keep her personal paranormal assets confidential. Like all smart, professional tuners, Lyra was always discreet about such matters. There was no quicker way to lose a client than to gossip about his or her psychic range. Those who generated the least wattage were always trying to make it appear that they were stronger. At the other end of the spectrum, the strong ones usually wanted to conceal their true power levels as well as the exact nature of their talents.

"What have you brought me?" Lyra asked.

"Take a look," Gloria said. She placed a green velvet jewelry box on the counter.

Lyra picked up the box and opened it. She gave an appreciative little whistle at the sight of the necklace inside. A brilliant carved stone of standard resonating amber glowed with the unmistakable luster characteristic of superior quality and resonating power. It was set in gold.

"Nice, Gloria." Lyra drew the necklace out of the box. "Very nice. Congratulations."

"Thanks." Gloria laughed with soft satisfaction. "Dear Hubert has been in a generous mood lately."

"I thought the bracelet he gave you last month was his

personal best, but this tops that piece. What put good old Hubert into such a gracious frame of mind?"

Gloria offered Vincent another cookie. "He thinks that now that Benson Landry is out of the picture, the Council will move to choose Douglas Drake as the new Guild boss."

"And that's important to Hubert?" Lyra asked.

Gloria winked. "Very important. He and Drake are friends from the old neighborhood near the South Wall. They joined the Guild together, and they've watched each other's backs in the organization ever since they were first-year hunters down in the catacombs. They've clawed their way up through the ranks, each one helping the other. Hubert's daughter is engaged to Drake's son. If Drake gets the top job, you can be sure he'll make certain that his good pal Hubert will be well taken care of."

Lyra rolled her eyes. "Gotta love Guild politics. Talk about democracy in action."

"There's another angle. Wilson Revere is trying to make it appear that he's above meddling in Guild politics, but the truth is he wants Drake to get the top slot. Figures it will give him an edge against Amber Inc." Gloria met her eyes in a very direct look. "Word is that Amber Inc. would prefer to see just about anyone other than Drake at the top of the Guild."

Lyra nodded. "Thanks for the update, Gloria."

"Any time. Now, about my lovely new necklace. I want the full treatment."

"I'll take care of it right now," Lyra said.

She held the pendant in her hand and focused delicately

through the amethyst amber of her charm bracelet. The majority of tuners used standard resonating amber because that was the only kind they could activate. Gloria and Jeff would naturally assume that she was using the amber that she wore so obviously in her earrings. But she had learned early on in her career that she could achieve an extra degree of clarity and focusing power in any piece of amber if she worked through amethyst.

She channeled psi delicately, feeling her way into the natural energy patterns of the stone. All amber—even a rough, raw chunk straight out of a mine—was capable of some focusing ability if you had enough talent to rez it and if you knew what you were doing. But the results were wildly unpredictable if the amber had not been tuned.

It did not matter how beautifully a piece of amber was carved and polished. If you wanted to use it to focus psi, tuning made all the difference. And the very finest tuners were those who could feel their way into the currents of latent power in a particular stone and align and stabilize them without loss of strength or clarity. A little distortion or a lack of full concentration on the part of the tuner at the critical moment, or simply insufficient talent, could ruin even the best amber.

It didn't take much to destroy the superior resonating power of a good stone such as the pendant. But it took real talent to bring out the full potential of such a piece.

She used dainty pulses of psi lightning to jump-start the currents of the pendant. The stone grew warm to the touch as she sent power into it. Once activated, the currents had to be carefully stabilized in a state of suspension. After that process was complete, anyone with even minimal psi, regardless of the type of talent, would be able to use the stone to focus.

But Gloria did not come to her just to get her amber tuned. If that was all she had wanted, she could have taken her business to any of a number of tuning shops in the city. It was the quiet word-of-mouth rumors of the very special services offered by Dore Tuning & Consulting that had brought the mistress of one of the most powerful men in the city into Lyra's shop.

She could do what very few other tuners were capable of doing, because it required nonstandard amber such as amethyst and a unique talent.

"Okay," she said. She held out the stone on her palm. "Touch the pendant."

Gloria obediently put one beringed and elaborately manicured fingertip on the amber stone.

"Ready?" Lyra asked.

"Say when."

"Focus," Lyra ordered softly. She jacked up her own senses, gently pushing more psi through amethyst, and concentrated on the pendant.

Virtually everyone possessed some degree of latent psychic talent, even if they weren't aware of it. But everyone's paranormal currents were unique to that individual, like fingerprints and DNA. Using her own talent, Lyra picked up the nuances of the wavelengths and intensity of Gloria's energy patterns and fine-tuned the pendant to resonate with them.

A moment later, she handed the pendant back to Gloria. "Done," she said.

"Excellent." Gloria slipped the necklace back into the jewelry case and opened her purse. "Same fee as usual?"

"Yes, thank you."

Gloria removed her wallet. Instead of extracting a credit card, however, she took out a few hundred dollar bills and put them on the counter. Lyra collected the money swiftly and made it disappear into the till. She was acutely aware of Jeff watching everything with a fascinated and rather shocked expression. She knew what he was thinking. No one paid this much just to get amber tuned. But he had the sense to keep his mouth shut.

Gloria gave Vincent one last cookie and closed her purse. "See you all next time."

She waltzed out the door on her sky-high heels and disappeared.

Jeff absently patted Vincent and looked at Lyra. "Excuse me, Miss Dore, I know I'm just the bodyguard, but is there any chance you might tell me what that was all about?"

She smiled. "I'll explain, but you have to promise you'll honor the code."

"Yes, ma'am, what code would that be?"

" 'What happens in an amber tuning shop, stays in an amber tuning shop.' "

His face fell. "Uh, well, the boss will probably ask me for a full report. And much as I'd like to know what you did for Miss Ray—"

"You're more afraid of what Cruz Sweetwater will do

to you if you don't tell him the whole truth and nothing but, right?"

Jeff made a face. "The boss is what you might call a little inflexible when it comes to some things."

"Yes, I know. He operates under a code, too."

Jeff exhaled heavily. "Yes, ma'am."

She smiled. "And so do you?"

"Guess you could say that's part of what being a member of the family is all about."

"You make being in the Sweetwater clan sound like being a Guild man or a member of a crime family. Lots of secrets and a private code."

Jeff flushed. "Yes, ma'am. Guess there are some similarities."

"Tell me. Don't you ever find it just a trifle stifling to be part of such a *close* family?"

"Yes, ma'am." Jeff shrugged. "But you know how it is with family."

"Not really."

Jeff was beyond red now. He was thoroughly chagrined. "Sorry, ma'am. I know your situation is a little, uh, different."

She took pity on him. "Hey, don't worry about it. I'm used to being on my own. Besides, I've got Vincent."

At the sound of his name, Vincent mumbled and fluttered down from the counter to the floor. He scampered to his painting, picked up the paintbrush, and went back to his favorite game.

"Yes, ma'am," Jeff said. He watched Vincent splash paint on the canvas with a slightly puzzled expression.

She did not need to be a mind reader to know what he was thinking. It was odd enough to be without any close relatives. Claiming a dust bunny as your next of kin was downright eccentric.

"And I've got friends," she added quickly. "Especially one very close friend. But never mind. I'll explain what I did for Gloria Ray a few minutes ago, and you can feel free to tell Cruz. Heck, it might be good for my business. I rely on word-of-mouth advertising to bring customers in for my special services, you see. It's not like I can advertise in the newspapers."

Jeff grinned, clearly relieved. "Thanks. So what did you do to Miss Ray's amber?"

"Essentially, I aligned the frequencies to her personal focus wavelengths. Other people could use the pendant, but they wouldn't be able to do what she can with it."

He frowned. "I don't get it. What can she do with her amber that someone else can't do?"

"Because the amber is tuned to her personal psi, its clarity and focus are greatly enhanced. The process doesn't make a person more powerful, but it does mean that the individual can use his or her talent with far greater precision. And that can sometimes be even more useful than a lot of raw psi talent."

Jeff made a face. "It sure can."

"The extra fine-tuning is especially important to people who possess strong talents, of course. They not only get better control; it takes less energy to work the amber. That, in turn, means that they are less likely to melt amber when they focus the full strength of their psi through a stone."

Jeff was definitely impressed. "So you're saying that Miss Ray has some kind of high-grade talent?"

"Let's just say that I do a lot of repeat business with Miss Ray."

Gloria Ray possessed an unusually strong level of intuition. She had confided to Lyra that it was an extremely useful asset in her career as the mistress of a wealthy, powerful man. Women in her position, she'd said, required an edge in order to stay on top of their games. They needed to know when they were in danger of getting dumped for a newer, younger model. More crucially, they needed to know when they were in real physical danger. Women who hung out with men like dear Hubert frequently learned the secrets of their lovers. And men with secrets sometimes concluded that the women they were sleeping with knew too much.

Gloria had come into Dore Tuning & Consulting the day after she had discovered that Hubert's former mistress had vanished under mysterious circumstances. Lyra had a hunch that Gloria was making plans to disappear under her own steam sometime in the near future.

Jeff glanced toward the door. "And here I thought she was just some councilman's arm candy."

"Never underestimate a woman, Jeff."

He nodded, very serious. "Yeah, the boss has been saying that a lot for the past three months." He frowned. "She paid you with cash. She didn't want a paper trail, right?"

"That was a very good observation. I'm impressed. As it happens, a lot of my special services customers prefer a degree of anonymity and discretion."

"Because they don't want others to find out about their talents?"

"Right."

"But why don't you want to advertise your special services in the usual way? It would give you a competitive advantage. There are a lot of tuners out there."

"The thing is, if I advertise, I'd have to offer the service to everyone who came through the door and asked for it."

He raised his brows. "I get it. You don't think everyone deserves the extra juice."

"There are some strange and dangerous people out there, Jeff. The last thing I'd want to do is fine-tune some amber for one of the bad guys and find out later that he used it to commit a crime or hurt someone."

He nodded somberly. "I'm with you."

"This way I get to vet my clients before I offer the service. If someone comes in asking about it, and I don't get good vibes, I can always say that the rumors about me are false."

He eyed her thoughtfully. "You can tell the good guys from the bad guys?"

"I can when I tune amber for them," she said. "There's another old saying in my business: 'It's in the psi.' "

"Like it's in the blood?"

"Yep. Every time a person uses amber, he or she leaves his psi prints in the stone. Bad psi isn't hard to sense."

"Any chance I could talk you into giving my amber your special service?"

"What's your talent?"

He shrugged. "Officially, I'm an amber talent, like the other men in my family. And it's true, I use a nonstandard amber."

She glanced at the blue green ring on his hand. "Tourmaline."

"Right. But the truth is, I use tourmaline to focus my real talent. I've got a variation of the para-hunter talent."

"Cruz explained it to me."

"Figured he would have by now."

She frowned. "What does that mean?"

Jeff looked embarrassed. "Sorry. Didn't mean to get personal. It's just that everyone in the family knows that you're the woman who broke the boss' heart, so it figures the two of you are pretty close."

She was so stunned she could hardly speak.

"What did you say?" she finally managed.

"I said, I assumed the boss had explained about the family talent."

She waved both hands to stop him. "Not that. The bit about the broken heart."

He shrugged. "It's no secret in the family."

"It's ridiculous. Some kind of stupid joke."

"We don't joke about that kind of stuff in my family," Jeff said.

"I don't know what Cruz told you, but I can assure you, I did not break his heart."

Jeff just looked at her, not speaking.

She sighed. "For Pete's sake. Forget it. Tell me about your version of the family talent."

"Right." Jeff was eager to change the subject. "I'm a para-hunter, so I've got the good night vision and the reflexes and all the rest. But what I'm really good at is reading a crime scene. I can walk you through the series of events that took place there. Something about the way psychic energy gets thrown off by acts of violence."

"Really? That sounds interesting."

A spark of excitement gleamed in Jeff's eyes. "Don't laugh, but I'd like to apply to the FBPI academy and become an agent."

"The Federal Bureau of Psi Investigation? Why would I laugh? Sounds like a fine and noble career goal to me."

Jeff made a face. "Not as far as my dad and the boss and Big Jake and everyone else in the family is concerned. We've always had sort of a weird relationship with official law enforcement. I can't figure it out, to tell you the truth. It's not like AI Security doesn't occasionally do favors for the FBPI, just like we do for the Guilds and the Arcane Society."

"Favors?"

"Well, sure, those agencies only come to us when they know they can't deal with the problem on their own, and they pay for the work we do, so I guess you can't really call it doing favors, but you get my point, right?"

"Uh, yes. Yes, I think so."

"The thing is, AI Security is a business. Bottom line is we work for people who can afford us. I want to be a part of real law enforcement, the kind that tries to get justice for everyone, even people who can't afford high-priced security agencies. I want to make a contribution."

"I understand," she said.

"More and more I feel like it's something I was meant to do."

"A calling."

He thought about that. "Maybe. In a way."

"Well, why not quit the family firm and follow your bliss? Apply to the FBPI academy."

He stared at her as if she had just suggested that he fly. "Quit Amber Inc.?"

She spread her arms wide. "It's a big world. Lots of opportunities for a motivated young man. Who says you have to stay in the family business for your whole professional career?"

"Well, that's sort of how things are at Amber Inc. If you're in the family, you work for the family firm. One way or another."

"Surely a few of your relatives have gone out on their own."

Jeff thought for a moment. "Well, there's my great-uncle Ned. He opened a travel agency."

"There you go."

"But mostly his company just handles corporate travel for Amber Inc."

"Oh."

Jeff cogitated for another moment. "The boss' father is a lawyer. So is his mother."

"Really? I didn't know that. Okay, it sounds like they didn't toe the family line."

Jeff sighed. "Their law firm has only one client."

"Let me guess. Amber Inc."

"Yeah." Jeff pondered briefly and suddenly brightened. "Aunt Brenda."

"What happened to her?"

"She's a doctor, a pediatrician at the Frequency Medical Center."

"The Frequency Medical Center was built by Amber Inc. Right. Well, Jeff, looks like you've got a problem. I'll tune some amber for you, but if what you really want is to become a genuine FBPI agent, you're going to have to kick over the traces and take a stand against family pressure."

He gave her a morose look. "You don't know my family."

"Are you kidding me? After what I went through since I met your boss? Trust me, I know your family."

He winced. "Yeah, I guess maybe you do. You know, you're not quite what I expected, Miss Dore."

She narrowed her eyes. A lot of men were prone to tasteless jokes about female amber tuners. The phrase *getting one's amber tuned* had multiple meanings in certain quarters frequented by males.

"And just what did you expect?" she asked coldly.

"I dunno," he admitted. "Should have known you'd be a little different, though."

"And why is that?" she demanded.

"Because you're the woman who broke the boss's heart."

Chapter 19

JEFF DROVE HER BACK TO HER APARTMENT SHORTLY before two so that she could change clothes for the auction preview appointment with Wilson Revere. They used a small, nondescript Float provided by Amber Inc. Security. The little vehicle did not call attention to itself in any way. If Jeff hadn't explained that beneath the boring gray paint job the car was discreetly armored with heavy-duty mag-steel, Lyra would never have known.

"Gets lousy mileage because of all the steel," Jeff said. "And it's sort of embarrassing to drive. But it has one big advantage. No one looks twice at it."

"Does Amber Inc. Security maintain a fleet of armored vehicles?" Lyra asked.

"The company garage always has a few on hand."

"To protect the executives? Not that I can envision

Cruz Sweetwater buzzing around in a Float, mind you."

Jeff laughed. "If you're in any of the executive suites at AI, it means you can take care of yourself. You drive whatever you want. Mostly we use the armored cars for clients."

"So now I'm an AI client?" She wrinkled her nose. "I hope no one plans on sending me a bill because, thanks to a recent lawsuit against a certain unnamed company, I can't afford a high-rez private security firm."

"Don't worry, there won't be any bill." Jeff slid the little compact into a parking space at the curb. "The boss is picking up the tab on this case personally." He glanced at the rearview mirror as he powered up the engine. "Speaking of the boss, looks like he's ready to take his shift."

"What?" Alarmed, Lyra twisted around in the front seat just in time to see a familiar black Slider glide into the parking space behind the Float. "Oh, no, no, this is a really, really bad idea."

Even as the sense of impending doom settled on her like a dark cloud, Vincent, perched on the back of the seat, started bouncing and chortling with anticipation. His red beret flapped wildly.

Lyra watched Cruz get out of the Slider and walk toward the Float. He wore another sleekly tailored black jacket, black trousers, and black bolo tie trimmed with a gleaming amber stone. The well-dressed assassin on his way to an upscale auction.

She grabbed Vincent and her tote, opened the door, and jumped out.

"No," she said. "Absolutely not, Cruz. You cannot go with me to the auction preview."

He halted in front of her. "Sure I can." He batted one of Vincent's paws a couple of times in greeting and kissed Lyra in a quick, outrageously proprietary way. Before she could protest, he straightened, braced one hand on the roof of the Float, and leaned in to speak to Jeff through the open window. "I'll take it from here. I'll give you a call when we need you back."

"Yes, sir. Bye, Miss Dore," Jeff said as he drove off down the street.

Lyra glared at Cruz. "Wilson Revere is an important client."

Somehow Cruz managed to look politely innocent, even a little confused.

"So?" he said.

"Look, you and Revere obviously have a history. If I walk into that auction with you, he might decide he doesn't need my consulting services after all."

"Revere reads the papers like everyone else. He knows that you and I are seeing each other again. He wouldn't have hired you if that was a problem. I told you, I think it's actually the reason he did hire you. He's going to try to use you somehow."

She ignored the last sentence and focused on the main point she wanted to make. "One night doesn't mean that you and I are involved," she warned.

"It does as far as the media is concerned."

"But it will look unprofessional if I arrive at that auction with you."

Cruz smiled. "Think of me as just another client."

SHE WAS STILL FUMING AN HOUR LATER WHEN SHE walked into the hushed, elegant atmosphere of the Fairstead Gallery with Cruz at her side. She consoled herself with the knowledge that at least she looked thoroughly professional in a skirted suit and pumps. Her hair was up in a businesslike twist. She wore her charm bracelet on her wrist. The usual pair of small, discreet amber earrings gleamed in her ears.

Vincent had been left at home. High-end auction houses did not welcome dust bunnies or any other species that possessed more than two legs. They were also highly selective when it came to the two-legged types. The only way a low-rent amber tuner turned part-time antiquities consultant could cross the threshold of the Fairstead was because she had been invited by one of the gallery's high-rent clients.

A number of well-dressed people circulated among the display cases, making notes about the various items that were slated to go on the block. Several uniformed guards stood watch. Lyra spotted two other amber consultants. Both moved routinely in these rarified circles. She knew they had noticed her, also. They gave her veiled what-the-hell-is-she-doing-here looks and then did double takes when they recognized Cruz. She returned the acknowledgments with a dazzling screw-you smile.

She heightened her senses and felt the familiar frisson that told her there was a lot of good amber in the room. She glanced at Cruz and knew he felt it, too. An affinity for amber was one thing they did have in common.

A suave, distinguished-looking man with discreetly enhanced patrician features and a wealth of unnaturally bright silver hair appeared as if by magic. Ignoring Lyra, he beamed at Cruz, displaying a lot of perfect teeth.

"Mr. Sweetwater," he gushed smoothly. "An unexpected pleasure. I'm Valentine Fairstead. I do not recall seeing your name on the guest list, but I am, of course, delighted that you decided to attend the auction."

"Thought I'd take a quick look," Cruz said, glancing casually around at the cases. "But I won't be bidding unless Miss Dore spots something of special interest. I rely on her for all my appraisals."

Horrified shock flashed in Fairstead's eyes. He looked at Lyra as if she were one of the multifooted species not welcome in the gallery.

"Miss Dore?" he repeated somewhat blankly.

"I wouldn't consider buying amber antiquities without her," Cruz said.

To his credit, Fairstead recovered quickly. He bestowed his gleaming smile on Lyra.

"Yes, of course, Miss Dore," he said. "Welcome to the Fairstead Gallery."

"Thank you," she said. It took effort to keep her voice

cool and polite, but she managed. "Actually, Mr. Sweetwater is here only because he very kindly offered to escort me today. One of your other guests has engaged my services this afternoon."

"I see." Fairstead was clearly thunderstruck. "Isn't that a little, ah, unusual?"

"I understand that you are going to be auctioning off some extremely unusual amber today," she said just as smoothly. "Rare amber is my specialty."

"Yes, of course," Fairstead said weakly.

Another man in an elegantly tailored business suit and a black and amber tie came toward them. He was tall and well-built with the refined masculine features that Lyra associated with rez-screen anchormen. There was nothing soft or genteel about his eyes, however. They were glacier blue. He gave Cruz a speculative glance and then smiled wryly at Lyra. She recognized him instantly. Wilson Revere was in the news a lot.

"I trust you're not going to tell me that I've already lost my new consultant to my competition, Miss Dore," he said. "I'll be crushed."

"No, absolutely not," she assured him swiftly. "I'm here to consult for you, as arranged, Mr. Revere. I mean, Wilson. Mr. Sweetwater offered to give me a ride, that's all."

Cruz looked amused at being relegated to the role of chauffeur.

"Not like I had anything better to do this afternoon," he said. He inclined his head with cool civility. "Got something special in mind here today, Revere?"

"Why, yes, as a matter of fact, I do." Revere smiled. "I'm looking forward to getting Miss Dore's opinion before I bid on it, however. I wouldn't want to make an expensive mistake."

"No," Cruz said, "you don't want to make any big mistakes."

He was using what Lyra thought of as his professional hit man voice, cold and laced with the promise of doom.

Infuriated, she swung around to face him. She should have worn higher heels, she thought. In her conservative two-and-a-half-inch pumps she was only a couple of inches above his shoulder. The lack of height was not an asset when one was trying to intimidate a man like Cruz.

"If you'll excuse me, I have work to do, Mr. Sweetwater," she said, infusing the words with as much authority as she could muster. Damn it, she was a professional, and she would not let him ruin things.

To her overwhelming relief, Cruz responded politely to the unsubtle hint. "Take your time," he said. "I'll have a look around on my own."

"You do that." Lyra bestowed a warm smile on Revere. "Why don't you show me the item that is of particular interest to you, Wilson?"

"Certainly." He gave Cruz a slyly amused smile and took Lyra's arm.

Together they walked off toward a distant display case. Lyra knew Cruz was watching their backs. She could feel his gaze the entire length of the room.

The Fairstead Gallery specialized in spectacular rare

amber jewelry of all descriptions. Rings, watches, cuff links, necklaces, and earrings glowed and glittered in the locked glass cases.

The gallery was also known for the gemstone quality of its raw, uncut, and untuned amber, the most valuable of which were the specimens of rare and exotic varieties.

"I assume the media was right for once?" Revere said in a conversational tone. "You and Sweetwater have resolved your legal issues?"

"There was nothing to resolve. Amber Inc. crushed my lawsuit."

"I trust Sweetwater made it worth your while to rescue that team that got trapped in the ruin?"

"We're still negotiating my fee," she said easily. "Now, why don't you show me the amber that caught your eye?"

"Right over here."

He guided her toward the row of cases set against the back wall. She experienced more than just a frisson of awareness when they got close to the specimens. All of her senses were fully rezzed by the unusual latent energies of the stones on display. The collection was, indeed, impressive. Chunks of rare emerald, ruby, and sapphire amber were arrayed on black velvet in the artistically lit cases. She also spotted some remarkable crystal, jade, and chalcedony amber, all of excellent quality.

"I'm interested in the amethyst piece in the last case," Revere said. "What do you think?"

She walked to the display case and studied the rough, uncut stone inside with all of her senses. The amethyst amber was attractive, showing good color and clarity. But when she probed for the latent energy of the stone, feeling her way into the untuned currents, disappointment whispered through her.

"It's a nice piece," she said. "It would make beautiful jewelry, but its resonating power is weak. Not that most people would notice, of course."

He watched her with a speculative expression. "Only someone who could rez amethyst would care one way or the other."

"Yes.

Revere studied the amber in the case. "You're sure about the latent energy in that stone?"

"Positive."

"Well, so much for that." But he did not look disappointed. Instead, he appeared satisfied, as if she had passed a test. "I'm not interested in making earrings out of that chunk of amethyst."

"I'm sorry, but you know how it is with amber. Not every piece is powerful." She cleared her throat. "Do you mind me asking how you planned to use it?"

"I'm looking for lab-quality stones. Your discovery of the ruin and those relics has fired up a lot of interest in amethyst."

"I see."

Revere glanced back toward the front of the room where Cruz was examining the contents of a case. "Can't let the competition get too far ahead of us. My people are convinced that the existence of the ruin is proof that there's a lot more power in amethyst than the experts have realized. Since we can't get our hands on any of the relics that Amber Inc. seized from you, I'm looking for some raw stones to use for research purposes in the Rez-Stone lab."

"Oh, geez. Sounds like an arms race."

"Amber is power," Wilson said. "In more ways than one." He did not take his eyes off Cruz. "As long as you're here, there is one other specimen that I'd like you to examine."

"Of course." She surveyed the rough stones. "The emerald is a nice specimen."

"I've got some good emeralds in the lab. The stone I want you to see is in Fairstead's private viewing room."

"This gallery isn't it?" she asked, looking around.

"No," Wilson said very softly.

Valentine Fairstead materialized again, white teeth shining.

"If you will follow me, Mr. Revere," he murmured.

He led the way past a guard and rezzed the lock of a door that Lyra had not noticed in the dim light. Revere ushered her into a small, windowless room. Fairstead followed, closing the door behind him.

"I keep this particular specimen in the vault," Fairstead said.

He crossed the small space and pulled aside a midnight blue velvet curtain, revealing a gleaming mag-steel bank vault–style door. Keeping his back to Lyra and Revere, he rezzed the lock.

The heavy door opened slowly. More steel glinted in the shadowy interior.

Energy pulsed from within the vault, lifting the hair on the back of Lyra's neck, thrilling and chilling her senses. She shivered with awareness and a sudden wave of fear. She knew those currents.

She watched Wilson out of the corner of her eye. She was sure she felt energy pulse around him, but there was no indication on his handsome face of any reaction. She reminded herself that men in his position were consummate actors.

Fairstead moved into the vault. "I'll bring out the piece," he said.

The door opened again, startling all three of them. Cruz walked into the room.

Fairstead rushed back out of the vault, empty-handed. He was clearly agitated and alarmed.

"I'm sorry, Mr. Sweetwater," he said. He slid an uneasy glance at Revere. "This is a private showing."

"Don't mind me," Cruz said. He gave Revere a truly dangerous smile. "I'm old-school. That means that Lyra leaves with the one she came with. That would be me."

"It was my understanding that Miss Dore was here in her professional capacity," Revere said. "Not as your date."

"Stop this," Lyra said tightly. "Stop it right now."

All three men looked at her.

"How dare you, Cruz Sweetwater?" She stormed toward him. "You asked me to give you another chance, but look what you've done to me."

He frowned. "I haven't done anything."

"Oh, yes, you have. You have humiliated me in front

of my most important client and the proprietor of the most respected amber gallery in the entire city. You've made me look like one of your bimbo girlfriends instead of a real professional consultant. How could you, after all the promises you made?"

She slapped his face hard, much harder than she had intended. The sharp crack of the blow resonated in the small space. For an instant she froze, shocked by her own small act of violence. She had been going for a theatrical touch, not a real blow. She had never before deliberately struck anyone in her entire adult life.

Cruz did not move. He just stood there, his jaw reddening from the blow. His eyes narrowed ever so slightly.

She burst into tears and rushed toward the door.

"I will never forgive you," she wailed. "This was going to be my big chance to recover from that mountain of debt I've been under, thanks to losing that lawsuit against Amber Inc. *I was going to consult for Wilson Revere.* You've ruined everything. Just like last time. I don't know why I let you talk me into trusting you again."

She yanked open the door and fled, sobbing. The clients, attendants, and guards in the outer room froze, transfixed by the sight of a hysterical woman running through the elegant establishment.

When she reached the front of the room, someone hurried to push open one of the thick glass doors for her. Dabbing at her eyes with the back of her hand, she rushed out onto the sidewalk.

She started walking briskly. As soon as she had put some distance between herself and the gallery, she stopped crying and started watching for a cab. It was typical of her luck, she thought, that there wasn't one anywhere in sight. She spotted a bus stop at the end of the block and hurried toward it.

Cruz appeared before the bus did. No surprise there, she thought. She watched as he eased the Slider against the curb.

He leaned across the seat to open the door.

"Get in," he said.

She thought about it for a few seconds, but there really was no point pretending he wasn't there. Cruz would not go away like one of her hallucinations.

She slid into the front seat, closed the door, and buckled her seat belt.

Cruz checked the rearview mirror and pulled away from the curb.

"What the hell was that about?" he asked.

"I slapped your face." She was still stunned by the anger that had momentarily turned everything red.

"Yeah, I noticed." He took one hand off the wheel and touched his jaw somewhat gingerly. "It was a little over-the-top, don't you think?"

"I thought it looked very realistic."

"Probably because it was realistic. Trust me, I felt it."

"I didn't mean to hit you that hard. I'm sorry. I got a little carried away."

"Forget it. What about the fake tears and the female hysteria?"

"I thought that all looked good," she said, not without some satisfaction. "Convincing."

"It was. I'm sure that everyone, including Fairstead, Revere, and half the top-tier amber collectors in the city, not to mention your competitors in the consulting world, bought it."

She struggled and failed to suppress a wry smile. "Everyone but you?"

"I know you better than they do. In a crisis you don't get hysterical. You file a lawsuit."

"Maybe you don't know me as well as you think you do." And maybe there were a few things about herself that she had been unaware of, too, until now. So much for having worked through all her anger with Harmonic Meditation. "In any case, I doubt that there's time for a lawsuit in this situation. Probably wouldn't do me any more good than it did the last time."

"Talk to me."

"There's an amethyst relic in Fairstead's vault," she said quietly. "I think it came from the ruin."

"Son of a ghost." He glanced at her. "You found the artifact that disappeared from the AI lab?"

"Maybe."

"What the hell does that mean? Aren't you sure?"

"I said I sensed *an* amethyst relic. The only question is, whose artifact is it?"

"There's no question about ownership," he said flatly. "It belongs to Amber Inc."

"We don't know for certain, yet, that the one in Fairstead's vault came from your lab." She cleared her throat. "There is another possibility."

He exhaled slowly. "Why do I have a feeling I'm not going to like this?"

"Probably because you know me so well."

"About this other possibility," Cruz said. "Just how many of the relics did you remove from that chamber before Amber Inc. took control?"

"Three. Figured you'd never miss them. And you didn't. Fortunately, the aliens didn't leave a detailed inventory of the artifacts they stored in the chamber."

"Please don't tell me you hid those three stones somewhere in your apartment."

"Do I look that dumb? I stashed them down in the tunnels, of course. As soon as we get back to my place, I'll change and go underground to see if any of them are missing. If all three are still there, I think it's safe to say that the relic in Fairstead's vault is the one from the Amber Inc. lab."

"You do realize I'm not going to let you go down to your secret hiding place alone, don't you?"

"If you go with me, it will no longer be a secret."

"No," Cruz said. "It won't be a secret. Looks like you're going to have to trust me."

Chapter 20

CRUZ CONTEMPLATED THE NARROW, JAGGED, HOLE-IN-the-wall entrance to the glowing catacombs. He did not know whether to be furious or impressed. But then, that was a typical state of affairs when it came to his relationship with Lyra.

They were standing in the sub-subbasement of an old, abandoned warehouse. The dank, concrete room smelled of mold and damp. The pitch-dark space was illuminated only by their flashlights and the sliver of green psi that filtered through the slim opening into the tunnels. Water trickled ominously somewhere in the darkness.

He looked at Lyra. She was back in her prospecting attire: trousers, boots, and a denim shirt. Vincent was perched on her shoulder, excited, as usual, about the possibility of an adventure.

"This is how you've been coming and going from the tunnels since I last saw you?" Cruz asked.

In theory, the only officially approved ways in and out of the underground world were via the main gates guarded by the Guilds. Those entrances were usually located within the great walls that surrounded the Dead Cities. But there were countless hidden hole-in-the-wall entrances to the catacombs throughout the Old Quarters of all the cities.

The holes were not man-made. The green quartz was incredibly strong. No human-engineered tools yet invented could make a dent in the stone. But at some point in the distant past, cracks and fissures had been created in the catacombs. One theory held that they were the result of earthquakes. Some experts were convinced that the aliens themselves had made them using the same technology they had employed to construct the tunnels.

Over the years the unofficial entrances had been discovered and used by a motley array of independent prospectors and treasure hunters—the so-called ruin rats—who made their livings on the fringes of the trade in alien artifacts. Such cracks in the walls were also the entrances of choice for drug dealers, criminals fleeing from the law, thrill-seeking kids, gangs, and the occasional serial killer.

Lyra's secret hole-in-the-wall was located below the streets of one of the seediest neighborhoods of the Quarter. Just the sort of place where a serial killer might bring his victims, Cruz thought.

"I had to find a new entrance after I made the mistake of showing you the last one," she explained, de-rezzing her own flashlight. "I figured you'd have it watched."

That hurt. He'd promised, after all.

"No," he said, determined to rise above the jab. "I didn't have your old entrance watched. I never told anyone else about it. I gave you my word that I wouldn't."

"Well, that's great, but given events at the time, I couldn't be sure you'd keep your word, now, could I?"

"You really don't trust me, do you?"

"Like I said, I trust you to do what you feel you must do, but that doesn't mean that I can trust you to do what I want you to do. Nancy offered to let me use the entrance below her gallery, but I thought you might have someone watching that one, too."

He reeled in his temper with an effort of raw willpower. Time to get a grip. There were priorities here. He had to stay focused. He de-rezzed the flashlight and started toward the gash in the quartz.

"Let's go," he said.

She must have picked up on his slightly savage frame of mind, because she gave him a startled, uneasy look. But she and Vincent followed him into the glowing green world.

They all paused just inside to run through the usual amber-rez locator checks and to verify that all the amber they were carrying was working properly. The safety precautions were overkill, but only idiots skipped them. Amber was the only way to navigate underground. If you got lost in the tunnels, you ended up wandering until you died from hunger or thirst or until you blundered into an energy ghost or an illusion trap.

"First left at the intersection," Lyra said briskly.

The intersection in question was a disorienting rotunda that connected thirteen passageways. Each branching corridor seemed to vanish into infinity. Cruz knew that part of that impression was due to the optical illusions created by the maze and the fact that everything underground was relentlessly green. In addition, while the heavy currents of energy that flowed through the tunnels gave you a pleasant buzz, they also did weird things to the senses, altering perceptions in subtle ways.

Lyra knew where she was going, of course. He might have issues with her lack of trust and independent ways, but she was a pro underground. She had been working the tunnels since her teens, and more recently she had made several successful forays into the rain forest. Like him, she had an affinity not only for amber but for the alien underworld.

"Did your security people learn anything from those two men who attacked us?" she asked in a clear attempt to change the subject.

They had been forced to change subjects a lot lately, he thought.

"Nothing helpful," he said. "They are just a couple of local street goons who got hired for their muscle, not their brains. They met their employer only once, in an alley behind a bar in the Quarter. Claimed they didn't get a good look at his face."

"Which is probably true," Lyra said. "If I set out to

hire a couple of thugs, I'd make sure they didn't see my face, either."

"You've got a point. But there was one unusual aspect to their story. I had intended to talk to you about it after you finished with Wilson Revere."

"I think it's safe to assume that particular consulting relationship has been permanently terminated," she said glumly. "Too bad. I coulda been a contender."

"A contender for what?"

"I have no idea. My grandfather used to say that a lot. He claimed it was a line from some Old World film. Never mind. Tell me about the thugs."

"I told you, they met the guy in an alley at night. They could have said it was too dark to get a good look at him. But when they were pinned down, what they actually told the interrogators was that there was something strange about him."

She frowned. "Physically, you mean?"

"They thought he was wearing some kind of mask, one that blurred and distorted his features."

"I've seen rez-screen films where the villain wears one leg of a pair of hose over his face. It changes his face in a really creepy way."

"They were asked about that possibility. They said it was more as if his face and his body were misshapen. And everything kept changing."

"What?"

"They said that sometimes it looked like the guy's head and body appeared elongated. At other times he looked too wide and twisted."

"Those two actually used a big word like *elongated*?"

"No, but you get my meaning. What they described was a man who managed to conceal his features by distorting them."

She thought about that. "Do you think he was projecting some kind of rez-film image of himself against the alley wall? One that looked real enough to fool the two thugs?"

"I considered that possibility. Both men had come out of a tavern to meet the guy. No question but that they'd been drinking. They were probably high on some street drug, as well. But the more they were questioned, the more their description of the meeting with the client sounded like an experience out of a dream." He paused deliberately. "What you might call a waking nightmare."

Lyra slammed to a halt and whirled to face him with such speed that Vincent almost fell off her shoulder.

"Are you saying that the man who hired those two thugs may be causing my hallucinations?" she demanded. A mix of hope, shock, and comprehension lit her intelligent face.

He stopped, too. "I think it's a possibility, yes."

"But how? Why?"

"I can't be positive about the how. Maybe the bastard found himself some handy-dandy bit of alien technology and figured out how to rez it to create hallucinations. Wouldn't be the biggest surprise in the world. More and more artifacts are coming out of the jungle every week. The other possibility is that he has a talent for it. There are records of similar abilities in the Arcane Society files."

"You mean like your talent for projecting that psi fog stuff?"

He did not like her lumping him in with the bastard, whoever he was. "A lot of talents came through the Curtain."

"But why come after me?"

"Not sure yet, but I think we can assume it's got something to do with the amethyst ruin."

"Oh, geez." She frowned. "The dreams have always taken place on one of the streets in my neighborhood. There are usually a few cars and other people around, but I've never noticed any one vehicle or person in particular."

"If this guy is employing a gadget that can generate hallucinations, he may also be able to use it to make sure you don't get a good look at him."

"But what's his goal?"

"I don't know. Maybe he's running some kind of experiment."

"That doesn't make any sense."

"Makes more sense than your theory," he said.

"The possibility that I'm going crazy? Well, of the two theories, I must admit I prefer yours. But I don't know, Cruz. You're getting pretty far out there."

"Wouldn't be the first time. Look, we're going to have to finish this conversation later. Right now we need to stay on task."

"Okay." She checked her locater again and then started forward once more. "The room is right around the corner."

Vincent got excited when they approached the entrance to the small antechamber. He mumbled enthusiastically.

"He thinks we've come down here to play with the amber," Lyra explained. "I told you, as far as he's concerned, they're my special toys."

"Hell."

"Brace yourself, Sweetwater. You're not going to like this."

She went through the vaulted doorway ahead of him. He halted briefly on the threshold, aware of the trickle of awareness that told him he was in the presence of a lot of powerful amber.

Three pyramids made of amethyst were arrayed on a cheap folding card table. Each relic was about a foot high and glowed gently with the latent energy trapped inside.

He whistled softly. "Son of a ghost." He was reluctantly impressed by her daring. "Those aren't like any of the others that we took out of the ruin."

"I found the pyramids the first time I went into the ruin. It was obvious that they were the most powerful stones. I think they are also potentially quite dangerous, so I hid them immediately. I knew that once I started selling the other relics on the underground market, there would be a risk that one of the antiquities gangs or the Guild or AI might get wind of the chamber and come looking. I didn't want them to discover these three artifacts."

"How are they dangerous?"

"I'm not sure, to be perfectly honest." She walked slowly around the card table and looked at him over the tops of the glowing pyramids. "But I can sense the power in them. Until I can figure out how to de-rez them, I don't want to risk letting them fall into the wrong hands."

"Meaning the hands of the Guild or the AI lab?"

"Or one of the underworld gangs. Power is just too seductive, Cruz. What if these pyramids turn out to be weapons of some kind? Everyone would want to control them: the Guilds, the government, criminals, the heads of large corporations like AI and RezStone."

"Okay, I get the point."

"I've come down here several times in the past three months and tried to find a way to safely neutralize the stones, but so far I haven't been successful."

"I don't suppose it ever occurred to you that if you had cooperated with Amber Inc. we might have found a way to render them harmless?"

"Even if you agreed with me that these stones should be destroyed, you know as well as I do that the authorities and the Guilds and the other AI execs would never go along."

He did not argue with her. She was right. Power was very seductive, and so was simple human curiosity. It was not hard to imagine what Big Jake and his brothers would have said if he had suggested that the stones be destroyed without first discovering their secrets.

He touched one of the pyramids very cautiously. Purple fire leaped under his fingers and flashed across his senses. His affinity for amber allowed him to sense the swirling currents of energy locked inside, but he knew at once that he could not rez them, let alone control them.

He took his hand away from the stone. The waves of energy subsided.

"You told me that the relics in the ruin were nothing more than alien art objects," he said.

"I think that's all they are. But these three pyramids are different."

"I can sure as hell see that." He looked at her. "Have you told anyone else about them?"

"Nancy knows about them. I described them to her, but I didn't tell her how powerful they are, and I didn't tell her where I hid them. I trust her completely, but I thought it would be safer if no one knew their location."

"I can't blame you for keeping secrets, given your opinion of Amber Inc. But we need to find out what these pyramids can do. Maybe they aren't weapons. Maybe they're actually components of some kind of high-tech engine. For all we know, we're looking at the power source of one of the excavating machines the aliens used to build the catacombs and the rain forest."

"No," she said, gravely certain. "I think they're works of art, like the other relics. But who knows what the aliens considered art? All I am sure of is that the energy in these stones is potentially very powerful and very dangerous."

"You said you've tried to run a few experiments on them."

"Yes."

"What happened?"

"Not much," she admitted. "I could stir the energy,

but every time I got close to aligning the currents, I got a really bad feeling and backed out fast."

He did not question the decision. "You're the only real expert on amethyst I've ever met. If you say the stones are dangerous, then we'll go with that conclusion. The good news is that they are all here."

"Yes. Which means that the energy I detected in Fairstead's vault was coming from one of the other relics."

"The one that was stolen from the lab."

"What happens now?" she asked. "Will you make the cops get a warrant so you can force Fairstead to open the vault?"

"I hate to break this to you. Wouldn't want to ruin your illusions about Amber Inc. But the company doesn't have quite as much influence with the Frequency PD as you seem to think."

She shrugged. "So you send in your own security people or you ask the Guild to do the job for you. Don't tell me you can't get into that vault."

"I could get in," he agreed. "But I've got a feeling it would be a lot more useful to have my people watch Fairstead and his gallery for a while before making any drastic moves. I'll call Flagg as soon as we get aboveground and have him set it up."

"Garrett Flagg? He was one of the people who was trapped in the chamber."

"Flagg is in charge of lab security. The theft and the murder happened on his watch. You could say he took it personally. Feels responsible."

She was intrigued now. "You want to find the connection between Fairstead's gallery and your lab."

"When I do, I'll be a whole lot closer to finding out who killed the technician and stole the relic."

"That's all you're going to do? Have your security people keep watch on Fairstead's gallery?"

"Well, there is one other pressing item on my agenda at the moment."

"What?"

"I've got a major family gig coming up at the end of the week. My grandfather's birthday party. I could use a date."

She stared at him, dumbfounded. "Me?"

"I'd consider it a huge favor."

"For heaven's sake, why?"

"Because everyone in the family is feeling sorry for me, and it's a little embarrassing, to tell you the truth. They think I'm depressed."

"Why?" she demanded a second time, suspicious now.

"Because you broke my heart three months ago."

"Good grief, Cruz. You don't expect me to believe that."

"Believe what you want. In our family we take broken hearts seriously."

"Hmm. What's in it for me?"

Chapter 21

THEY WALKED THROUGH THE DOOR OF LYRA'S APARTMENT an hour later. Vincent scurried into the kitchen, tumbled up onto the counter, and gazed worshipfully at the cookie jar.

"We've got a deal, then?" Lyra asked. She went into the kitchen and raised the lid of the jar. "If I go with you to your grandfather's birthday celebration, you promise to let me keep the pyramids until I can figure out how to de-rez them?"

There had been little chance to discuss the terms of the bargain since they had left the antechamber. As soon as they had reached the surface, Cruz was on his phone issuing a string of terse orders to Garrett Flagg, setting up the twenty-four-hour surveillance of the Fairstead Gallery. He hadn't finished making the arrangements until they had arrived at her apartment building.

"You have my word that I'll let you decide what to do with them." He went around the counter and took down the bottle of Amber Dew. "Meanwhile, I won't tell anyone else about those stones."

"Okay, I guess," she said.

"Your enthusiasm is heartwarming," Cruz said.

Vincent chose a cookie with the air of a connoisseur selecting a fine wine. When he had picked out the perfect treat, he bounced up to the top of the refrigerator to eat it.

Lyra replaced the lid. "I still don't get it, though. Why are you suddenly so willing to leave me in possession of the pyramids?"

He poured a measure of the liqueur into two balloon glasses. "Think about it."

After a moment, it clicked.

"Of course. You've concluded that, at least for the time being, those stones are safer down there in my personal safe-deposit box than they would be in your company's lab," she said.

"One man is dead, and one relic has been stolen. Obviously the lab's security isn't as good as yours."

"In other words, you were planning to leave the pyramids down there, regardless of whether I agreed to go with you to Big Jake's party tomorrow night." She made a face. "I should have known better than to bargain with a Sweetwater."

"Well, sure. Sweetwater luck and all that. But that doesn't change one fact."

She took the glass of Amber Dew he held out to her.

"And what fact is that?" she asked.

"You really did break my heart, and everyone in my family knows it." He swallowed some of his drink. His eyes were as dark as midnight in the Quarter, green flames burning in the obsidian depths, just like the fire in his ring.

Her pulse skidded, and her senses fluttered. She could almost believe him. She desperately wanted to believe him. She sipped the heady liqueur and lowered the glass, trying to look cool and just a tad amused.

"You're good," she said. "You're really good."

"It's the truth." He turned and walked back out into the living area. "Heartbreak is bad enough. Knowing that your entire family is worrying about you and feeling nothing but pity for you doesn't help."

"Ah, the pride factor."

"It's the only thing you left me."

She grinned and held up one hand. "Stop. Now you're the one who's guilty of going way over the top."

"I thought I told you, in my family we don't have a problem with going over the top. Not when it comes to love." He stopped at the coffee table and looked at the vase of purple orchids. "Are those new? They don't look like the ones I saw here yesterday."

"Those were delivered this morning."

"Same damned note?"

"Same note," she agreed. "But I wouldn't necessarily use the word *damned* to describe it."

"Mind if I take a look?" He already had the envelope in hand and was extracting the card.

"Help yourself," she said dryly.

Vincent had finished his cookie. He tumbled down from the refrigerator and fluttered across the room to the corner where his current canvas lay atop the stack of newspapers. He hopped up onto the wooden chest that contained his painting supplies and made enthusiastic noises.

"All right," Lyra said. "You can play with your paints for a while."

Vincent jumped down from the chest and hovered eagerly while she took out his supplies.

Cruz contemplated the card with a grim expression.

" 'We were meant for each other,' " he read aloud. He shoved the card back inside the envelope and dropped it onto the pile. "Same message as on all the others."

"Umm-hmm."

For a moment he stood there, looking at the orchids. "Does it strike you as a little weird that the orchids are always purple?"

She opened the lid of the chest. "At first, when I assumed they were from you, I thought that the color was meant to be a sentimental reference to amethyst amber."

"Maybe it *is* a reference to amethyst," he said, his voice low and very thoughtful.

Vincent jumped up onto the rim of the chest and surveyed the selection of brushes inside. After some deliberation, he chose a magenta one and bounced back down to the floor. He used two paws to remove the top of the paint tube, exposing the attached brush.

"Remember, we only paint on the canvas," Lyra said firmly. "Not the walls or the floor or the refrigerator."

Vincent chortled and began smearing paint on the canvas. She closed the lid of the chest and looked at Cruz.

"I don't think you can read too much into the color of the orchids," she said. "Not after the storm in the media during the lawsuit. The only way you could *not* connect me with amethyst would be if you were living in a cave."

"Maybe it's a stalker who fixated on you after the media frenzy."

A chill drifted through her. She winced. "Thanks. Take all the romance out of it for me, why don't you?"

"Who the hell is he, Lyra?"

She sighed. "I don't know. Since I found out you weren't the one sending them, I've been making a list of the men in my life. It's sort of a short list."

He drank some of the Amber Dew. "Good to know."

"I started with the deliveryman. He has been known to flirt with me from time to time. But somehow, I just can't see Dave sending such expensive flowers. I also considered Mr. Martinson."

"Who's Martinson?"

"He owns the bookstore next door to my tuning shop. But he must be eighty, if he's a day."

"Age doesn't have a thing to do with it," Cruz said. "Trust me."

"I suppose that's true. But, again, we come back to the cost of the flowers. I doubt that Mr. Martinson could afford twice-weekly deliveries of rare orchids, either." She paused. "I've got a few male clients who might be possibilities, I suppose. You know how some guys are about tuners."

"I'll need a list."

"Forget it." She laughed. "I'm not ready to turn you loose on any of my customers. Got a feeling that would be real bad for business."

"Damn it, Lyra—"

She held up a hand, palm out. "To tell you the truth, I'm starting to wonder about the plumber."

"What plumber?"

"The one the landlord sent to check out my bathroom sink last month. Something about a problem with a leak in the empty apartment next door. He told me that he thought the trouble was here."

"What makes you think he might be the one?" Cruz asked.

"Vincent didn't take to him, and I must admit there was something about him that bothered me, too."

"Did he make a pass?"

"No, he behaved himself. But he spent a lot of time fussing with the sink in the bathroom and then the one in the kitchen. He was here for quite a while before he decided that there was nothing wrong. And there's something else."

"What?"

"From time to time these past few weeks I've had that creepy feeling you get when you know someone is watching you."

"I'll check out the plumber tomorrow," Cruz said.

"How? I don't know his name or the name of his company."

He smiled faintly. "I run a security business, remember? We find people. I'll call your landlord tomorrow."

Alarm jolted through her. "Promise me that you won't frighten my landlord. I don't want to give Mr. Ashwell an excuse to kick me out. I'm a little behind on the rent."

"You make it sound like I deliberately go around scaring people."

She smiled wryly. "I don't think you realize how scary you can be at times."

He looked at her, his expression hard. "Do I scare you?"

She wrinkled her nose. "No, of course not. I wouldn't have let you through the door the first time if I had been afraid of you. And I certainly wouldn't have let you back into my apartment a second time."

"I'd never hurt you, Lyra."

"I know."

"That's something, at least." He put his unfinished drink down on the coffee table and walked to the wall where he de-rezzed the lights.

A frisson of sensual energy shivered across her senses, stirring her deep inside.

"Cruz?" she whispered, suddenly uncertain.

He did not respond. Instead he came toward her, gliding through the emerald shadows of the room. The psychic energy of passion flared in the atmosphere. Her fingers trembled. Afraid that she might drop her glass, she set it on the nearest end table and forced herself to breathe.

"It could be that what is between us is nothing more than sexual attraction," she reminded him.

"Sex is involved." He stopped in front of her. "And sex is good. It certainly works for me. But when it comes to this kind of energy, you're talking about a lot more than sex. Sweetwaters understand that."

"Because you're into over the top?"

"Right."

He was so close now that she could inhale his scent and feel the heat, not only of his body but also of his aura. Memories of all the sleepless nights she had endured during the last three months came flooding back. The price she would pay if he went away again would be even higher this time, she thought. Because this time she would have to face the bitter knowledge that she had known the risks. There would be no excuses.

"And just how did your family come to be such experts on the subject?" she asked.

"I told you, it's in the talent."

In the psi, she thought.

He pulled her into his arms and kissed her with a slow, relentless deliberation that burned through all of her hesitation and uncertainty. She could do this, she thought. She was a Dore. She knew how to take risks.

And she could trust Cruz, at least when it came to passion. He had his priorities, and he had an agenda, but when he held her like this, she knew that the intoxicating exhilaration and the incredible sense of intimacy were real for both of them. It was all there in the way the invisible currents of their auras resonated together across the spectrum. She had never experienced this kind of psychic rush with any other man, and she knew that she never would, no matter how long she lived.

She put her arms around him and abandoned herself to the embrace. He deepened the kiss until she parted her lips for him. Then he moved his mouth to her throat. Her head fell back; her eyes squeezed shut against the heady euphoria of his need and her own.

"You take my breath away," he whispered.

"Oh, *Cruz*."

He picked her up in his arms and carried her toward the bedroom. She heard a faint scurrying sound in the outer room. *Vincent,* she thought. It occurred to her in a fleeting way that she had left the chest of paints unlocked.

But in the next moment she forgot all about the paintbrushes. Cruz was undressing her, and she was wholly occupied with the task of trying to get him out of his shirt.

In a matter of moments their clothes were relegated to a soft heap on the floor. She thought she saw him kick something out of sight under the bed, but there was no time to question the small action. Cruz fell back across the comforter, taking her with him. She came down on top, astride. The rising tide of her own feminine power made her wild and reckless.

Cruz was fully aroused, hard and rigid. She braced herself for the first thrust. But he used his hand on her instead, stroking her until she was soaking wet and breathless with need and anticipation. When he showed no inclination to finish what he had started, she lost patience.

She grabbed his wrists and pinned them on the bed on either side of his head. His teeth gleamed briefly in a wicked smile.

"Speed isn't what we're going for here," he said.

"Well, in that case, maybe I should slow down."

She lowered herself very, very slowly onto his erection. Cruz laughed a little at first, but soon he was groaning. She rose even more slowly. Soon he was slick with his own sweat, and his breathing was harsh. She could feel him straining to hang on to his control.

"Then again, there are times when there's something to be said for speed," he said, his voice a low, sexy growl.

He freed himself, tumbled her onto her back, and came down between her legs.

She laughed, and then he was back inside her, plunging deep, and laughter gave way to the sounds of hot, urgent need. The fever built swiftly within her. She clutched at his damp shoulders.

The tightness inside her came undone in shivery currents that flooded through her and through her aura.

He followed her over the edge with a hoarse shout of exultant release.

Chapter 22

SOME TIME LATER HE FELT HER STIR BESIDE HIM.

"Where are you going?" he asked without opening his eyes.

"I forgot to lock up Vincent's paints," Lyra said.

He opened one eye and watched her pull on a robe. "You're afraid Vincent is going to get carried away?"

"Painting is just a game to him. Everything's a potential canvas. That's why I keep his brushes padlocked when I'm not around to supervise. One of these days, though, he's going to figure out how to de-rez the lock the same way he discovered how to get the caps off the brushes."

She disappeared through the sliding screens. A moment later a light came on in the kitchen. He heard a horrified wail.

"*Vincent.* What have you done? Do you realize how

hard it's going to be to get all this paint off the floor? If Mr. Ashwell sees this, we'll be sleeping in the alley."

A cupboard door opened.

"I just hope it hasn't had a chance to dry completely," Lyra said. "If that's the case, I may be able to get most of it up with water. If I have to resort to paint remover, it will mean refinishing the floors. Do you know how much that will cost?"

Water ran in the kitchen sink.

Cruz got to his feet and pulled on his trousers. Force of habit made him pause to collect the knife sheath from under the bed and buckle it around his lower leg. Sweetwater men always felt naked when they were unarmed. There was an old saying in the family: talent is great, but never forget the backup.

Lyra was at the sink, speaking sternly to Vincent, who was sitting on the counter.

"We talked about this," Lyra said. "You can't just paint everything in sight."

Vincent bounced up and down and made cheerful chittering noises, evidently unconcerned.

Lyra sighed. "I know, it's my fault. I should have locked up the brushes."

Cruz grinned. "Need some help cleaning up the new masterpiece?"

He was halfway across the room when he felt the dark energy whisper through him. He jacked up his senses. At the same instant Vincent sleeked out. His hunting eyes appeared.

"Hit the lights," Cruz said quietly.

Lyra did not question the order.

Faint noises sounded from the balcony of the adjoining loft.

Cruz reached the kitchen in two strides. He put his mouth very close to Lyra's ear. "You said the apartment next door was empty."

"Yes," she said, speaking just as quietly.

"There's someone on that balcony. Stay down. Don't move."

He pushed her into a crouching position behind the counter and crossed the short distance to the sliding glass door. There he flattened himself against the wall and quietly unlocked the slider.

Vincent disappeared from the counter and reappeared on the floor near Cruz's left foot. He crouched there on his hind legs, attention fixed on the balcony.

Together they waited.

There was a soft thud when a dark figure jumped from the neighboring balcony onto Lyra's balcony. A few seconds later a second man landed.

Cruz slid open the window and moved outside. Vincent darted past him, going straight for one of the would-be intruder's ankles.

The man yelped in shock and pain. He kicked out wildly. Vincent went flying through the air and landed nimbly on the railing.

"What the hell?" one of the men hissed. "What was that?"

The second man spotted Cruz.

"Shit," he snarled. He raised a mag-rez.

Simultaneously, green fire flared on the balcony as the first man generated an energy ghost.

Cruz laid down a blanket of psi fog, more than enough to douse the intruders' senses. The ghost went out immediately. This time, at least, Lyra was out of range.

Both men yelled in panic as their senses evaporated. They floundered wildly. Vincent, clearly unaffected by the fog, just like last time, leaped from the railing onto the shoulder of the nearest man, going for the throat.

"Vincent, no," Cruz said. "I need them alive."

Lyra appeared in the doorway. "My God, *Cruz*."

She was too close, Cruz thought. She should have been swamped with the psi fog. But she was on her feet.

Deprived of their senses, the two men continued to reel about. One stumbled and collapsed. The other groped for the railing, missed, and nearly went over the edge. Cruz grabbed him just in time.

"I need something to secure them," Cruz said. "Get your jungle pack. There's some rope inside."

"Right," Lyra said. She turned to hurry toward the bedroom.

She should have been reeling and flailing.

"How are you doing that?" he demanded.

"Turns out amethyst is good for a few things besides making jewelry. It just took me a couple of tries to figure out how to use it to counter the effects of your talent on my aura."

She disappeared back into the loft.

He wanted to demand more of an explanation. She

was, after all, the only person he had ever met who could resist the effects of the senses-numbing fog. But he had priorities.

He moved in on the first man, but before he could strike the blow that would have rendered the attacker unconscious, the nightmare struck.

The world suddenly warped around him. He was plunged into a bizarre dreamscape.

The buildings and rooftops of the Quarter came alive, twisting into strange, unnatural shapes that melted and folded in on themselves. Some rose to impossible heights. Others shrank and wavered out of existence. The familiar glow of the Dead City wall grew more intense, illuminating the world with ultraspectrum hues that pulsed in eerie patterns. The ethereal towers inside the wall acquired ever more fantastical and distorted shapes. The balcony undulated like a churning ocean. He staggered to his feet and grabbed for the railing. He missed and went down hard on one knee.

His hand brushed against the mag-rez. Instinctively he swiped at it. He could not use it in his current state, but he had to keep it out of the hands of the attackers. He heard the gun skid across the tiles, but he could not tell if it had gone over the side of the balcony as he had intended.

The next thing he knew, he was staring at the stars, seeing them as he had never before. The twin moons were too bright, too close, threatening to sear his senses. He turned his head to the side to avoid the intense light and found himself looking through the bars of Lyra's balcony straight across to the balcony of the adjoining apartment.

Something moved on the other balcony, a creature unlike anything he had ever seen. Whatever it was, it melted and re-formed and melted again.

Aliens, he thought. *They have finally come back. Maybe they have been here all along.*

"Ghost shit," one of the attackers whispered, awed. "He's down."

The strange being on the other balcony spoke, its voice echoing darkly as though it came from the depths of a crypt.

"Destroy him," the voice ordered. *"Get the woman."*

Two distorted forms loomed over Cruz, blocking his view of the alien on the other balcony.

"You deal with him," one of the men said. "I'll grab the woman."

"Shit, there's that rat again. It bit me once. I'm probably gonna need shots."

"Shoot it. Shoot it."

"I can't. The gun's gone. The SOB pushed it over the side of the balcony."

"Cruz." Lyra's voice rose in a scream of fear and rage. "What did you do to him, you bastards?"

"Forget the rat," one of the men said. "Drop the SOB over the side. I'll get her."

The second figure started toward Cruz. He halted abruptly. "Watch out. She's got something in her hands. A lamp."

Glass exploded.

Forget the alien, Cruz told himself. The two men were trying to grab Lyra. He had to stay focused here. Time to prioritize.

Ignoring the nightmarish shapes and images around him, he rezzed all the psi he could summon and pushed it through the black amber of his ring. Somehow he knew, with his hunter's intuition, that the only hope he had of protecting Lyra was to push back the strange energy that was being used to keep him locked in the eerie hallucination.

"Let me go," Lyra shrieked.

"The rat is back," the first man yelled. "It bit me."

"Hell with the rat, the woman just bit me."

Cruz pulled more energy, reaching for his limits and those of the obsidian.

The nightmare landscape wavered and suddenly dissolved. The world came back into focus. The creature on the balcony fled back into the adjoining apartment and disappeared.

Cruz knew the precise instant when the obsidian shattered into myriad shards. He shut down his senses, cutting off the rush of heavy energy as fast as possible, but he was a heartbeat too late, and he knew it.

The shards of fractured obsidian had already had a chance to act as individual psychic mirrors, reflecting his own energy back at his aura in chaotic waves that were already starting to inundate his senses. He'd been warned of the theoretical risks involved with pushing obsidian too far. Now he was going to find out the hard way if the experts were right.

But first he had to save Lyra.

He staggered to his feet and saw the two men trying to maneuver a wildly struggling Lyra toward the front door of the loft. One of them had a hand over her mouth. They were both using their boots to try to fend off Vincent.

Cruz jacked up what was left of his exhausted senses, hoping for one last surge of adrenaline to help him push more energy through the backup amber in his watch. Nothing happened. He knew then that he had five, maybe ten minutes left before he went unconscious.

He yanked the knife out of his ankle sheath and went forward.

"I don't believe it," one of the attackers snarled. "The son of a bitch is back on his feet. Something went wrong. He was supposed to stay down."

"Shit, he's got a—"

Cruz reached the first man before he could finish the sentence. He drove the knife deep, aware even as he struck that his aim was off. The aftereffects of the psi drain were already hitting him, playing havoc with his coordination and strength.

There was, nevertheless, a satisfying grunt of pain and fear. He jerked the knife out. Blood flowed over his hands. The man collapsed.

The second man dropped Lyra and ran for the door, Vincent on his heels.

"Vincent, come back," Lyra shouted. "Let him go."

Cruz was vaguely aware of the sound of the front door slamming open. He heard heavy boots pounding down the stairs. The second intruder was gone.

He sank slowly to his knees, the bloody knife still gripped in his hand. The green-hued shadows of the loft started to turn gray.

"Cruz." Lyra crouched beside him. "Oh, my God, you're hurt. What happened? Did they shoot you? I didn't hear a gun. Cruz, stay with me, here. I'm calling an ambulance."

There was a familiar chittering sound in his ear. Vincent sounded anxious. Cruz forced himself to concentrate. There was one more thing he had to do, something important; the most important thing he had ever done in his life.

"No ambulance," he whispered. "Call Jeff."

"But Cruz, you're bleeding."

"Not my blood. The other guy's. Call Jeff. Tell him I shattered obsidian. Tell him to take you to Amber Island."

"I can't go to your family's compound."

"Yes," he said, "you can and you will. I need to know you're safe, and that's the only place I can be sure you will be. Get your phone."

He heard the soft, melodic clash of the charms on her bracelet as she hurried across the room. A moment later she was back. She gripped his hand.

"Got it," she said. "But let's get something clear here. I'm staying with you. If we go anywhere, we go together. Do you hear me, Cruz Sweetwater?"

He thought he felt a gentle surge of energy through her hand; her energy, not his own. For a few more precious seconds the darkness retreated. He was probably hallucinating again.

"Call Jeff," he repeated.

"I'm calling Jeff." With her free hand, she fumbled with the phone. "But whatever you do, don't let go. Do you hear me, Sweetwater?"

"I hear you." He closed his eyes. "Nag, nag, nag."

"I've got a talent for it."

The night engulfed him. The anxious chittering of a dust bunny and the sound of Lyra's charms followed him into the darkness.

Chapter 23

MOMENTS AFTER SHE MADE THE CALL TO JEFF, LYRA HAD a front-row seat from which to observe the dazzlingly efficient and astonishingly powerful machinery of the Sweetwater empire in action.

Jeff burst through the open front door of her apartment ten minutes after she called. He was not alone. He had a phalanx of Amber Inc. Security operatives with him.

"Hurry," Lyra said. She was still crouched beside Cruz, gripping his hand.

"Got another man down over here," someone said. "Still alive."

"That's one of the bad guys," Lyra said. "The other one got away. Cruz is the one who needs help."

Someone threw the lights. Lyra saw a lot of blood on the hardwood floor. She wondered, in a distant way, if it would be harder to remove than Vincent's paint.

A stoutly built woman with short, spiky blonde hair went down on one knee beside Cruz and took out a stethoscope. A stretcher appeared. Within seconds there were so many people in the small loft that Lyra was afraid Vincent would get squashed beneath an Amber Inc. Security boot. With her free hand she picked him up and plopped him on her shoulder. His red beret had evidently come off during the battle with the intruders. He clutched it tightly in one paw.

"How is the boss?" Jeff said. His face was grim. "Is he still alive?"

Lyra realized that he was speaking to the woman holding the stethoscope to Cruz's chest. Alarm zapped through her.

"Of course Cruz is alive," she said before the med tech could respond. "Why wouldn't he be? He's going through some kind of burn-and-crash syndrome just like ghost hunters do when they melt amber. He needs some time to recover, that's all."

"The boss didn't just melt amber," Jeff said, his voice unnaturally flat. "When you called me you told me that he had shattered obsidian."

"That's what he said to tell you, but I assumed that meant he had melted his obsidian amber."

"He told you that he uses black amber?" Jeff said, sounding startled.

"I'm a Dore. I know amber."

"Sure," Jeff said. "That figures. Thing is, black amber is so rare most people don't recognize it. When they see it, they assume it's some other gemstone."

"What's the problem here?" she asked tightly.

"Maybe you don't know as much about obsidian as you think," Jeff said. "You don't melt it when you over-rez it. You shatter it."

"What do you mean?" She looked down at the black stone in Cruz's ring. "There are no fractures in the obsidian."

"Never mind; I'll explain later. We've got to get him to the clinic."

"You mean an emergency room," Lyra said.

The med tech looked up. "No, a regular ER won't know what to do with this kind of situation. The Arcane Society runs a private clinic. The doctors there are his best chance."

Lyra tightened her grip on Cruz's hand and pulsed a little more energy through her fingers.

"Okay, you're starting to scare me," she whispered. "The clinic sounds like a good idea. But I'll warn you, Cruz was adamant about both of us going to your family's compound on Amber Island, Jeff. When he wakes up and finds out that he's somewhere else, he's liable to be pissed."

"Hell." Jeff hesitated but only for a fraction of a second. "He must have been really worried about you."

"Yes, well, those two men *were* trying to kidnap me," she said quietly.

"In that case you are definitely going to Amber Island. We'll take the boss to the clinic."

"Sorry," Lyra indicated the hand she was using to hang on to Cruz. "Where he goes, I go. Take your pick, Amber

Island or the clinic, but either way, we stick together, at least until he wakes up."

The med tech sat back on her heels. Lyra could see her name tag. *Benson.*

"I think that's a good idea," Benson said. "I'm not sure what's going on here, but Mr. Sweetwater appears to be stable. I vote we don't disrupt the situation. If you take them both to Amber Island, the clinic can send a team to meet you there."

"Right," Jeff said. "Amber Island it is."

The med tech who was crouched beside the fallen attacker spoke. "What do you want us to do with this guy? He's alive. I've got the bleeding stopped. He'll probably make it if he gets to an ER."

"He goes to the Guild clinic," Jeff decreed. "They can handle him without having to notify the cops."

He continued giving orders with a precision and speed that would have done credit to a professional Federal Bureau of Psi Investigation agent.

There was one more skirmish a short time later when Lyra got into the back of the unmarked ambulance with Vincent on her shoulder.

"Sorry, ma'am, I can't let any animals ride back here with the patient," one of the techs said.

"The bunny's with me, and I'm with Sweetwater," Lyra said.

The tech opened his mouth to argue, but Benson shook her head.

"It's okay," Benson said.

"Yes, ma'am." The tech stood back.

Benson got in and went to work slapping monitors on Cruz.

Jeff vaulted up into the rear of the vehicle and sat down beside Lyra. The doors slammed shut, and the ambulance pulled away from the curb.

"What happened back there?" Jeff asked.

She gave him a quick rundown of the events.

"Two men?" he asked. "Are you certain?"

"Yes."

"That doesn't sound right. How the hell did two men manage to take down the boss?"

"I don't know. He got both of them under control almost immediately. Then he sent me back inside the apartment to get something he could use to secure them. That's when everything must have gone wrong. The next thing I knew, the two intruders were trying to drag me out the door. Cruz was just lying there on the balcony, not moving. I thought at first they'd shot him, but I didn't hear a gun go off. Then, all of a sudden, Cruz was back on his feet coming at one of the men with a knife."

"If he had to resort to the knife, it was because he could no longer use his talent," Jeff said grimly. "For some reason he had to jack up so much psi he shattered black obsidian just to deal with a couple of street thugs. It doesn't resonate."

"That's all I can tell you. Things happened so fast."

Jeff took a phone out of his pocket. "You're sure there were only two men?"

"Yes."

Jeff spoke quickly into the phone, issuing more orders.

"Get a PF team inside Miss Dore's loft immediately," he said. "They'll be looking for psi traces of two men, probably ghost hunters. At least one of them generated a ghost. One got away. We have the other in custody. Point of entry was the balcony. Exit was the front lobby of the building. Make sure all those locations get covered. I want a full report as soon as you have anything."

Lyra touched his arm to get his attention. He looked at her, one brow raised in inquiry.

"There may be more blood from the one who got away," she said. "I think Vincent bit both of them."

Jeff glanced at Vincent, who was huddled on Lyra's shoulder.

"Nice work, big guy," Jeff said.

Benson smiled. "They say that with dust bunnies, by the time you see the teeth, it's too late."

"It's a predator thing," Jeff said.

He went back to the phone and spoke tersely for another minute before he ended the connection.

"What's a PF team?" Lyra asked.

"Short for para-forensics."

"Good grief, you mean AI Security has its own forensics lab?"

"Keeps things simple," Jeff explained. "And also quiet. Remember what you said about discretion being important in the amber tuning business?"

"Yes."

"Amber Inc. Security has a similar business philosophy." He looked at Benson. "How's he doing?"

"Believe it or not, he seems to be fine." Benson checked

the instruments. "Looks like just a real serious postburn crash but nothing worse."

"I told you so," Lyra said. But she was more relieved than she wanted to admit. "What's the problem with obsidian amber?" she said. "I know very few people can rez it, but it can handle a lot of power, can't it?"

"Sure, it will take a lot of psi," Jeff studied Cruz. "The problem is that when it does get overloaded, it doesn't just shut down the way regular amber does. Instead, the pattern of the waves breaks up in weird and unpredictable ways."

"That's what you call shattering obsidian?"

"Right. It's like suddenly you're pushing energy through a zillion little psychic mirrors. The psi gets reflected right back at your aura. Sets up an unstable resonating pattern that fries the senses of whoever is generating the currents through the stone." He paused a beat. "The theory is that the effect is probably permanent."

"Theory?" she said, alarmed all over again. "You mean you don't know?"

"The problem is that we don't have enough experience with black amber to be able to predict the outcome in a situation like this," Benson explained. She did not look up from the monitor. "Very few people can even rez it, let alone actually generate enough power to fracture a stone. So, yes, mostly, all we've got to go on is theory."

"Mostly?" Lyra whispered.

"I checked the Arcane Society files on the way to your address tonight," Benson said. "There are only two other cases on record. In each instance the victim lapsed into a coma after shattering obsidian. One died. The other survived, but his para-senses were destroyed. He eventually committed suicide." She paused a beat. "They were both Sweetwaters."

Lyra tightened her grip on Cruz and pulsed more psi. "He's not in a coma."

"No," Benson said.

"And he's not going to slip into a coma," Lyra said. "He needs to recover from the psi drain, that's all. When he wakes up, he'll be fine."

Benson studied her for a moment. Then she switched her attention to Jeff.

"This is the one, I take it?" Benson said.

Jeff smiled slightly. "Yes."

"Not quite what I expected," Benson said.

Lyra glared at both of them. "What one?"

"The woman who broke Cruz Sweetwater's heart," Benson said.

Chapter 24

HE'D LOST THE BIGGEST SALE OF HIS CAREER. THE AMEthyst relic was worth a fortune.

Valentine Fairstead's hand shook as he opened the back door of the gallery. Frustration, rage, and anxiety coursed through him. It had been so close. He'd had Wilson Revere, himself, right there in the vault room. When it came to high-end clients, it didn't get any richer. Well, with the exception of a Sweetwater, of course.

But he'd never even tried to court the Sweetwaters. For one thing, rumor had it that their private vault was already overflowing with priceless amber of every kind and description, both archaeological relics and laboratory-grade specimens. He had never come across any piece that he thought would interest anyone in that family.

Truth be told, he had always been relieved by that

knowledge. For some reason, he had never wanted to deal with the Sweetwaters. Something about that clan made him nervous.

Wilson Revere, however, was another matter entirely. Revere was a sophisticated, polished, well-educated man with exquisite taste, just the sort of client that the Fairstead Gallery preferred to cultivate.

He got the door open and hurried into the back room. Turning, he swiftly unlocked the rear door. He breathed a little sigh of relief. The dark alley behind the gallery always made him nervous. You never knew who might be hiding behind a trash container. The Quarter was not the safest place in the city at night.

But the man he had come here to meet insisted that he arrive at midnight and use the back door. There were other instructions as well. He was not to turn on any lights until they were in the windowless vault room.

He made his way by feel into the main sales room. From there he groped a path between the ranks of display cases until he reached the door of the vault room. He de-rezzed the lock and moved into the small space. Finally, he was able to switch on a light.

The door opened a moment later. A man entered the room.

"About time you got here," Fairstead growled. "I still say this is unnecessary."

"You're the one who screwed up the deal," the newcomer said. "Now I have to clean up your mess. Open the vault."

"Sweetwater never even saw the relic, I tell you," Fairstead insisted. He went to work on the lock. "There's no way he could have known it was in here."

"He must have suspected something. Why else would he have turned up at your gallery today? He's not one of your regular clients."

"It was the woman, I tell you. He was with her, and she was here because Revere wanted an outside opinion. The fact that Sweetwater was present had nothing to do with the relic."

"I don't like it. Too much of a coincidence. We've got to cut our losses and fast."

Fairstead pulled the heavy vault door open and stepped inside. "What are you going to do with the amethyst?"

"Make sure it gets found so that Sweetwater will stop looking for it. We need to get him off our trail. At the rate he's going, he's liable to uncover our little sideline. We can't afford that."

Fairstead picked up the amethyst relic. The stone was warm in his hand. It glowed faintly. For a moment the connoisseur in him surfaced. He savored the strange, elegant carvings that covered the purple amber.

"Exquisite," he breathed. "If only we knew how to activate the energy inside. Is it true that Lyra Dore can rez up images inside these stones?"

"That's what they say. Give it to me."

Fairstead sighed and handed him the relic. "Pity. It would have been the biggest sale we've ever made."

"Some risks aren't worth taking."

"I agree."

Fairstead walked out of the vault. He turned to close the door.

He never saw the mag-rez gun in the other man's hand. The first shot struck him in the back, flinging him halfway into the vault. The second shot took him in the head.

Chapter 25

CRUZ AWOKE TO A WARM, SILKEN BREEZE THAT CARRIED the familiar scents of the ocean and the feel of Lyra's fingers entwined with his own. Satisfaction flooded through him.

He opened his eyes and saw her. She was sitting in a chair positioned very close to the bed, holding his hand and looking out the open glass doors of the bedroom, watching the sun-flashed sea. She was dressed in a pair of jeans and a snug little black T-shirt. She looked incredibly sexy. The shirt hugged her breasts and emphasized the sleek curves of her shoulders and upper arms. Then, again, she always looked incredibly sexy.

For a moment he did not speak or move. He just watched her, fascinated by everything about her. It had been like this the first time he saw her, he thought. And it would be like this every time he looked at her for the rest of his life. The psychic connection between them was real, and it was intense, just as everyone in the family had promised it would be when he finally found the right woman.

Vincent chortled exuberantly and bounded up onto the bed. His beret was at its usual rakish angle. He fluttered up the quilt to perch on the pillow.

Startled out of her reverie, Lyra turned in the chair. It seemed to Cruz that everything about her glowed.

"Hey," she said, smiling. "About time you woke up."

"How long was I out?"

"It's a little after nine AM. You've been in la-la land since late last night."

He looked out the open doors again, taking in the lush green gardens and the view of the sea. He knew the setting as well as he knew his own name. They were in his personal cottage on the island, the one above the cove.

"You got us to Amber Island," he said. "Good."

"Jeff took care of everything. How much do you remember?"

He thought about that for a moment. "The two men on the balcony. The hallucinations—"

She blinked. "What hallucinations?"

"Yeah," Jeff said from the doorway. "What hallucinations?"

"That's the interesting part." Cruz gave Lyra's hand a quick squeeze and then shoved aside the covers and swung his legs over the side of the bed. He looked down and discovered that he was still wearing the pants he'd put on just before the intruders had arrived. The trousers were splashed with dried bloodstains. More memories slammed into place. "Someone used some kind of psi on me last night. It created a dreamscape like the waking nightmares that you described, Lyra."

"You're kidding," she said. Her eyes widened. "You think one of those attackers created those hallucinations?"

"Someone is responsible for inducing them. I'm not sure who, yet. One thing I do know, you can be certain you aren't on the verge of a mental breakdown, Lyra. And neither am I. Life is good."

She stood, picked up Vincent, and hugged him close. Her eyes were shadowed, but he could see the relief shining in them.

"I don't know what to say," she whispered. "After all these weeks of wondering."

"We've still got a problem," Cruz pointed out. "We need to find out why that pair was trying to kidnap you." He looked at Jeff. "What have you got?"

"The man you took down last night will probably make it, but he's still zoned out on the drugs they gave him for the surgery. We picked up the other one last night, but I gotta tell you, he doesn't seem to know much."

"Just more dumb muscle off the street." Cruz rubbed his jaw. "Like the first two someone sent to take me out."

"Looks like it. Same vague description of whoever paid them. Guy was wearing some kind of face-distorting mask."

"Not a mask," Cruz said. "He was generating a hallucination that concealed his features—" He broke off as another memory slammed home. "Damn. He was there last night. I saw him."

"What are you talking about?" Jeff said.

"There was a third man. Last night I thought he was just part of the dreamscape, but he must have been real. Make sure the PF team checks out the adjoining loft. He was on the other balcony."

"I've got people there now." Jeff took out his phone. "But they're only looking for the psi traces of the two men who left residue in Lyra's place. I'll tell them to go next door and search for a third guy."

Cruz headed for the bathroom doorway. "I need a shower, and then I need food."

Jeff looked at Lyra. "See? That's why they made him the boss of AI Security. He knows how to prioritize."

Lyra gave him a weary smile. "I could use a shower, myself. I'll see you gentlemen later."

With Vincent tucked under one arm, she walked out of the bedroom.

Jeff watched her go and then turned back. "She spent the night sitting beside you, holding your hand. At first she wouldn't let go of you at all. Benson, the med tech, finally convinced her that you were okay. But aside from changing into some clothes that we picked up for her at the loft and using the powder room a couple of times, she wouldn't leave your side."

"She saved my life," Cruz said. He went to the sink. "Or, at least, my senses."

Jeff said nothing. He didn't need to. They both knew that, for anyone in the family, it amounted to the same thing. The thought of having your psi senses permanently fried was harrowing. Over the years more than one strong talent in the Sweetwater clan had opted to take his own life when some rare catastrophe had deprived him of the psychic side of his nature.

The thought reminded Cruz that he'd ruined a perfectly good piece of obsidian. Automatically he glanced down at his hand and saw that he was still wearing his ring. The black stone glinted in the light.

"I need to get some fresh amber," he said. He glanced at Jeff through the open doorway. "I destroyed mine last night."

Jeff grinned. "No problem. Lyra retuned your ring for you while you were sleeping."

He frowned. "She tuned obsidian?"

"I get the feeling she can tune just about any kind of amber."

Cruz thought about that for a moment. "She uses amethyst. Within the Society there have always been a few rumors about people who can work that kind of amber."

"I know," Jeff said. "They're supposed to be descended from Old World crystal workers."

Officially, all types of psychical abilities were considered equal within the Arcane Society, but human nature being what it was, some forms of talent got more respect than others, just as some were more feared than others.

Historically, those who worked crystals had always occupied one of the bottom rungs of the Society's social ladder, ranking below aura readers and low-grade intuitives. They were right down there with sleight-of-hand talents, another bunch who tended to make their livings in less than legal ways. A psychic skill with sleight of hand usually pointed one toward a career as a pickpocket or card shark. Those with the ability to read crystals had often ended up as carnival fortune-tellers who took advantage of the gullible.

But the Sweetwater family talent hadn't always been considered respectable, either, he reminded himself. And just as Harmony had produced some interesting twists in the clan's various psychic abilities, it had probably had some unpredictable effects on people like Lyra.

"You know, sir," Jeff said, "if you're really nice to her, she might give you her special amber tune-up service. She did my amber and, wow, what a difference."

Cruz swung around and started toward him.

"What the hell is that supposed to mean?" he asked softly.

"Hey, don't look at me like that," Jeff retreated toward the open doors. "I didn't mean anything like what you're thinking, honest."

"Yeah? What was I thinking?"

"Haven't got a clue," Jeff said quickly. "Look, I'm just trying to tell you that Lyra has this really cool thing she can do when she tunes amber. I saw her do it for one of her clients. I asked about it, and she did it for me."

Cruz closed the distance between them. "What kind of really cool thing are we talking about?"

Jeff took another step back. "She locks the frequencies on to your specific wavelengths. It makes the focus more precise. When you use the amber, you don't have to generate as much raw power to get the same effect. Think about what that might have meant last night. You wouldn't have had to push so much energy through your ring. Maybe it wouldn't have shattered."

Cruz stopped, frowning a little. "Assuming she can do that special tuning thing to obsidian."

"Right. Assuming. But I use tourmaline, and she did it for me. You know how complicated tourmaline is. I ran some experiments yesterday. Works like a charm. Not only do you get more bang for the buck, you get incredible precision. It's the difference between driving a tractor and a Slider. Both will get you from point A to point B, but the tractor requires more fuel, and it squashes a lot of stuff along the way."

"The woman never fails to surprise me," Cruz said.

He headed into the bathroom and contemplated the image in the mirror. The guy staring back at him looked like he'd just surfaced from a weeklong bender. His eyes were bottomless pits, and he really needed a shave. But mostly he needed to find the SOB who had tried to kidnap Lyra.

One thing at a time. Got to prioritize here. Always with the damn priorities when all he really wanted to do was settle down with Lyra and get started on the next generation of Sweetwaters.

He opened the mirrored cabinet and took out the razor. "Any news from the people watching Fairstead's gallery?"

"I talked to Flagg a few minutes ago. We've got another situation."

Cruz rezzed up some lather. "Why?"

"Fairstead was seen returning to the gallery around midnight last night. He let himself in through the alley entrance. He never came out. The gallery employees found his body in a little room at the back of the main showroom this morning."

"Huh." Cruz thought about that while he went to work with the razor. "But Flagg's people didn't see anyone else enter or leave the gallery last night?"

"No. There may be a reason for that. The cops found a hole-in-the-wall entrance to the tunnels inside Fairstead's office."

"The killer came and went from underground." Cruz angled the razor for another stroke. "I assume the vault was opened?"

"Yes. But here's the weird part. My friend in the Frequency PD says that the gallery employees did an inventory and told him that nothing was missing."

"The killer took the relic. It wouldn't have been on any inventory list."

HALF AN HOUR LATER, CRUZ WALKED OUT OF THE BEDroom wearing a fresh shirt and trousers from the selection of clothing he kept at the cottage. He headed toward the kitchen, thinking of Lyra and coffee, in that order.

Jeff appeared in his path. "Bad news. We have what you might call a situation."

"What?"

"Big Jake arrived by boat while you were in the shower."

“Should have known he’d find out what happened last night. Now that he’s supposed to be retired, he’s got way too much time on his hands, and he likes to meddle.”

“That’s probably what he’s doing as we speak. He grabbed Lyra.”

“*Grabbed* her?”

“Okay, maybe that’s a little over-the-top,” Jeff conceded. “Here’s the deal. After Lyra got out of the shower, she decided to take the path down to the cove. Big Jake came here as soon as he got off the boat. He wanted to know where she was. Someone told him. He went looking for her.”

Cruz headed for the front door. “You’re right. We’ve got a situation.”

Chapter 26

VINCENT WAS ENCHANTED WITH THE COVE. HE DARTED and frolicked about, red beret flapping. Lyra smiled as he chased waves, investigated stray bits of seaweed, and played with seashells. Dust bunnies could teach people a lot about the art of enjoying life, she thought. As far as they were concerned, almost anything could be turned into a game.

She was watching Vincent dip a paw into a tide pool in an effort to capture a tiny crab when she felt the tingle of awareness that told her she was no longer alone. She turned and saw a man coming toward her.

He was a lot older than Cruz, his hair gray and thinning. A pair of wraparound sunglasses concealed his eyes, but she knew who he was. The family connection was obvious in the hard profile and the prowling, specter-cat way he moved, even though he used a cane. She would know that well-dressed-assassin look anywhere.

Big Jake Sweetwater.

He reached the bottom of the path and started toward her. She was glad that she was wearing sunglasses, too. He couldn't see her eyes any better than she could see his.

Vincent paused long enough to give the newcomer a cursory glance, but he lost interest immediately and went back to his fishing.

Jake came to a halt in front of her. "So, you're Lyra Dore."

"Good morning, Mr. Sweetwater. Fancy meeting you here."

"I own this island," he said gruffly.

"Oh, right, I forgot. Did you come down here to ask me to leave? I wouldn't want to get arrested for trespassing. I'm still trying to pay off the lawyer I used to try to sue your company. I can't afford another attorney."

His jaw turned to granite, but he rose above the taunt. Lyra was impressed.

"They tell me you saved my grandson's life last night," he growled.

"Between you and me, I think he would have pulled through on his own. He's a very strong talent, as I'm sure you're well aware, and amazingly stubborn. Can't imagine where he got that, but there you have it. Those are useful traits when it comes to dealing with psi trauma."

"You think?"

"Yes. But I'm going along with the story that I saved

his life, because I like the idea of having a Sweetwater in my debt."

"I talked to the med tech on the scene. She said Cruz might have survived, but he sure as hell wouldn't have made it through with his senses intact without some outside intervention. She thinks it was the energy you were generating through physical contact that was the deciding factor. It stabilized his aura until he could recover from the trauma."

"Guess we'll never know for sure, will we?"

"I'm sure," Jake said. "So is the med tech and everyone else who knows what happened. Like I said, you saved his life."

"His senses, maybe."

"Amounts to pretty much the same thing as far as a Sweetwater is concerned."

"Whatever. It's nice to know the Sweetwaters owe me."

Jake grunted. "If you care about Cruz enough to save his life, why in the hell did you have to go and break his heart?"

She nearly choked on her outrage. "Let's get something straight here. What I did for Cruz last night I would have done for anyone, if I thought just holding my hand would save a life. As for the heartbreak part, geez. Don't even try to convince me that you actually fell for that crazy talk."

"What's crazy about it?"

"You're Big Jake Sweetwater, for Pete's sake. I can understand some of the younger, more impressionable members of your family like Jeff buying into that romantic nonsense, but not you. Never you."

"Or you?" he asked, the words barely audible above the crash of the waves.

"Of course not. Look, I don't know who started that story about me breaking Cruz's heart, but I'm sure it was intended originally as a joke."

"We don't joke about true love in this family. We take it seriously. You broke my grandson's heart, and that really pisses me off."

"Yeah, well he stole that amethyst chamber from me. If it hadn't been for him and Amber Inc. I'd have been rich by now."

"You'd have been plenty rich if you'd just taken the damned settlement our lawyers offered you."

"That money came with way too many strings attached."

"What strings, damn it?" Jake's voice rose to a roar.

Vincent abruptly responded to the escalating tension in the atmosphere. He didn't go all sleek and predatory, but he abandoned his fishing and fluttered across the rocks toward Lyra. She picked him up and tucked him under her arm, grateful, as usual, for the comfort of his furry little body.

"If I had taken the money, I would have had to give up my claim on the chamber," she said.

Jake whacked a nearby rock with his cane. "That was the general idea."

"I'll never do that. As far as I'm concerned, that ruin was my discovery, and it belongs to me. In addition to giving up my claim, your lawyers actually demanded that I sign a nondisclosure clause and stop doing interviews with the media. I wasn't about to agree to that, either. Bad press was the only weapon I had to use against you."

"Why the devil did you care so much about that ruin in the first place?"

"Ask Cruz."

"He gave me some ghost crap about you probably being worried that the amethyst relics inside the chamber might prove to be weapons. Said you didn't trust Amber Inc. or the Guilds with them."

She nodded once. "You've got that right. And now your lab has gone and lost one of the artifacts. Which only goes to prove that my concerns were justified."

"And you claim you're not a romantic. Only a romantic fool would turn down the kind of money we offered you just to keep those relics out of what you thought were the wrong hands."

"That wasn't a romantic act," she shot back. "It was my insider knowledge of how things operate at Amber Inc. that made me do it."

"Next you're going to tell me you got that so-called insider knowledge from your grandfather."

She raised her chin. "That's right."

Jake studied her in silence for a moment. Then he exhaled heavily.

"Arthur Dore raised you on poison," he said. "He was the one who challenged me to that game of poker. We each owned claims. Both deeds went into the pot. Winner take all."

"He was drunk. You took advantage of him."

"He'd had a few drinks, but he knew what he was doing." Jake's voice softened a little. "But I'm willing to allow that his memory of events wasn't real clear."

"Cruz told me that there was a woman involved," she said.

"There was. Madeline. My wife. Dore challenged me to that game because he had some crazy notion that if he won and wound up owning both mines, Madeline would marry him instead of me. But that was never even a remote possibility."

"What makes you so sure of that? Oh, wait." She held up a hand, palm out. "Cruz said that when it comes to love, you Sweetwaters have some kind of special intuition."

"It's part of our talent. The first time I met Madeline, I knew she was the one. She and your grandfather had been seeing each other, but there was nothing serious on either side. At least not until Dore realized that Madeline was going out with me. He was furious but only because it was just one more thing he had lost to me, not because his heart was broken."

"You're sure of that, are you?"

"Damn sure. I knew your grandfather better than you did, at least back in those days. Hell, you weren't even born yet. I'm damn sorry you lost your parents, and I'm glad you had Arthur Dore to take you in, but it sounds like he gave you a somewhat revised version of history."

She gave him a bright, shiny smile. "Well, one thing's for sure, there's no way to prove his version now, is there? History is written by the winners, and you were the winner."

"What the hell did you expect me to do? Give him back the deed to the mine?"

"Yes," she said. "That would have been the right thing to do."

Big Jake's hard face darkened with outrage. "Like hell. I won that claim off Dore fair and square. He knew it, and I knew it. If I'd turned around and tried to give it back to him, he would have refused it."

"Why would he have done that?"

"For the same reason you wouldn't take the settlement money Cruz offered you as compensation for that amethyst ruin. Pride. Arthur Dore would have seen any attempt to return the deed as an act of pity."

She felt the familiar shiver of awareness and turned to look at the path that led up the bluff. Cruz was making his way down to the cove, moving with his characteristic sure-footedness. Dark glasses veiled his eyes, but even from here she could see the grim set of his jaw.

She switched her attention back to Jake.

"You know, I never gave it much thought, because there wasn't any point to imagining how things might have been different," she said. "But you're right. Granddad would have turned down your offer."

"I did not cheat him out of that claim," Jake said quietly. "And even if I had, it still wouldn't give you the right to break my grandson's heart. If you had a problem with me, you should have come to me about it."

"Ah, but I didn't have a problem with you," she said politely. "I was doing just fine without any Sweetwaters in my life. My problem is with Cruz. And if anyone calls me a heartbreaker one more time, I swear I'm going to swim back to the mainland."

The corner of his mouth edged upward slightly. "That would be a very long swim," he said.

"So, I'll steal one of your boats. Now, if you don't mind, I'm going back to the house for breakfast."

"I'm hungry, too. I'll come with you."

"Your island. Suit yourself."

"Thanks, I'll do that." He fell into step beside her, driving his cane into the sand with each step. He looked toward the path. "Looks like the rescue mission has arrived."

"I don't need rescuing from you."

"Nope, you sure as hell don't. You can take care of yourself. So what's with the dust bunny?"

"His name is Vincent."

"I hear they bite."

"Oh, yeah."

Jake chuckled. "Like you."

It was not a question, so Lyra saw no need to respond.

Cruz came to a halt in front of them.

His dark glasses glinted in the sun. He looked at Lyra and then at Jake.

"Is there a problem here?" he asked in his dangerously neutral voice.

"Yes," Jake said. "But I'm told the problem is with you, not me, so we're going to have breakfast. You can join us if you like."

Cruz smiled at Lyra. "Thanks, I'll do that."

Chapter 27

THEY ATE BREAKFAST OUTDOORS ON THE VERANDA THAT overlooked the spectacular cove. The cook came down from what everyone on the island referred to as the Big House, a large, airy mansion about a mile from Cruz's cottage. There were platters of succulent fruits and berries, fluffy cheese-and-vegetable omelets, and endless piles of toast and pots of coffee.

Vincent went into full cute mode and charmed the cook into providing him with his own plate heaped with samples of everything on the table. He crouched on the foot-wide railing with his hoard and, like every other male in the vicinity, went to work on his breakfast with gusto.

"Here's what we've got," Cruz said, forking up a bite of omelet. "Valentine Fairstead was murdered last night, and the murder is probably linked to the missing relic, which we know was in his vault as of yesterday afternoon."

"How do we know the relic was in his vault?" Jake demanded.

"Because Lyra was there with a client who wanted her opinion on a special piece of amethyst," Cruz said. "They were escorted to a private room by Fairstead, and the vault was opened. She didn't get a chance to see the relic because I walked into the room at that moment, and Fairstead immediately closed and locked the vault. But she had time to sense it."

Jake eyed Lyra. "You're sure that relic was in Fairstead's vault?" he demanded.

"Yes," she said. She picked up her coffee cup. "I'm good with amethyst, remember? And I know those relics. I spent a lot of time with them before AI stole the ruin from me. They resonate on some very unusual and distinctive wavelengths."

Jake's eyes narrowed. "We did not steal that damn ruin."

"Moving right along," Cruz said smoothly. "Since nothing else was stolen out of the vault, it's clear that whoever killed Fairstead was after the relic. That means he knew it was there in the first place. I'm betting the list of suspects is a short one."

"With Lyra's client at the top?" Jake asked.

"It's a possibility," Cruz conceded. "But on the whole I'm inclined to doubt it."

"Who the hell is this client, anyway?" Jake demanded.

There was a short silence. Jeff concentrated on some toast. Cruz ate his omelet.

Lyra smiled, drank some coffee, and lowered the cup. "Wilson Revere."

Stunned outrage flashed across Jake's face. "What the hell? You're consulting for Revere?"

"Past tense, I'm afraid." She sighed. "Cruz made a scene. I was humiliated. I burst into tears and managed to create a spectacle of myself in front of a very large group of the most important amber collectors in Frequency. I think it's safe to say that I won't be getting any more high-end clients like Revere for a while."

"Revere is our biggest competitor," Jake roared. "He's a complete and total son of a bitch. You can't trust him any farther than you can walk without amber in the tunnels."

"Really?" She gave him a quizzical look. "I never had any problem with him."

Evidently sensing that he wasn't going to get far with her, Jake rounded on Cruz.

"Did you know she was working for Revere?" he demanded.

"Yes," Cruz said patiently. "That's why I went along. But as Lyra said, the situation became somewhat untenable, so we left. The bottom line is that we were able to determine that the relic was in Fairstead's vault. That's why I set up surveillance on the gallery."

Jeff leaned back in his chair. "We think the killer came and went via the catacombs, and that's where we are now."

Jake grunted, clearly unsatisfied. But he picked up his coffee. "You're going to take a look?"

"I've got the plane standing by," Cruz said. "Jeff and I will leave right after breakfast."

Lyra lowered her cup. "What about me?"

Cruz looked at her across the table. "You're staying here."

She pretended she had not heard the command.

"What, exactly, are you going to be looking at?" she asked instead.

It was Jeff who answered. "The Frequency PD won't let us into the crime scene. They're still working it, and they can be kind of territorial. But no one can stop us from going into the catacombs beneath the gallery. The boss and I are going down to see if we can pick up any traces of the killer."

"Right," Lyra said. She crumpled her napkin and got to her feet. "You'll be needing me, then."

Cruz gave her a hard look. "And why is that?"

"Even if you do manage to track the killer through the catacombs, that doesn't mean you'll be able to find the relic. But if it is anywhere in the vicinity, I'll be able to sense it."

"Huh," Jake said and looked at Cruz. "She's a Dore. She knows what she's doing when it comes to amber."

Chapter 28

CRUZ JACKED UP HIS SENSES AND STUDIED THE JAGGED tear in the glowing green quartz wall. At once the whispers of violence—hot, ravenous, haunting and, yes, darkly thrilling—lifted the hair on the nape of his neck and sent a shot of adrenaline through him. The dirty little secret of every man in the family was that it felt good, really, really good. Until he had met Lyra, the sensations of the hunt had always ranked as the most enthralling rush he had ever experienced. Now it was the second most enthralling rush.

Vincent, perched on his shoulder, made a low, rumbling sound. He was still fully fluffed, but he seemed to understand that they were engaged in some kind of hunting game. He was having a good time, too. What's more, he obviously did not feel the need to try to appear politically correct about it.

"The killer came this way, all right," Cruz said. "And he used the same route out."

He moved through the ripped quartz into the dense darkness of the underground cavern. Jeff followed. They both used their flashlights.

"Hot when he arrived," Jeff said. "He was planning the kill. Hotter when he left."

Jeff was doing his best to hide the effect the spoor of violence was having on him. His voice was so unnaturally level and uninflected he sounded as if he were making an observation on the weather.

They were both fully rezzed, fighting the same battle to maintain a facade of cool control, not only because control of one's talent was considered priority number one in the Sweetwater family, but also because of Lyra. She was strong and she was gutsy, but even strong, gutsy women had been known to run screaming in the opposite direction when they found themselves in the presence of men whose talents predisposed them to be stirred and deeply aroused by violence. Couldn't blame the ladies, Cruz thought dourly. Just the old survival instinct kicking in.

There was only one way a woman could come to trust such a man with absolute certainty, and that was if she experienced and accepted a psychic connection with him. That was the only way she could comprehend at the very core of her being that he would never be a threat to her, that he would die to protect her.

"The first question that comes to mind," Jeff said, "is how did the killer know about this entrance to Fairstead's gallery?"

"He wouldn't have discovered it by accident," Cruz said. "Fairstead must have shown it to him."

Lyra stepped through the torn quartz and rezzed her flashlight. "Maybe the killer had a long-standing business relationship with Fairstead, and this is how he came and went from the gallery on a regular basis."

Cruz and Jeff looked at her. She did not appear to notice. Her attention was on the cavern.

Jeff cleared his throat. "If he was a regular business associate of Fairstead's, why would he come and go underground?"

"He probably supplied Fairstead with artifacts that had what you might call somewhat murky provenances," she continued. "Fairstead had an image to uphold in the high-end antiquities trade. He would not have wanted his clients or his competition to see him buying antiquities or valuable specimens from a tunnel rat or a low-level independent like, say, me."

Jeff's cool demeanor slipped a little for the first time. He was torn between astonishment and laughter.

"No offense, but you seem to know a lot about the underground amber market, Miss Dore," he said.

"I do," she agreed. "Just ask the boss."

Jeff looked at Cruz.

Time to take charge, Cruz thought.

"We are not going there," he said. "And that's an executive decision. Back to our problem here. The killer may or may not have been a regular supplier of illegal amber to Fairstead, but it's a good bet either way that Fairstead knew him."

"The police have that much, already," Jeff said. "They're going with a falling-out among thieves scenario."

Cruz glanced at him. "Is that from your buddy in the Frequency PD?"

"Uh-huh."

Cruz nodded, impressed. "Nice work. Always good to have contacts like that inside regular law enforcement."

Evidently encouraged, Jeff kept going. "They're talking to low-end dealers throughout the Quarter, trying to find out who might have been selling to Fairstead. What they can't figure out is why nothing was taken from the vault."

"In other words, they still don't know about the relic," Cruz said.

Jeff shook his head. "No."

"That's something, at least. Let's see if we can pick up anything else here."

The cavern was a natural cave, but at some point in the past two hundred years, someone had constructed a steep flight of stone steps that led upward into the darkness, presumably ending in the basement of the Fairstead Gallery.

Cruz walked to the staircase and touched the handrail. The miasma of recent violence washed through him again. This time he rezzed a little energy through his newly tuned ring, trying to see if he could get any more details.

He was expecting the escalation of the intensity of the psychic traces. What caught him off guard was the way the violent energy came into sharp, clear focus.

"What the hell?" he asked. Automatically he looked down at his ring.

Jeff grinned. "Told you. It's that special precision tuning thing that Lyra does. Makes a difference, doesn't it?"

Cruz glanced at Lyra. "Yes, it does."

She smiled. "I usually charge extra for that."

"Why didn't you ever tell me that you could do that with amber?" Cruz asked.

"You never asked."

"Got any more tuning secrets?"

"Certainly. But a tuner never tells all her secrets. What are you finding there on the stairs?"

"One man," he said, going back to the business at hand. He glanced at Jeff. "Do you agree?"

Jeff seemed briefly taken aback at having been asked for an opinion. But he recovered quickly.

"Yes," he said. "Just one going up the stairs and one coming back down. The same guy, I think."

Cruz touched another section of the railing. He rezzed a little more energy and was once again amazed by the clarity of what he sensed. "He was excited, but he was also a little rattled."

"He knew he was taking a big risk killing Fairstead," Jeff offered. "That was bound to produce a high-profile murder investigation."

"Something I'm not getting here," Lyra said. "We're talking as if the same guy who sold the relic to Fairstead came back later to murder him and retrieve the artifact. But why would he do that? He and Fairstead had done the deal."

Cruz looked up toward the top of the steps. "Given the timing of Fairstead's death, I think the killer may have heard about your dramatic little scene in Fairstead's gallery yesterday afternoon. He panicked after he found out that I was there in the same room as the relic. He doesn't believe in coincidences."

"Makes sense," Jeff said. "If he knew that you were not only at the gallery but also in the vault chamber where the amethyst was hidden, he might have freaked. Figured you were getting too close."

"So he goes in last night and kills the one person who could identify him," Lyra said. "Valentine Fairstead."

"And while he's at it, he retrieves the artifact," Cruz concluded, satisfied with the logic. "Let's go; we've seen enough."

"Where are we going?" Lyra asked.

"Now that we have his psi spoor, we might be able to follow the killer's path through the catacombs. Normally the heavy psi inside the tunnels makes it very difficult to track someone underground, but with this new tune-up job on my amber, things may be different."

Jeff grinned. "I think you may be right."

"Are you serious?" Lyra asked. "You can actually track a person by following their psychic spoor?"

"Only if he's still riding the waves of energy that accompany acts of violence," Jeff explained. "Once he's calmed down, the traces become indistinguishable from other kinds of psi."

"Tuners aren't the only ones with a few secrets," Cruz said. "Sweetwaters have some also."

"I've got to tell you that does not come as a huge surprise," Lyra said.

Cruz focused through his amber. The currents of violent psi leaped into clear definition immediately.

"Got him," he said quietly to Jeff.

"Same here," Jeff said.

Vincent rumbled excitedly and leaned forward so far, Cruz wondered if the dust bunny would fall off his shoulder. But Vincent did not seem the least bit worried about that possibility. He stared straight ahead with all four eyes, riveted.

"It's like he knows we're hunting," Jeff said. "Like he's hunting with us."

"He's a good dust bunny to have at your back in a fight," Cruz said. "Trust me. I saw him in action last night."

"Oh, great," Lyra said. "I sense male bonding and a pack mentality developing here."

An uneasy jolt sliced through Cruz. Maybe she was making a joke. Maybe not. Either way, he did not want her to start classifying him as some kind of predatory beast. Her opinion of his character was shaky enough as it was.

"Think of the three of us as a team," he said, "not a pack."

"Whatever," Lyra said.

The killer's spoor led through three disorienting intersections, each with multiple connecting hallways, past countless vaulted chambers and anterooms. It dead-ended in front of a solid wall of quartz.

When they all stopped, Vincent chittered impatiently

and bounded down to the floor. He scampered eagerly to the wall. A dust bunny–size hole in the quartz opened. Vincent went through it and promptly vanished. The hole closed.

"Well, that answers that question," Lyra said. She studied the wall. "The killer escaped into the jungle. He's long gone."

"Damn," Jeff muttered. "We'll never be able to track him down in the rain forest, not even with our new, improved, highly tuned amber. You can't track anyone in the jungle unless you've got their locator frequency. The psi in there is just too heavy and way too freakish."

Cruz studied the blank quartz wall. "He's gone, and you're right, we can't track him. But I'd really like to have a look around on the other side of that wall."

"Why?" Lyra asked.

"Last night after the murder he was in a real hurry. Maybe he got careless and dropped something."

Vincent reappeared. He made encouraging sounds and promptly disappeared again.

Jeff contemplated the wall. "We need to get someone down here who can open a people-size jungle gate."

"That would be me," Lyra said.

Chapter 29

SHE MOVED TO STAND IN FRONT OF THE BLANK WALL. She could feel Jeff's intense scrutiny and curiosity.

"The boss never mentioned that you could open this kind of gate," he said.

Lyra looked back over her shoulder at Cruz. "He was trying to protect me."

Jeff frowned. "From what?"

"Whoever killed the lab tech and stole the relic was believed to have disappeared into the jungle, using a gate he had opened," Lyra explained. "That person was also doing his best to set me up. If it got out that I could open jungle gates, it would be one more piece of evidence against me."

"Right," Jeff said, obviously satisfied.

She gave him a quick, sidelong look. He did not appear the least bit startled, let alone appalled, by the knowledge that Cruz had deliberately concealed evidence that might have been used against her. Just the opposite, in fact. Jeff was acting as if such an action was perfectly normal, the sort of thing he would have expected Cruz to do under the circumstances. It was enough to make you wonder if there might be something to all that nonsense about the deeply romantic nature of the men of the Sweetwater family.

Jeff's eyes lit with sudden excitement. "Hey, that means the killer probably knows you can open jungle gates. Right? How many people are aware of that?"

"Not many," she assured him.

"Well, that could narrow the list of suspects," he said, glancing at Cruz for support.

Cruz moved forward to stand beside Lyra. "Maybe, maybe not. It may have just been a coincidence."

Lyra and Jeff looked at him. Neither said a word.

"Okay," he said. "Probably isn't a coincidence. But either way, we know one thing for sure about him now."

"Right," Jeff said. "*He* can open them."

Vincent reappeared and bounced up and down at Lyra's feet, red beret flapping wildly. He was impatient to get on with the game.

She concentrated for a moment, rezzing energy until she caught the latent patterns within the quartz wall. They became crystal clear to her senses almost immediately. She went to work tuning the wavelengths with her amethyst charms until they resonated in such a way that she could control them.

A large section of wall dissolved, revealing a luminous, almost impenetrable mass of green. Warm, humid air and the sounds and smells of the verdant world on the other side greeted them. Vincent dashed forward and tumbled up onto a fallen log, all four eyes open. Cruz and Jeff followed more cautiously.

"Don't forget the killer has a mag-rez," Lyra reminded them quickly.

"Guns are like any other high-tech gadget," Cruz said somewhat absently. "They won't work in the rain forest, just like they won't work in the catacombs, because of the heavy psi."

She relaxed a little. "Right. For a moment there I forgot."

Vincent muttered and hopped off the log. He disappeared into a maze of green vines.

"He's onto something," Lyra said.

"Looks like it," Cruz agreed. He slipped a jungle knife out of its sheath on his pack and went toward the vines. "But it's going to be tough to follow him."

Jeff freed his own knife and went after him.

Lyra followed the rough path the men created. Vincent was no longer in sight, but she could hear him chortling excitedly.

A few minutes later, Cruz and Jeff came to a halt. Lyra heard the roar and splash of water. She pushed aside a veil of green orchids.

"Careful," Cruz said. He put out a hand to keep her from moving forward. "It's slippery up here."

They were standing at the top of a waterfall. Vincent was on a nearby rock, all four eyes fixed on the pool below. Cruz and Jeff were studying the bottom of the falls, as well. There was the same air of fixed intensity about them. *Hunters,* Lyra thought, *all three of them.*

She took a cautious step closer to the edge and looked down. A body floated in the grotto pool at the foot of the cascading water. Shock reverberated through her. There was no mistaking the standard-issue Amber Inc. jungle uniform.

"Good grief," she whispered. "Who is it?"

"Let's find out," Cruz said.

He and Jeff made their way down the rocky incline to the pool. Wading knee deep into the water, they caught hold of the body and hauled it back to the edge of the grotto. When they got the man onto dry ground, they turned him onto his back. His neck flopped at an unnatural angle. Several hours of soaking had taken its toll, as had a bad gash in the forehead, but the features were still recognizable. So was the distinctive goatee.

"That's Dr. Webber," Lyra said. "The head of the AI lab. The one who kept calling me, demanding that I assist with his experiments."

Cruz crouched beside the body and went swiftly through the pockets. Within seconds he withdrew a drenched mag-rez gun. "What do you want to bet this is the weapon that was used to kill Fairstead?"

"That would be a sucker bet," Jeff said.

Lyra collected Vincent and scrambled down the rocky incline. "What happened to him?"

"Looks like in his hurry to escape, he didn't see the grotto until it was too late," Jeff said. "He fell, hit his head on the rocks, and drowned."

"That's sure what it looks like," Cruz said, straightening.

A familiar tingle fluttered Lyra's senses.

"It's here," she said.

"What?" Jeff asked.

"The amethyst artifact that was taken from Fairstead's vault. It's somewhere nearby."

Vincent made excited little sounds and wriggled free of her grasp. He hopped onto the rim of the pool, jumped into the water, and promptly disappeared beneath the surface. A moment later he reappeared, the relic clutched between his two front paws. He paddled with his other four feet to the edge of the pool. Cruz leaned over and took the relic from him.

"Thanks, Vincent." Cruz examined the softly glowing block of carved amethyst. "This is it, all right. The one that went missing from the lab."

"Looks like that's a wrap," Jeff announced. "Webber stole the relic. He didn't have the kind of connections needed to sell such a valuable artifact, so he took it to Fairstead. Fairstead tried to sell it to Wilson Revere yesterday, but you showed up, and everyone involved got nervous."

Lyra frowned, thinking. "Dr. Webber got scared because he thought that Cruz was closing in on Fairstead and that Fairstead would lead straight back to him. So he retrieved the relic and killed Fairstead, the one person who could identify him. He escaped through the gate. But he was in a rush. He didn't see the waterfall until it was too late. Broke his neck."

"Works for me," Jeff said.

Cruz studied the relic. "Doesn't work for me."

"Why not?" Lyra asked.

Cruz looked up. "It's just too damn neat."

"Got another theory of the crime?" Jeff asked.

Cruz raised his brows. " 'Theory of the crime'? Have you been watching *Psi Crime Investigation* again?"

Jeff reddened.

Lyra glared at Cruz. "I love that show. All that psi forensics stuff is fascinating."

"They say it's very accurate," Jeff said earnestly. "Real cutting-edge psychic crime-scene investigation techniques."

"I can't believe we're talking about a rez-screen program." Cruz slid his pack off his shoulder, unzipped it, and shoved the relic inside. "Forget I even mentioned it and start looking for some indication that someone else was here."

Jeff surveyed their foliage-choked surroundings. "That's going to be a little tough. You know how this place eats evidence. Drop a gum wrapper on the ground, and the next day it's gone."

"Webber's body is still in pretty good shape," Cruz said. "The rain forest hasn't turned him into compost yet. That means he must have died recently. If the killer got careless and dropped something, it will still be here."

"Assuming there is a killer," Lyra said.

Cruz looked at her with eyes that burned with a cold emerald fire. Energy seemed to shiver in the air around him.

"This was no accident," he said quietly. "There was a killer. The spoor is still on the body. You can't wash off the taint of murder with water."

A chill of awareness slipped through her. He was fully rezzed, she thought, running on his talent.

Jeff studied Vincent. "Maybe the bunny can find some evidence for us the way he found the body."

They all contemplated Vincent. He was still on the rim of the pool, busily fluffing his wet fur. The little red beret was soaking wet.

"I don't think that will work," Lyra said. She leaned down to remove the wet cap. "I'm pretty sure that he thought this was a game of fetch the relic. As far as he's concerned, it's finished."

She squeezed the excess water out of the beret and pinned it to Vincent's damp fur.

"Looks like we get to do this the old-fashioned way," Cruz said. "We'll establish a search grid and walk it shoulder to shoulder. Nobody moves out of visual range of the others. Understood?"

Jeff grinned at Lyra. "That means don't go wandering off on your own."

"Thanks," Lyra said. "I did sort of wonder. All that technical jargon, you know. A girl gets confused."

Cruz ignored her and started up the steep incline. "We'll try the top of the falls first."

"Why?" Jeff asked.

"Because regardless of where he killed Webber, the killer had to drop the body from that point in order to make the accident look real."

"Sure," Jeff said. "And maybe there was a struggle. That would be good."

"Yes, it would," Cruz agreed.

Lyra grabbed a trailing vine and used it to haul herself up the incline behind the men. "Why?"

"Because where there's a struggle, you often find some evidence," Jeff explained.

"Oh, right," she said. "I knew that."

"Except where there's a lot of water and a lot of jungle," he added grimly. "Talk about a great place to hide evidence and bodies."

"We found Webber's body," she reminded him.

Cruz looked back over his shoulder. "That was because someone wanted us to find him."

"How could the killer have known that we would find the jungle gate in the catacombs?" she asked. "Let alone conduct a search?"

"He must have assumed that I'd check out the murder scene with a PF team and pick up the psi trail," Cruz said. "He knew that trail would dead end at the gate and that I'd figure it out from there. Once inside, it would have been hard to miss the waterfall. No offense, but we didn't really need Vincent."

"Don't say that." She looked at Vincent, who was already at the top of the falls, playing with a palm frond that dipped into the water. "He thinks he won the game."

Cruz came to a halt at the edge of the falls and gave Vincent another considering look. "Are you sure you can't convince him to play a new game?"

"Yeah," Jeff said, scrambling up to stand beside him. "One that involves finding evidence of some kind."

"I don't know how to go about it," she said. She watched Vincent bat the palm frond with his front paw. "It's not like he's telepathic or anything. He's a dust bunny."

"Forget it," Cruz said. "Let's start the sweep. We'll stick to the area immediately around the perimeter of the falls."

They moved out side by side, arm's length apart. Vincent tumbled after them but showed no interest in the new game until they passed a small cave in the rocks. At that point he chortled to them and disappeared into the shadowed opening.

They stopped.

"Now, what?" Jeff asked.

"I don't know," Lyra said. "Maybe he spotted some small animal that passes for dust bunny prey."

Vincent reappeared with a piece of foil in one paw. He looked quite pleased with himself.

"He's into bling," Lyra explained.

"Will he give it to you?" Cruz asked.

"Sure." She picked up Vincent. "Can I see that?" she asked.

Vincent let her take the scrap of foil. She handed it to Cruz.

"It's a wrapper," he said. "The kind used to package candy and snack bars."

Jeff whistled softly. "Someone dropped it. The killer?"

"Yes." Cruz smiled his cold smile of satisfaction. He

rubbed the wrapper between his thumb and forefinger. "His psi is all over it."

"Could be a piece of foil from something Webber ate," Jeff said. "If there was a struggle, the killer's psi could have ended up on the snack bar or anything else in the vicinity."

Cruz moved to the edge of the rocky opening and crouched to study the interior. Then he reached inside and withdrew what looked like a plastic sack emblazoned with a familiar logo.

"That's an AI rain poncho pouch," Jeff said. "The rain gear is standard issue in every AI pack."

"Same psi traces," Cruz said.

"Again, could have belonged to Webber," Jeff said. "Maybe he got caught in a downpour, put on the poncho, and waited out the storm inside that cave. You know what it's like when it rains in the jungle. You can't move. Maybe he was wearing the rain poncho when the killer attacked."

"On *Psi Crime Investigation* they make it clear that, although the courts are starting to admit testimony from psychics, it has to be backed up with hard evidence," Lyra said.

Cruz gave her and Jeff a narrow-eyed look. "That does it; no more *PCI* for either of you. You want proof that the poncho and the snack bar wrapper didn't belong to Webber? Fine. I'll give you proof."

Jeff frowned, curious. "How will you do that?"

"Watch and learn, Mr. Hotshot Psi Crime Investigator," Cruz said.

He went back down the side of the falls to the body, removed Webber's pack, and unzipped it. A few seconds later he pulled out an unused rain poncho still tucked neatly inside its plastic pouch. Next he went swiftly through the remaining contents of the pack. After a moment, he straightened.

"There aren't any energy bars missing, either," he announced.

"Oh, yeah," Jeff said. "I should have thought of checking out the pack. Okay, it's pretty clear that the killer left the pouch and the wrapper. Now we know something else about him."

"He was carrying AI equipment, so he probably works for AI," Lyra said.

"We know more than that." Cruz started back toward the top of the falls. "He's cutting his losses and getting rid of his partners. Cleaning up."

Chapter 30

"SOMETHING I'VE BEEN THINKING ABOUT," CRUZ SAID.

"Just something?" Lyra settled down onto the lounger and took a sip of her wine. "Funny, I had the impression that you've been thinking about a lot of stuff lately. You know, finding the artifact, hunting a killer."

They were sitting on her balcony, a bottle of wine and a plate of cheese and crackers on the small table between them. Vincent was on the railing, munching on a cracker. The night was balmy and warm, and the great wall cast its eerie green glow over the Quarter.

"The particular stuff I'm thinking about is the way the gate of the amethyst chamber closed, trapping five people inside," Cruz said.

"You're back to wondering if it was something other than an accident?"

"I am." He ate a cracker. "You said the gate could have been closed by either stray waves from a psi river or a storm. You also said that someone working certain nonstandard amber could have done it deliberately."

"Right. In addition to amethyst, I'm pretty sure diamond or silver amber would do it. My grandfather told me that they have some distinctive properties. He said they could disrupt the currents generated by most of the other ambers. But both are extremely rare. I've never come across a single specimen of either in my work. So even if the killer could work one or the other, how would he get hold of a chunk to use on the gate?"

"I can think of one place. The vault at the lab."

"Wow." She raised her brows. "You've actually got some diamond and silver at the lab?"

"Sweetwaters and their employees have been collecting specimens and artifacts of rare amber for decades. Everything goes into the vault, but almost nothing comes out. It's like the basement of a big museum in there. Things go into storage and get forgotten."

"But presumably access to the vault is limited."

"Sure."

"Got a list?" she asked.

"It's a short one." Cruz drank some wine. "Felix Webber was right at the top."

"Well, that fits. He was at the ruin when it closed." She paused. "Assuming he could work diamond or silver."

"If he was able to work it, he sure as hell kept the information to himself. It wasn't in his file."

"Wouldn't be the first time someone with an unusual talent kept the data out of an employment file."

"True."

She considered for a moment. "Originally you thought that whoever triggered the gate did it to frame me."

"That theory still fits. But I'm starting to wonder if there was an additional goal."

"What?"

"Another murder. I have a feeling that one of the five people trapped inside that chamber was the real target."

"You sound very sure of that," she said.

"I am."

"But how can you know something like that with such certainty?"

"The same way I know we were meant to be together."

"Your talent?"

"Uh-huh." He ate another cracker.

She pursed her lips. "You know, I can buy the idea that you have a talent for hunting bad guys. But this thing about the men in your family being able to know when the right woman comes along? Not so much."

"You get used to it after a while."

"Me, I'm going to sign up with a professional matchmaker."

"Why bother? Just be a waste of money."

"Maybe," she said. "But now that I'm going to be getting this big check from Amber Inc. as my fee for opening the ruin, I can afford to experiment with a really high-end matchmaker."

"This is all about making me suffer isn't it?"

"No," she said. "It's about me being really, really careful the second time around."

"Okay," he said.

Chapter 31

CRUZ WAS AT HIS DESK WHEN JEFF STROLLED INTO THE office early the next morning.

"I've got Webber's parapsych profile," Jeff said. "There's nothing in it about the doc being able to open jungle gates, just like there's nothing in it about his ability to work unusual amber."

"That doesn't come as a shock." Cruz closed the file he had been reading and took the folder Jeff held out to him.

Jeff dropped into a chair and stretched out his legs. "I don't get it. If Webber was helping himself to relics from the lab vault, why didn't we pick up on it?"

"Like I told Lyra, there's fifty years' worth of amber in that vault. Every drawer is crammed with relics and samples. No one would notice if a few items went missing now and then, especially if whoever took them knew how to bypass the security alarms."

"Something Webber would know how to do," Jeff said.

Cruz rocked back in his chair and clasped his hands behind his head. He contemplated the three paintings hanging on the wall across the room.

"Here's what I think happened," he said. "Webber had a nice little part-time racket going for himself. Probably teamed up with Fairstead and the third man a few years ago. They kept the thefts small, taking pieces no one would miss. But the amethyst relics from the ruin were different. Each was worth a fortune on the underground antiquities market. Got a hunch they had never before risked swiping something that valuable out of the vault."

"Security was a hell of a lot tighter around the relics, too," Jeff observed. "Unlike some of the other stuff housed in the vault, one of those artifacts would have been missed immediately. They needed to make it look like someone else had stolen the artifact. They picked the obvious suspect."

"Lyra. But something went wrong the night of the theft. One of the lab techs must have discovered them. They had to kill him to keep him quiet."

"They?" Jeff repeated.

"Webber and the third man."

Jeff eyed the files spread out on the desk. "Do you have a name for this third guy?"

"I think so, yes." Cruz picked up one of the files and handed it to him.

Jeff glanced at the name and whistled softly. "Well, this is sort of embarrassing. How did you figure it out?"

"Process of elimination. There were five people caught in the amethyst chamber the night the gate closed. I'm almost-certain Webber was trying to kill one of them."

"So the Frequency PD was right? This is a falling-out-among-thieves scenario after all?"

"Feels like it. The problem for the police is that they haven't got a clue where to start looking for the other two thieves. But we found one dead in the jungle."

Jeff tapped the folder on the edge of the desk, looking thoughtful. "And this is the third guy. He looks good for it, all right."

"Looks good for it?" Cruz repeated. He sighed. "You've really got to lay off *PCI.* It's ruining your vocabulary."

Jeff rose, an unusually determined expression on his face. "I'm getting into practice."

"For what?"

Jeff started toward the door. "Guess I forgot to mention it, but I'm going to be handing in my resignation soon. I'm leaving AI Security."

"Is this some kind of joke?"

"No joke." Jeff opened the door and turned partway around. "I'm applying to the Federal Bureau of Psi Investigation."

"The hell you are."

"Thanks for your support, sir. I really appreciate it."

Cruz exhaled slowly, reining in his impatience. "Come back here. Sit down. We'll talk."

"Some other time maybe."

"Damn it, Jeff, Big Jake will have a fit. Not to mention your father and my brothers and everyone else in the clan. In this family we don't take up careers in regular law enforcement."

"No, we just work for people who can afford to pay for protection, and sometimes we do things that law enforcement can't or won't do."

"Including occasional favors for the FBPI," Cruz reminded him coldly.

"You know what that makes us? Mercenaries."

"That's ghost crap. This is a private security agency, but we're not mercenaries, damn it. We don't take money for that kind of work. Not anymore. Sweetwaters have rules. We've always had rules. What's more, we've never worked for the bad guys, even when there was money on the table."

"Okay, I'll give you that much. Here's the thing. I want to work for the *little* guy. You know, the folks who can't afford high-end private protection."

"That's exactly what we do when we accept a contract from the FBPI."

"It's not the same thing," Jeff insisted.

Cruz studied him for a long moment.

"How long have you been thinking about joining the FBPI?" he asked.

Jeff shrugged. "For about as long as I can remember. Ever since I was a kid."

"But you're just now making this career decision?"

"It's a little tough to make a career decision in this

family, unless the career path in question involves an Amber Inc. subsidiary."

"So why now?"

"Why not now?" Jeff shot back.

"You need to give this a little more thought, Jeff."

"Why bother? That won't convince anyone in the family that it's a good idea. I've wasted enough time as it is. I'm tired of being a bodyguard."

"Is that what this is about? You want to move up? Hell, ambition isn't a problem in this family, and you know it. In fact, it's about time you showed some. There's plenty of opportunity here at AI Security."

"I've already made my decision. I'm not changing my mind. At least I've got one person on my side."

"Yeah? Who?"

"Lyra."

Jeff went out into the hall and shut the door with exquisite control.

Cruz looked at the closed door for a long time. After a while he got to his feet and went down the hall to the accounting department.

Chapter 32

SOME TIME LATER, CRUZ WAITED FOR HIS PREY IN A shadowed office. He sat, booted feet propped on the corner of the desk, and thought about the implications of Jeff's unexpected outburst of rebellion. Lyra could not be blamed entirely, he decided, but the odds were excellent that she had served as catalyst and cheerleader.

Probably only the beginning. No doubt about it, when she became a member of the family, she was going to rattle the mag-steel barricades that had always encircled the close-knit Sweetwater clan.

Footsteps in the hall pulled him out of his reverie. The familiar rush of the hunt crackled through him.

The door marked AI LAB SECURITY opened. Garrett Flagg walked into the room and rezzed the lights. He stopped short when he saw Cruz sitting behind his desk. He managed to keep his expression one of polite confusion, but he could not mask the flare of sudden panic that snapped in the atmosphere around him.

"My secretary didn't tell me you were in here, Mr. Sweetwater," he said.

"That's because she doesn't know I'm here. I arrived while she was in the ladies' room. Close the door and sit down."

Flagg hesitated. Cruz could almost taste the currents of fight-or-flight energy pulsing in the other man's aura. But Flagg shut the door and took the seat on the other side of the desk.

"Am I being fired?" he asked. He managed to inject a little dry amusement into his voice.

"No," Cruz said. He took his feet down off the desk. "You're going to be arrested. But I want some answers first."

"Arrested." Flagg's face went slack with shock. For an instant the panic surged higher. Then it metamorphosed into a tightly controlled rage. "What the hell is this about?"

"It's about three murders and a stolen artifact."

"You're accusing me of murder? You're insane."

Cruz smiled a little. "Aren't you even going to ask me why I mentioned three murders instead of two?"

"I don't know what the hell you're talking about."

"Sure you do, but I'll walk you through it, anyway. A while back—hell, maybe a few years back—you and Webber came up with a nice little racket. The AI vault was filled with rare and exotic amber. You figured no one would miss the occasional missing artifact or specimen.

Stealing the relics was no problem, but you and Webber needed someone to sell them for you, so you hooked up with Valentine Fairstead."

"This is crazy."

"Things went swell for a while. Who knows how long you could have kept your little sideline going if you hadn't gotten greedy and decided to go for the really big score with one of the amethyst artifacts that were coming out of the new jungle ruin?"

"I don't know where you're getting this crap. I want a lawyer."

"The sight of all those blocks of carved amethyst sitting in the vault was just too tempting. But you knew that, unlike the other trinkets you had swiped, the amethyst would be missed. You needed someone to take the fall. Lyra Dore was perfect."

"You think I set her up? Shit, she's really rezzed your amber, hasn't she? I always figured you were way too smart to get suckered by a woman. Hell, she doesn't even have great tits. I don't know what you see—"

Cruz vaulted over the desk, jerked him out of the chair, and slammed him against the wall.

"You make one more comment like that about Lyra, and you won't be needing a lawyer, because you will not leave this office alive," Cruz said softly. "Do you understand me, Flagg?"

"Yeah, sure. Take it easy, man. I'm telling you I didn't have anything to do with that stolen artifact."

Cruz released him. "Let's return to our story. Fairstead set up the big score. Wilson Revere was interested in the artifact. It was perfect. But somewhere along the line, Webber started getting nervous. The deal was just too big. Way beyond anything the three of you had handled before. He was probably afraid that after it was concluded, you would get rid of him and take his share of the profits. It was a reasonable assumption. So he decided to try to take you out first."

"This is crazy."

"He was scared of you, though. He knew that if he failed and you realized what had happened, you'd kill him. So he tried to concoct an accident at the amethyst ruin. He could work either diamond or silver amber, and he knew from his research that it could be used to interfere with amethyst currents. So he took a chance and closed the gate at the ruin while you and the others were inside."

Flagg looked startled. "Webber closed that gate? That little bastard. I should have guessed. I didn't think he had the guts to pull a stunt like that."

"His big plan fell apart when I brought Lyra down into the jungle to open the gate. He had no way of knowing that I would go to her for help, let alone that she would actually agree to rescue anyone connected to Amber Inc."

"Webber was a fool."

"The three of you knew I was getting close. You must have been pretty damn desperate to hire not one but two pairs of lowlifes off the street to take me out. Two clumsy attempts. Two failures. The second time around, there was another man on the scene who used his talent to take me down. I'm assuming that was Webber working diamond amber again. That stuff has got some very weird properties."

"You're making this up as you go along," Flagg growled.

"In the end, after you discovered I had been in Fairstead's vault room, you realized the whole situation had become just too hot. You decided to pull the plug. You killed Fairstead and Webber and tried to stage the scene so that it looked like only the two of them were involved in the theft. You even tossed in the amethyst relic, just to make it look good. Nice touch, throwing it into the grotto pool. But it wasn't much of a risk. You were pretty sure it would be found in the course of a thorough search of the area."

"You can't prove I killed Webber or Fairstead or anyone else."

Cruz went behind the desk and picked up the backpack he had stashed there earlier.

"This is yours," he said. He set the pack on the desk. "I found it in your locker this afternoon."

"So what?"

"There's a poncho inside. It's still damp. There's no pouch, because you got careless and left it in the little cave above the waterfall in the jungle. One of the energy bars is missing, as well. You ate it while you waited out the rainstorm. I found the wrapper. You were still hot from the kill when you put on the poncho and ate the energy bar. Your psi was all over both."

"You can't prove anything with an empty plastic pouch and an energy bar wrapper. Psi evidence won't hold up in court unless there is corroborating physical evidence."

"Hell, everyone watches *Psi Crime Investigation.* Okay, you want proof? Let's talk about the money."

"What money?"

"All three of you—Webber, Fairstead, and yourself—left nice, neat money trails every time you sold an artifact. One of the folks down in Accounting got into your bank records and into Webber's an hour ago. The cops will find Fairstead's soon enough. Let's see, I've got motive, means, and I can put you at the scene of the crime." He thought about what he had just said. "You know, this is kind of fun. I think maybe I understand what Jeff sees in this whole law enforcement career path thing."

"Son of a bitch." Flagg yanked a pistol out of the pocket of his leather jacket. "Damned Sweetwaters. You always think you're the smartest guys in the room. I've got news for you. I ran that little amber skimming operation for over three years, and no one suspected a thing."

"You're right. What's more, you probably could have gotten away with it for a while longer if you hadn't tried to move that amethyst relic. That was stupid, Flagg. No other word for it. Just plain stupid."

"Shut up." Flagg walked to the table and picked up the pack. The nose of the pistol was leveled at Cruz's midsection. It never wavered. "You think I didn't plan for a worst-case scenario like this?"

He went swiftly across the room and pushed a lever that had been concealed in the wall. A section of paneling slid aside. Soft currents of alien psi whispered through the opening.

"You're going to disappear into the tunnels?" Cruz asked. "That's your big escape plan? Good luck with that."

"I'm going into the jungle. Everyone knows you can't track a man in the rain forest who doesn't want to be found. When I come back to the surface, I'll have a new identity, and I'll be in another city-state. But you won't have to worry about that, because you'll be dead."

"So you're the one who opened the gates," Cruz said. "I assumed it was Webber. Okay, that answers that question. Couple more before you disappear into the underworld. Where's the amber that Webber used to close the ruin entrance and generate those hallucinations?"

"You're so damned smart, figure it out for yourself."

"And why the hell did Webber stalk Lyra in the first place? Or was that your idea? Maybe you decided that if everyone, including Lyra herself, thought she was going crazy, it would make it easier to pin the crimes on her."

"I couldn't care less about your little tuner girlfriend. But I can tell you this much. Webber was furious with her because she wouldn't help him run his experiments. He was obsessed with those relics. I'd tell you to save your questions for him, but I guess that won't work, seeing as how he's dead. And now, so are you."

Cruz sensed the slight elevation of energy that accompanied the almost invisible tightening of Flagg's finger on the trigger. He sent out a wave of muffling psi fog, enveloping Flagg in a senses-disorienting haze.

Flagg screamed. He floundered wildly in the psychic mist, lost his balance, and sprawled on the floor. The pistol roared. The bullet smashed into the ceiling. He tried to get off another shot, but Cruz kicked the weapon out of his hand.

The door slammed open. Jeff and several people wearing Frequency PD badges charged into the room.

Cruz quickly shut off the hot energy he had been generating, afraid that the fog would sweep over the others, even though he had been using the increased focusing power of the obsidian to direct the currents only toward Flagg. There was another reason for caution. He did not want the police questioning the nature of his talent. As far as the world was concerned, he just had a strong affinity for amber. It was Sweetwater family policy to keep it that way.

But no one coming through the door seemed to notice anything out of the ordinary. The cops surrounded Flagg. One of them pulled out a pair of handcuffs.

Jeff walked over to Cruz. "You okay, boss?"

"Sure." Cruz glanced down at his ring. "Did you feel anything when you came through the door?"

Jeff lowered his voice. "You mean that psi fog you generate? Nope."

"You know something? Lyra's special tuning service really works."

"Told you so. Get everything?"

Cruz reached inside his shirt and removed the recording device. "Every last word."

The cops had Flagg on his feet.

Cruz looked at him. "You were wrong."

"About what?" Flagg muttered.

"Nobody ever said Sweetwaters were always the smartest guys in the room. But we do tend to be lucky."

"I want a lawyer," Flagg said.

Chapter 33

LYRA BALANCED THE PAPER BAG FILLED WITH COFFEE and tea supplies in one arm and opened the back door of the gallery with her free hand. The first thing she noticed was that the lights were off. The second thing was that there was no illumination coming from the main sales room, either. Nancy had said that she was going to close early in order to set up for the private auction, but it was late afternoon, and the sun had gone down behind the green wall. The early twilight was descending rapidly on the Quarter.

There should have been lights.

"Nancy?" Lyra hovered in the doorway. A cold, prickling sensation slithered through her. The darkness in the back room seemed unnaturally heavy. "I brought the extra cream and coffee. I also threw in some more cookies, just in case."

Master Quinn appeared in the doorway that separated the back room of the gallery from the sales room. He was dressed as usual in his long amber robes, several chains of amber beads around his neck.

"Your friend won't be needing the cookies," he said in his serene guru tones. "Close the back door, put the sack on the table, and come with me."

He walked across the room and opened the door of what looked like a closet. The top of the underground stairwell loomed in the darkness. Paranormal currents wafted into the room.

The sensation chilling the nape of Lyra's neck metamorphosed into outright dread. She knew the feeling all too well. Her fight-or-flight instincts were surging. Something was terribly wrong. It wasn't just Quinn's presence here in the gallery or the lack of proper lighting. It wasn't even the fact that Nancy was nowhere in sight. It was the strange pulses of energy she was picking up. They were coming from Quinn.

Instinctively she readied herself to run. It was unfortunate that she was dressed for the auction in a tight, narrow-skirted black dress and three-inch heels, she thought. Not the best attire to wear when called upon to run for your life. But that was the Dore luck for you.

"Where's Nancy?" she said, fighting to keep her own voice calm.

"You will see her soon enough." Quinn motioned toward the stairwell with a graceful flourish. "After you, Lyra."

"I don't think so."

She dropped the sack and spun around, intending to run out into the alley, screaming. There had been no one loitering out there when she had entered the shop a moment ago, but maybe someone in one of the rooms above the shops would hear her.

But before she could take a single step, the world skewed and warped around her. The rear door of the shop narrowed and elongated. The ceiling was suddenly impossibly high. The three little steps down into the alley twisted endlessly in a terrible, writhing, Möbius strip. The pavement below was a winding river filled with heaving waves.

The floor beneath her feet fell away, and she went down hard amid the items that had spilled from the sack. She looked up and saw a specter bending over her.

"I have been patient with you," Quinn said. His voice seemed to come from a vast cavern. "But I will wait no longer."

"You're crazy."

"You still do not comprehend, but you will soon. Come with me."

The room snapped back into proper focus with dizzying suddenness. Lyra sat up cautiously, breathing deeply to control the nausea.

"You're the one who was causing the hallucinations," she said. "It was you all along. You've been doing something to me to make me believe that I was going crazy."

"My talent for inducing hallucinations is extraordinary. A rare gift that runs in my family." He reached into his robes and pulled out another chain. A pale stone caught the light. "I have been able to enhance it and control it with crystal amber."

"Why use your talent against me?"

"I have watched you in my class. I knew that you would try to resist me. Your will is strong. I had to demonstrate my power over you. I knew that it would be necessary for you to understand that I can control you utterly before you would submit."

"Submit to what, for Pete's sake?"

"To me. I am prepared to offer you what no other man, including Sweetwater, can give you."

"What?"

"Power." He gave her a scary, whimsical smile. "You could say that we were made for each other, Lyra Dore. Ours will be the ultimate in harmonic relationships."

"This is just so frickin' romantic. But I gotta tell you, you've got the wrong woman, Quinn. I'm not the romantic type."

"There is no mistake. I recognized you as the one the first day you entered my classroom."

"Is that so?" she managed. "How?"

"It was very simple, really. You were the only one in any of my classes who was not affected by the low dose of energy I use on the students," he said.

"Damn. No wonder everyone else was getting so much more out of those meditation classes. You were hypnotizing them with your amber."

"I brought them into harmonic balance. At least for the period of time they were in my studio. But not you. Never you."

Outrage swept through her. “And here I thought I was just a slow learner, a meditation class failure. You’re a scam artist, that’s what you are.”

“That’s a lie.” For the first time, strong emotion lit Quinn’s eyes. “I am no con man. I really can control the minds of others.”

“Maybe. For short periods of time. But at the high level of power required to induce hallucinations, I doubt that you can maintain a focus for more than a few minutes before you exhaust yourself. Talk about a heavy psi drain.”

Quinn smiled again, unconcerned. “I have found that even two or three minutes of a nightmare is long enough to control anyone I wish. No one can withstand such visions for long.”

“Let’s get back to Nancy. Where is she?”

“I told you, she is waiting for us.” Once again, Quinn swept out a hand, indicating the doorway to the underworld. “And I can promise you that she will wait forever in the catacombs if you do not accompany me. I took the precaution of removing all of her amber.”

“I can’t believe that you would leave her down there without amber. That’s a death sentence.”

“One that only you can commute.” He tossed a flashlight to her. “Get up.”

She picked up the flashlight and got unsteadily to her feet. The nausea had receded, but she was still shaky. It wasn’t just the aftereffects of the hallucinations, she thought. This was fear, pure and simple. She hated feeling afraid.

And from anger came strength.

She rezzed the flashlight and went toward the dark stairwell. "What, exactly, do you want from me, Quinn?"

"I know your secret, Lyra," he said. He followed her, his voice once again serene and assured. "I know your true power. You are so much more than a mere tuner. With me you will explore your true and full potential."

Another chill tightened her insides. She started down into the darkness. "What are you talking about?" she whispered.

"When you walked into my classroom shortly after your discovery of the amethyst ruin, I knew beyond a shadow of a doubt that you were the woman I needed."

"So I can tune amethyst," she said. "That's no secret. So what?"

"Do not try to deceive me. I know what the scientists and the researchers at the AI lab do not know. You found three of the pyramid stones."

She was stunned. "I don't know what you're talking about."

"Of course you do. What's more, you can work the stones."

"How do you know that?"

"The only reason you would have taken care to conceal those particular stones from Amber Inc. is because you recognized their power. As soon as I researched your genealogical records, my conclusions were confirmed."

"You researched my ancestry?"

"It's all there in the records of the Arcane Society, my

dear. As is the information that only one who is descended from a long line of crystal workers can rez the full latent energy of the stone. You are that woman."

She stopped halfway down the staircase and turned to look at him. "You're a member of the Arcane Society?"

"Yes."

"Wait a second. Are you telling me that the Society has my genealogical records?"

"One of your ancestors who came through the Curtain was Arcane. Didn't you know that?"

"No, I sure as heck did not know that."

"She evidently lost her connection with the Society during the Colonial era," Quinn said. "That was not unusual. Life was hard and chaotic in those early years. People were focused on survival. Many members of the Society drifted away. Their descendants have forgotten their roots."

"I can't believe this. The Society lets just anyone use their records to research someone else's family tree?"

"There is nothing private about an individual's family tree, either within the Society or outside of it," Quinn said.

"There sure as heck ought to be."

"Anger is a destructive emotion."

"No shit."

She arrived at the last step. On one side of the subbasement wall psi light glowed through the ragged crack in green quartz. She clicked off the flashlight and went toward it. Quinn followed.

"All right, I'm here with you in the tunnels," Lyra said, moving through the opening. "Where is Nancy?"

"Patience, Lyra. That was always your problem in meditation class. You never achieved a proper degree of harmonic balance." Quinn checked a locator. "Take the first turn to the right."

Obediently she went toward the first intersection. The heels of her shoes clicked lightly on the quartz floor of the tunnel. "What is it with you, anyway? Amethyst is just a pretty gemstone. Okay, I can generate some attractive images in the relics that came out of the ruin. But when you get right down to it, those chunks of amber are nothing more than alien sculptures."

"Raw amber may have its limitations, but some of the amber artifacts that were created by the aliens are imbued with great power."

"I'm telling you, they're just a bunch of carved rocks."

"Not all of them," Quinn said gently. "Not the pyramids." His voice sharpened abruptly. "Move, woman."

When she did not follow instructions quickly enough, she got another taste of a psychically induced dreamscape. This one warped the already odd proportions of the catacombs into a deeply disturbing world. She froze, terrified that in her disoriented state she would stumble into an alien illusion trap or an energy ghost.

"Remember, your friend's life depends on you," Quinn said, voice sharpening again.

He released her from the hallucination. She sucked in a deep breath and continued down the hall.

"What, exactly, do you want from me?" she said. "Aside from the ultimate harmonic relationship thing, I mean."

"Don't pretend to be naïve, Lyra. It doesn't suit you. You're going to tune those three very special amethyst relics for me."

"What makes you so sure I've got them? I'm telling you, AI confiscated everything in that ruin."

"Your friend Nancy tells a different story. She said you stashed the pyramids somewhere underground. Unfortunately, she did not know the location."

Another wave a fury swept through her. "She would never have told you that willingly. What did you do to her?"

"Calm yourself. I did not hurt her. There was no need. I simply put her into a trance and asked her a few questions about you."

"What kind of questions?"

"Shortly after I began to comprehend your true potential, I wanted to know more about you. The only person you are close to is Miss Halifax. She was the obvious one to interrogate. She remembers nothing of the session, of course. I made certain of that."

"You really are a lowlife."

"The news that you had concealed three pyramids of amethyst came out quite accidentally, I assure you. But once I had it, I knew for certain that you were the right woman."

A creepy sensation trickled through her. "What, exactly do you know about the pyramids? Why are you so interested in them?"

"The three you discovered are not the first amethyst pyramids to be found. My grandmother also discovered one. She, too, had a great affinity for amethyst. She understood that there was enormous power in the stone."

"What happened to her pyramid?"

"In the end she destroyed it." Quinn's voice flashed with rage again. "She was a weak woman. She wrote in her journal that she considered the stone extremely dangerous. She was convinced that once it was tuned to a specific individual, it could be used to generate and focus enormous power, regardless of whether he or she could work amethyst."

"I get it. You think you can work the pyramid stones, but you can't do that unless they are tuned to your frequencies."

"My grandmother refused to tune the pyramid for me because she concluded that I was psychically unstable."

"Gee. Wonder how she got that impression."

Quinn drew a deep breath and visibly steadied himself. Once more he slipped into his serene, guru voice.

"When I found out that she had rendered the stone powerless, I had no choice, of course," he said. "I had to kill her."

"You murdered your own grandmother?"

"What else could I do? She deliberately tried to keep me from fulfilling my destiny. She was even planning to notify the authorities of the Arcane Society that I was unstable. They would have tried to smother my talent with drugs. If that hadn't worked, they would have made certain that I disappeared. I could not allow those fools to interfere with my destiny."

"And just what is this high-rez power you think you're going to get?"

"My grandmother believed that whoever could master just one of the pyramid stones would gain the ancient powers of the aliens."

"Hmm."

"Think what that means." Quinn flattened one of his palms against a glowing tunnel wall. "I will have the powers of those who built these catacombs and the underground rain forest. Who knows what I will be able to achieve once I have that level of talent?"

"Not to rain on your parade, Quinn, but the aliens are gone. They couldn't make it here on Harmony. Maybe their powers weren't so great, after all."

"You have no imagination. I have searched for more pyramid stones for years, and at last I have found them."

"You know, I think your grandmother was wrong about those pyramids—"

"Silence."

"This is so typical of the Dore luck. I join a meditation class to reduce my stress levels, and what do I get? A mad guru."

"Enough. I will not allow you to provoke me. You would do well to remember that you will remain alive only so long as you serve me."

"*Serve* you?"

"Well, I had planned to offer you marriage," he conceded. "But when Sweetwater returned, you rushed straight back into his arms, in spite of how he had betrayed you. It was obvious that you are incapable of appreciating what I could give you. So, yes, instead of sharing my power, you will serve me."

"What made you think there might be more pyramid stones?"

"My grandmother was convinced that there were others. She did not believe that the one she found was the only stone of its kind. But I knew that only another amethyst worker was likely to find others. Do you realize how rare your talent is?"

"I've heard that a lot lately," Lyra said.

"For the past six weeks I have tried to drive you closer to me. To woo you. Twice a week I sent you the most exquisite amethyst orchids."

"So you're the one. Well, that figures. I finally get a secret admirer, and he's a nutcase. And here I was blaming the plumber. Tell me something. If you wanted me to like you, why did you try to scare the crap out of me with those damned hallucinations?"

"I wanted you to turn to me for help. I wanted to show you that I and I alone could save you from the nightmares. But you kept resisting. For a time I saw it as a tribute to your spirit. I even admired your strength of will. I enjoyed proving that I was your master. But then Cruz Sweetwater came back into your life. I tried to remove him."

"You were the one who hired those thugs to try to kill him," Lyra said. "You tried to take him out not once but twice. The second time you were there, on the other balcony, generating one of your stupid dreamscapes. But that didn't work either, did it? You're a real, all-around screwup, aren't you, Quinn?"

Quinn's normally serene features twisted into a demonic mask. "And you're a real bitch."

"Does this mean that the ultimate harmonic relationship is off?"

"Turn left."

"Sure."

She rounded another corner and saw the vaulted entrance of a small antechamber. Nancy stood there, scared, her arms tightly wrapped around her waist, but under control. Quinn had not bothered to tie her up. He had taken her amber. That was more than enough to confine anyone underground.

"Lyra." Relief and panic mingled on Nancy's face. Her eyes glittered with tears. "I'm so sorry."

"This is my fault, not yours." Lyra rushed toward her, hugging her fiercely. "It's going to be okay. I promise you."

"Enough," Quinn said. He looked at Lyra. "You have seen her. She is alive, and she will stay in that condition if you do exactly as I say. Take me to the three stones."

Lyra released Nancy, stepped back, and kicked off her heels. "It's a long hike from here. I'm not going to last much longer in these shoes."

"Hurry," Quinn hissed.

Lyra looked back at Nancy. "Stay right where you are, okay? It will be all right, I promise you."

"Trust me, I'm not going anywhere without amber," Nancy vowed.

"Move," Quinn ordered. He backed up the command with another disorienting wave of energy.

"You know, if you don't stop doing that," Lyra said, "I'm going to throw up on your fancy robes."

Quinn blinked, startled. He took a hasty step back, scowling. "Let's go."

"I'll need a locator," she said to Quinn.

"Give me the frequency coordinates. I'll enter them in my locator."

She rattled them off quickly and waited while he punched in the numbers.

"Now," Quinn said. A feverish excitement glittered in his eyes. "Take me to the stones."

"Yeah, sure, whatever," Lyra said.

Chapter 34

CRUZ LOOKED AT THE TELEPHONE RECORDS THAT JEFF had just tossed down in front of him. Vincent dropped the red crayon he had been playing with and drifted across the desk to see what was going on.

"How did you end up with Vincent?" Jeff asked.

"He's keeping me company while Lyra helps Nancy set up for an art auction tonight. They were afraid he would get into the hors d'oeuvres." Cruz studied the records. "What did you find?"

"Those are Valentine Fairstead's calls for the past three years." Jeff dropped into a chair. "I circled the ones he made to Flagg and Webber and those that he received from them. They tend to occur in clusters."

"Probably corresponding with the times when they were setting up thefts and sales of the artifacts out of the vault."

"That's what it looks like." Jeff leaned forward. "In which case we're looking at twenty-eight different thefts during the past three years. Fairstead also made some calls to various high-end clients at those times, letting them know that he had something special, probably. I tracked down the names and wrote them in the margin. For the most part they're the usual suspects."

Cruz moved his finger down the list of calls. "Here's the one he made to Wilson Revere last week."

"There are other familiar names there, as well. Like I said, most are collectors who have been known to dip into the underground antiquities market."

"Something I'm having trouble with here," Cruz said.

"What?"

"The street muscle that we've been assuming Flagg hired to whack me."

Jeff's brows shot up. "I thought it was more than an assumption."

"He denied it when I asked him about it."

"Well, sure. He's not going to admit he tried twice to have you killed."

"Everything else about this scam was well-managed for over three years. But hiring those four thugs was sloppy and unsophisticated."

"I don't know about that. If it had worked, you'd have been dead, and the antiquities scam would still be humming along."

"It just doesn't feel like Flagg."

"Maybe Webber hired the guys who tried to take you out."

"Maybe. But regardless, there's another question. Whoever used amber to generate those hallucinations that forced me to shatter obsidian was there that night. What's more, he's been stalking Lyra for about six weeks. Flagg told me that Webber was furious with her because she refused to cooperate with the amethyst experiments, but I just can't see Webber as a stalker."

"You'd be surprised by the profiles of the men that turn into stalkers."

"Whoever this guy is, I think he may also have been sending twice-weekly deliveries of purple orchids to Lyra."

"Okay, you've got me there. That definitely doesn't sound like Dr. Felix Webber."

Cruz sat forward and folded his arms on the desk. "In which case, we're looking for a fourth man, someone who had nothing to do with the antiquities scam."

"Someone who can generate hallucinations?"

"Yes." A familiar frisson of icy awareness shot through Cruz. "Lyra."

"What about her?" Jeff asked.

"Something's wrong." He reached for the phone and punched in Lyra's number. There was no answer. He was trying the number for the Halifax Gallery when Jeff suddenly looked at Vincent.

"Hey, what's up with the bunny?" Jeff asked.

Vincent had sleeked into full predator mode. All four

eyes were open. He leaped to the floor and dashed toward the door.

"Vincent," Cruz said.

To his amazement, Vincent paused, looking back. His small body was vibrating with urgency.

"Wait for us," Cruz said.

Chapter 35

LYRA WALKED INTO THE CHAMBER AHEAD OF QUINN. The three pyramids of amethyst amber glowed gently on the card table where she had left them.

Quinn stopped short in the entrance. Wonder, awe, and an unhealthy excitement battled for control of his features.

"It's true," he whispered. "You really did find the pyramid stones. And they are stones of rare power, just like the one my grandmother discovered. I can sense the energy in them."

Lyra stopped near one of the pyramids and rested a hand casually on the surface. The stone glowed a little brighter at her touch.

"Now what?" she asked softly.

"Now you will tune all three of the pyramids to my wavelengths so that I can access their power." Quinn walked to the card table and touched one of the pyramids with reverent fingers. "I will be the master of the stones."

"I should tell you that I agree with your grandmother. These stones are dangerous."

Rage flared again in Quinn's face. "Tune the stones, or you will die in this chamber."

"You know, I usually get paid extra for my special tuning services."

"Shut up and tune the stones."

Quinn was practically spitting with fury. The temperature inside the tunnels was always comfortable, but there was a greasy sheen of perspiration on his shaved skull.

"Okay, okay, take it easy," Lyra said. "I'll tune your amber for you. Just so you know, there won't be any refund if you're not satisfied with the service. Place the pyramids so that they are all touching. They must be in physical contact with each other."

She was winging it now, but Quinn did not appear to notice. He arranged the stones as she had instructed.

"Now what?" he demanded eagerly.

"Put your hands on the stones and concentrate, just as you do when you use your talent."

Again, he obeyed, splaying his fingertips on the sides of the pyramids.

She touched one of the stones with a forefinger. Energy pulsed.

"Focus," she commanded softly.

Currents shifted subtly in the pyramids as though some

long-dormant power had been disturbed. The stones brightened. She identified Quinn's patterns almost immediately. *Crazy, all right.* A moment later she had the wavelengths that pulsed in the heart of each stone.

The latent power she sensed in the pyramids chilled her to the core. Energy shifted, writhed, and uncoiled. Whatever was happening was not meant for the human mind.

"Concentrate harder," she whispered. "Give it everything you have."

"Yes." Quinn was nothing short of enraptured now. He stared into the glowing pyramids. "I can see things, amazing things. It's music. Who ever thought you could literally *see* music? Energy is pouring through me, making me stronger. This is incredible."

She tweaked the patterns a little more so that the energy in the stones began to pulse in the same pattern as Quinn's natural psi currents. But the currents in the pyramids were far more powerful than his. They seethed and coiled and burned, seeking a channel.

"Now I can see colors in the music," Quinn whispered. "No, I can *feel* the colors. There are no names for the shades of purple and green and blue I am able to see. The music is everywhere. Can't you hear it?"

"No," she said. "Only you can hear it and see it and sense it, because I have tuned the stones to your personal wavelengths. The power of the pyramids is yours and yours alone, now."

"Mine to control," he gasped, ecstatic.

"If you can," she added very quietly.

Quinn did not hear her. He was enthralled, his face awash in waves of wildly fluctuating purple light.

"Enough," he said finally. He sounded suddenly exhausted. "This is too much to absorb in one session. It is clear that I must do this in stages."

She took her fingertip off the stone and stepped back. But the pyramids continued to glow hotter. The entire chamber was pulsing with amethyst light.

"Stop it," Quinn ordered.

But there was no stopping what she had unleashed. She could no longer bear to look directly at the pyramids. The purple fires were too intense. Every instinct she possessed urged her to run. She whirled, turning toward the door.

Cruz, Vincent, Jeff, and Nancy arrived in the opening at that moment. Cruz and Vincent rushed toward her. She reached down and scooped up the sleeked-out dust bunny.

"Let's get out of here," she said. "I think the curtain is about to come down on this performance."

Cruz caught her hand.

"Go," he said to Jeff.

"What's happening?" Quinn shouted. "I can't release the stones. I'm trapped in the currents. Make them stop. *Make them stop*."

Jeff seized Nancy's wrist.

They ran down the quartz corridor. Cruz halted them in front of a vaulted entrance.

"Inside," he said.

They ducked into the antechamber.

The explosion, when it came, was accompanied by an unearthly scream. The shriek of horror seemed to go on forever before it was cut off.

And then there was only the eternal silence of the catacombs.

Chapter 36

"WE GOT TO THE GALLERY JUST AS NANCY WAS COMING up the stairs from the hole-in-the-wall below her basement," Cruz said. "She filled us in on what had happened."

"I went back to the surface to get help," Nancy explained. "The amber in the heels of your shoes was good enough to help me make my way back here, Lyra, but I knew I'd need a locator and some manly assistance to find you and deal with Quinn."

"The amber in my shoes is not my best," Lyra said. She glanced at the clock. It was nearly seven. The auction was due to start in an hour. "It's strictly for emergencies."

Jeff looked at her. "You keep tuned amber in the heels of your shoes?"

"Every last pair I own," she said. "I'm a tuner and an

indie prospector. Trust me when I tell you that the combination has made me downright obsessive about amber."

They were in the main sales room of the Halifax Gallery. She and Nancy were rushing through the last-minute preparations for the auction, setting out the hors d'oeuvres and napkins. Vincent was on the counter eating some of the cookies that had been intended for the attendees.

Cruz and Jeff lounged against the counter on either side of Vincent. They had recovered Quinn's body and hauled it back to the surface, where they had quietly summoned the forces of Amber Inc. Security to make things go away. Quinn's death would be attributed to a stroke, according to Cruz. Lyra did not doubt him.

"It all started with that damn amethyst ruin," she grumbled. She arranged neat rows of champagne flutes on the buffet table. "I swear, everything went wrong after I found it. The Dore luck struck again."

There was a stark silence behind her. She turned and realized they were all looking at her.

"What?" she asked.

Cruz cleared his throat. "Well, you and I met because of the ruin, and I like to think that wasn't all bad luck."

She glowered. "You know what I mean. If I hadn't discovered that ruin, I would never have ended up in Quinn's Harmonic Meditation class. He wouldn't have started stalking me and sending those purple orchids."

Nancy fanned out some napkins. "You have to admit, the flowers were beautiful. Very pricey, those amethyst orchids."

Lyra shuddered. “I never want to see another purple orchid as long as I live.”

“The problem was that we had two things happening at the same time,” Cruz said. “The theft of the artifact and Quinn trying to make Lyra think she was going mad so that she would turn to him as her savior.”

“But she never went that route,” Nancy said. “She was too strong-willed. I’m the one with the weak mind. I can’t believe that bastard put me into a trance and questioned me about the artifacts without me even knowing it. I still can’t remember the incident.”

“It’s not your fault,” Jeff said. “I pulled the Society’s ancestry records on Quinn. He comes from a long line of powerful and very unstable psychic hypnotists and illusions talents. The only reason Lyra was able to resist his attempt to put her into a deep trance was because her affinity for amethyst gave her some limited immunity to his talent. But even she couldn’t escape the hallucinations he induced.”

“Neither could I,” Cruz added. “So don’t blame yourself.”

Nancy wrinkled her nose. “Well, I guess that does make me feel a little better. I mean, if even a Sweetwater had a few problems fending off Quinn, I can accept the fact that I allowed myself to get hypnotized and spilled my best friend’s secrets.” She looked at Lyra. “Good thing you never gave me the coordinates of that chamber where you stashed the pyramids. I’d have blabbed those, too.”

“Wouldn’t have made any difference.” Lyra stepped

back to admire the array of glassware. "One way or another, he needed me to tune the stones."

Cruz looked at her. "What do you think happened there at the end?"

"I think that I was right all along," she said, straightening a plate of canapés. "The pyramid stones were some sort of psychic art form, just as the other objects that came out of the ruin are, but on a grander, more powerful scale."

Nancy picked up a tray of tea sandwiches. "A whole symphony orchestra for the psi senses instead of a single violin?"

"Exactly," Lyra replied. "The tremendous power of the pyramid stones may have been no big deal to the aliens. The equivalent of going to a rock concert, maybe. They were clearly more adapted to the psychic side of their natures than we are to ours. But for a human, the performance was literally overwhelming."

"Why the explosion of psi energy there at the end?" Cruz asked. "Why didn't the currents from the pyramid simply zap Quinn's senses? Instead, all three pyramids were destroyed."

She looked at him across the row of champagne bottles. "He wanted my special service. He insisted that the pyramid stones be tuned to his personal wavelengths. I gave him what he wanted. But he could not channel so much energy. No human could. The wavelengths rebounded back into the stones and overloaded them."

Cruz smiled slowly, a feral smile that said more than words ever could. "You set a trap, and he fell into it."

She swallowed hard. "I tried to warn him that the stones were dangerous, but he refused to believe me."

Jeff frowned. "But how did you know what would happen when you tuned the pyramids for him?"

"I couldn't be absolutely certain of the outcome," she admitted. She looked down at the plate of canapés she had put on the table. "I'd never actually tuned one of the pyramids before. But I'd experimented a little with them, and I had a sense of how the currents in the stones would react if they were channeled into a human mind."

"Well, that does solve the problem of what to do with the three pyramid stones," Cruz said. "They're just so much pretty amethyst now. Good for nothing more than making jewelry."

"But there may be others," Lyra said. "Quinn kept talking about his grandmother's journal. Evidently she believed there might be a number of pyramids."

"We'll deal with that problem if and when it arises," Cruz said. "Right now you and Nancy have an auction to run."

Jeff looked at the three paintings hanging on the wall. "Those are the pictures that you're putting on the block tonight?"

"That's right," Nancy said. "They're by a very hot new artist named Chimera. I'm expecting all three to go for top dollar."

"Huh," Jeff said. "If you ask me, Vincent can paint as good as that Chimera guy."

Cruz studied the paintings. "You know what? I think you're right."

Lyra exchanged a quick, uneasy glance with Nancy. Some things were a little too complicated to explain in a short period of time, especially to a couple of men who were in the security business. In addition, there was no way to know quite how Cruz and Jeff would view the facts of the situation, given the strict Sweetwater code.

She put on a breezy smile.

"That only goes to show how much you two know about modern art," she said. "It's all in the eye of the beholder, remember?"

Chapter 37

"A HUNDRED THOUSAND DOLLARS." LYRA TUCKED VINcent under one arm and drew her key out of her small black clutch. "I still can't believe it. A hundred grand for those three pictures, thanks to Mr. Anonymous. That dear, sweet man. I can't believe the way he kept upping the bid on the phone."

Cruz took the key from her to unlock her door. "Nothing like auction fever setting in to drive up the price."

"I know, but one hundred thousand hot smackaroos," she said, unable to contain her glee. "Nancy didn't think she'd get anywhere near that much for the pictures. Do you realize what this means?"

Nancy had been giddy after the auction. Jeff had invited her to a nearby tavern for a celebratory drink. She had not needed a second invitation.

"There's a standard split at art auctions," Cruz said.

"A certain percentage goes to the seller, in this case, the artist. The gallery takes a hefty commission."

"Right, the artist." Lyra kissed Vincent's furry little head and plopped him on her shoulder. "He gets his cut, of course." *As many cookies as he wants for the rest of his life,* she thought. She moved briskly through the doorway. "But Nancy and I are splitting the commission, since I'm the one who introduced the artist to her. My share will be more than enough to pay off that dumb-ass lawyer. I'll even have enough left over to get my car fixed, pay off my debts, and buy some new furniture."

Cruz followed her through the doorway. "Let the good times roll."

He sounded amused. She rezzed a light and turned to look at him. He had worn formal black for the auction, once again the well-dressed assassin. His presence had been quickly noted by the other attendees.

"It was very kind of you to make that first bid," Lyra said. "It gave the whole event a lot of cachet. Once the others knew a Sweetwater was interested, they couldn't wait to start bidding."

"Glad I could get things rolling." He shrugged out of his black jacket and dropped it over the back of the reading chair the way he always did. Making himself at home. "Is there any of my Amber Dew left?" he asked, unknotting his tie.

A frisson of intimacy flickered across her senses. Once again they were acting like any other intimate couple after an evening out, although this particular evening out had begun with getting kidnapped by a crazy guru.

Given all the excitement, she should have anticipated that Cruz would insist on sticking around for the main event, the auction. His presence had made both Nancy and her nervous at first, in spite of the beneficial effect on the bidding. But after a while it became clear that he did not recognize the three paintings as Vincent's work. That was modern art for you, she thought happily. No one could tell the difference between a picture done by a human artist and one done by a dust bunny.

"I think of it as *my* Amber Dew, but the answer is yes," she said lightly. She set Vincent on the counter, opened the lid of the quartz jar, and took out a cookie. She gave the treat to Vincent and then headed for the bedroom to slip off her heels. "I wonder who he is," she said through the opaque screens.

A cupboard door opened in the kitchen. Glasses clinked.

"Who?" Cruz asked.

"The anonymous bidder." She walked out of the bedroom barefoot. "The one who got the three paintings."

Cruz came around the counter and handed one of the glasses to her. "Obviously someone who has expensive taste in modern art."

She raised her glass. "Here's to Mr. Anonymous. May he continue to collect modern art for decades to come."

Cruz touched his glass to hers. "To Chimera."

She managed, just barely, to avoid glancing at Vincent.

"To Chimera," she said smoothly. She raised the glass to her lips.

"And to us," Cruz added before she could take a sip.

She hesitated, searching for any and all possible traps. But, really, where was the harm in acknowledging their affair?

"Okay," she said.

"Nothing like a little enthusiasm in a woman," Cruz said.

She smiled. "To us."

They each took a sip. Cruz touched her lips with one finger.

"You are one of the gutsiest people I've ever met," he said gently. "Why are you so afraid of what's between us?"

"I'm not afraid," she said. "Oops. Almost forgot. There's something I've been meaning to do ever since we got out of the tunnels this afternoon."

She put the glass of Amber Dew on the counter, crossed the room to the coffee table, and picked up the vase of purple orchids.

"What are you going to do with those?" Cruz asked.

"Dump them in the garbage." She went into the kitchen and used the foot pedal to raise the lid of the trash can. She crammed the orchids inside and let the lid slam closed. "So much for modern romance."

"Quinn really called you his chosen bride?"

"Oh, yeah. Said we were destined to rule together with the power of the pyramids, or something quaint along those lines." She picked up her glass and went back across the room to the sofa. She sat down and propped her bare feet on the coffee table. "But you came back and ruined everything. Don't you dare laugh."

"Believe me, I'm not laughing. Got a hunch the bastard

was going to kill you after you tuned the stones for him, though. I could feel his intent when I saw him with you in the chamber."

"Sadly, it turned out that I wasn't quite what he wanted in the way of a bride."

Cruz crossed the room and sank down beside her. "You're everything I want."

A shiver went through her.

"Cruz—"

"You are afraid to give us a second chance. Admit it."

She drank some of the liqueur. "The Dore luck, you know. Just can't depend on it."

His jaw tightened. "The Sweetwater luck doesn't seem to be working real well at the moment, either."

She stopped smiling. "Did you really think it would be that easy, Cruz?"

"No, I knew there would be a price to pay. I wouldn't have come here if I hadn't been prepared to pay it." He contemplated the liquid in his glass. "Which reminds me, I think the time has come to tell you a little more about my family."

She chuckled. "Okay, now you're starting to make me really nervous."

He did not say anything. Instead, he removed his shoes and put his feet up on the table beside hers.

She looked down and noticed the bottom edge of the leather knife sheath showing just below the cuff of his trousers. Her mouth went dry.

"And exactly why do you feel it necessary to have this conversation?" she asked.

"I'm serious about us. You and me. I'm hoping for a future together. That means you have a right to know everything."

"Is this some more of the dark family secret thing?" she asked warily.

"Yes," he said and lowered the glass. "I told you that my family has a long history in the security field."

She put her own glass down on the table. "You did mention the old family business. Out of pure curiosity, why was Big Jake so determined to get out of that line of work, anyway? Sounds like Sweetwaters had been successful in it for a few hundred years."

"We were." He looked at her. "But that kind of work eats away at your soul, even when you think you're doing it for all the right reasons."

"Yes," she said. "I can see where there would be a huge psychic price to pay. Nobody except a total sociopath gets away with killing another human being without getting hit with some blowback, even when the killing is justified." She shuddered. "I found that out, myself, this afternoon. I don't think I'll be sleeping well for a while."

"No," Cruz said. He covered her hand with one of his own. "But you won't be alone."

In the highly charged hours following the scene underground there had been no time to process the events, no time to absorb all the implications. Now it was hitting her hard.

She sighed. "I didn't know for sure that the pyramids would kill him."

Cruz just nodded. His hand tightened on hers.

"Right up until the last few seconds, I thought maybe the energy in the stones would just shatter his senses, probably permanently. Whatever happened, I knew he would never be the same. But I didn't know for certain that he would die."

"It's okay," Cruz said again. "I've been there. I understand."

She stilled. "You mean you've—?"

"Yes." He swirled the last of the Amber Dew in his glass and drank it down. He turned his head on the cushion to look at her. "The Sweetwaters' decision to go mainstream didn't change everything. The really bad guys, the psychic sociopaths, are still out there. And sometimes just finding hard evidence against them isn't enough. Sometimes the Arcane Society drugs aren't enough. Sometimes only a really powerful talent can track and take down another powerful talent."

She exhaled slowly. "What you're saying is that occasionally you still get called back into the old family business."

"Occasionally." He watched her. "But I swear to you we no longer take money for those jobs. I know it's a fine line, but to the family it's an important one."

"I see."

"You don't look all that shocked."

"You forget," she said quietly. "I've had some experience with the Sweetwater family, namely you and Jeff. I've tuned amber for both of you. You're arrogant, stubborn, and inclined to be annoyingly dictatorial, but you were obviously born with a psychic predisposition to serve and protect. You're the good guys. Like we in the tuning business say, it's in the psi."

"That's not what you were saying three months ago."

"I told you, I understand that you did what you thought you had to do three months ago."

"And I came back because there's something else I need to do now."

"What?"

"Make love to you."

He leaned over her and kissed her, a long, deep, aching kiss. Passion, heat, and energy swirled in the atmosphere. She felt the rush across all her senses and throughout her body. The sense of rightness shimmered through her.

Maybe she couldn't trust the Dore luck when it came to love, but the energy of desire between her and Cruz was real. The bond between them was real. It might not last forever, but she knew in her bones that she would never find another man like Cruz Sweetwater again. Dores might not be the luckiest people on the planet, but they weren't stupid. What was it Nancy had said? *Time to go for the amber ring.*

She put her arms around Cruz and kissed him back. He crushed her lightly down onto the cushions and started to move over her. A soft skittering sound from somewhere in the vicinity of the kitchen made her freeze, her fingers buried in Cruz's hair.

"What?" he said, his lips on her throat.

"Vincent. We can't do this in front of him. He'll be embarrassed."

"He's a dust bunny. I doubt if he knows the meaning of embarrassed."

"Okay, *I'll* be embarrassed."

There was a few seconds of stillness before Cruz finally moved.

"Right," he said.

He rolled to his feet, picked her up, and carried her into the screened bedroom. In the shadows he undressed her slowly, sliding the black gown down over her hips. The dark fabric pooled on the floor around her bare feet. He unhooked the lacy black bra next and tossed it onto the dresser.

When he put his powerful hands on her breasts, a tremor of exquisite delight surged through her. She undid his shirt with shaking fingers and slipped her hands beneath the fabric. His skin was warm, the muscles of his chest sleek and hard.

He went down on one knee in front of her and kissed her stomach. She felt him hook his thumbs in the waistband of her black panties and draw them down to her ankles. And then his hand was between her legs, urging her thighs apart. She could feel her own liquid heat and knew that his fingers were already slick with it. The flare of urgent tension inside her made her dig her nails into his shoulders.

"Cruz." She closed her eyes against the surging energy. She could barely stand.

He rose, picked her up, and settled her on the bed. She opened her eyes and watched, enthralled, as he unbuckled his belt and stripped off his clothing and the knife sheath with a resolute efficiency and speed that spoke volumes about his own level of arousal.

And then he was on the bed with her, his rigid erection pressed against her hip, his lips on her breast.

"Trust me," he whispered against her throat. "We're meant for each other."

At least for tonight, she thought. And maybe tomorrow night, maybe for a week, a month. Who knew? She refused to look any further into the future.

She moved her hand down his hard, lean body, savoring the tautness of muscle and skin. He shuddered when she wrapped her fingers around him and stroked gently. She sensed his aura flaring, hot and dark with desire. *For me,* she thought. Of that much she could be certain. Tonight Cruz wanted her as badly as she wanted him.

The heat flaring between them was so intense that it left a sheen of perspiration on their bodies and dampened the sheets. When Cruz finally moved on top of her, looming over her in the darkness, gathering her close, all of her senses were thrilled. And then he was pushing slowly, heavily into her, stretching her, filling her, joining with her in ways that swept far beyond the physical.

This was so much more than sex. The shatteringly intense intimacy stole her breath. Nothing had changed since he had left three months ago. She loved this man. She would love him all of her life, regardless of what happened between them tomorrow or next week.

"Tell me that you know that what we have together is real," he whispered against her throat. "Give me that much tonight."

"This is real," she said.

It was the truth. She knew he must have sensed it in her aura. Out of the corner of her eye she caught a glimpse of his ring. Green fire glowed in the depths of the black amber.

Moments later her release flashed through her in small shock waves. Her climax triggered his own. He followed her into the glorious aurora.

Chapter 38

LYRA CAME AWAKE TO THE SOUND OF CHIMES. IT TOOK her a moment to identify the source of the irritating noise.

"I think someone's at the door," she mumbled into the pillow.

"Good guess," Cruz said.

His voice came from across the bedroom, not the other pillow. She opened her eyes and saw him standing at the foot of the bed. He had his trousers on and was in the process of buckling his belt. She glanced at the clock on the bedside table.

"It's not even seven o'clock," she said. "Who in the world can it be at this hour?"

The doorbell chimed again and again.

"Whoever he is, he isn't going to go away quietly," Cruz said. He shrugged into his shirt. "I'll take care of it."

He went out into the main room. Alarm jolted through her. She leaped from the bed, grabbed her robe, and hurried after him.

"Wait," she hissed. "It could be some bill collector's goon. Did I mention I'm a little behind on the rent and a few other things?"

"I'll take care of it."

Cruz did not slow down. He kept going toward the door. Vincent was already there doing his happy dance and chortling a greeting. Lyra relaxed. Whoever was out in the hall was a friend.

Cruz opened the door. It took Lyra a few seconds to recognize the woman on the other side. Nancy's eyes were concealed behind oversized dark glasses. It promised to be another warm day, but she was wearing a heavy winter coat. The hood was pulled up around her face. She clutched a newspaper in one hand.

"About time," Nancy muttered. She glanced anxiously back down the stairs and rushed into the loft. "Close the door. Quick. I parked in the alley. I don't think anyone saw me on the street, but sooner or later they'll find this place."

"What's wrong?" Lyra asked. "Are you all right?"

"No, I'm not all right. I'm freaked out of my mind. You should be, too. We've got to get out of town. Throw some things into a suitcase, grab Vincent, and let's go. We can hide out at my parents' house on the lake."

"Take it easy," Cruz said. He closed the door with an air of great calm and went toward the kitchen. "How about some coffee first?"

"We don't have time for coffee," Nancy said. She jerked off her sunglasses and pushed back her hood. "Haven't you two seen the morning papers?"

"Not yet," Lyra said. "Why?"

"This is why." Nancy held up the copy of the *Herald*, displaying the front page.

Lyra stared with mounting horror at the photographs positioned just below the fold. The first was a picture of Vincent, clearly identifiable by his red beret. He was sitting on the kitchen counter, a cookie in one hand, a paintbrush in the other. The second photo was of one of the three paintings that had been auctioned off the night before.

The headline read, "Art Scam at Local Gallery?"

"Oh, my Lord," Lyra whispered. She yanked the newspaper out of Nancy's hands. "The plumber. I *knew* there was something off with that guy. The son of a bitch was a spy. That critic at the *Frequency Herald* must have hired him to watch your gallery. He probably saw me bringing Vincent's paintings in through the back door. Later he hired someone to pose as a plumber to get into my loft."

"I knew that critic was determined to find out the identity of Chimera," Nancy said, "but who would think that he would stoop to this? And how did he figure out that Vincent was the artist and not you?"

Lyra sighed. "Vincent was playing with his paints the day the plumber arrived. In fact, he was working on one of the paintings we sold last night."

"We're doomed," Nancy said darkly. "Get your things."

"I keep a pack ready," Lyra said. "Give me a few minutes to shower and get into some clothes."

"I strongly suggest coffee and breakfast before you two hightail it out of town," Cruz said from the kitchen. "You'll need the energy."

Nancy glared at him. "You don't understand. When Mr. Anonymous picks up the morning paper and finds out he bought six paintings that were done by a dust bunny, he's going to raise holy heck. We can't even refund all of his money. We spent what we got for the first three. Whatever happens, the reputation of the Halifax Gallery will be in ruins."

Lyra paused in the bedroom entrance. "And so will the reputation of Dore Tuning & Consulting. You know what people say about small-time tuners like me. A lot of folks think we're low level scam artists even on a good day. When it gets out that I was involved in this fiasco, I might as well close my doors for good."

Cruz set a large frying pan on the stove. "Wait until you taste my scrambled eggs. I don't do a lot of things in the kitchen, but I'm good with scrambled eggs."

Lyra narrowed her eyes. "You don't seem to grasp the gravity of the situation, Cruz."

"Probably because the situation is not grave." Cruz opened the refrigerator door. "Mr. Anonymous is satisfied with his paintings. He won't be suing the Halifax Gallery or anyone else."

"How do you know that?" Nancy demanded.

Understanding slammed through Lyra. She watched Cruz take a carton of eggs out of the refrigerator.

"Oh, geez," she whispered. "You're Mr. Anonymous, aren't you? You bought the first three paintings, too."

Cruz smiled. "They're all hanging in my office as we speak. I don't think the three I picked up last night will fit in that space, though. I'll probably put them up in my house, instead. The walls are pretty bare. The place could use some color."

"Wait a second," Lyra said. "You were at the auction last night. You stopped bidding early on. The winning bid came in by phone."

"It was placed by the same person who bought the first three paintings," Nancy said. "I recognized the voice."

"That would be because I used the same person to bid last night that I did to pick up the other paintings."

"Who?" Lyra demanded.

"A friend who owns a gallery in my section of the Quarter. He owed me a favor."

"Holy dust bunny," Nancy breathed. "Give me a minute here. I need time to wrap my brain around this thing."

"Good grief." Lyra stared at Cruz. "How did you find out that we were selling Vincent's paintings?"

"I knew Nancy was your best friend. I subscribed to the Halifax Gallery's e-mail newsletter. When the first pictures went up for sale, I recognized Vincent's work immediately. They were all from his blue period, remember? He was just getting started with that color when you kicked me out. I figured, hey, what are the odds?"

"So you bought all three paintings?" Nancy said, still looking stunned. "Even though you knew they were done by a dust bunny?"

He cracked an egg into a bowl. "Art either hits you on a personal level, or it doesn't. Vincent's pictures were like little slices of Lyra's life. Whenever I looked at them, I thought about being here with her in her loft. Talk about personal. The paintings gave me something to cling to while I waited for her to forgive me."

"That is so romantic," Nancy said in a breathy voice.

Cruz cracked another egg. "Sweetwaters are good at romantic."

Lyra gave him a warning look. "We are not going there."

"Okay, you two can deal with your personal issues some other time," Nancy interrupted briskly. "We've got a major crisis here. Evidently Mr. Anonymous, aka Cruz Sweetwater, will not be suing the Halifax Gallery for fraud. That is one thing we no longer have to worry about. But that still leaves Lyra and me with some problems. The critic at the *Herald* has smeared us all over the front page of the paper."

"To say nothing of Vincent," Lyra said indignantly. "The guy at the *Herald* was the first to applaud his pictures when you put them up in your gallery. He's pissed off now only because he discovered that they were painted by a dust bunny. We made him look stupid."

"So now you make him look sharp and insightful," Cruz said. He cracked another egg into the bowl.

Lyra and Nancy looked at him.

"How do we do that?" Lyra asked.

"You and Lyra will give an interview to the *Herald* critic congratulating him for spotting the little art joke that the Halifax Gallery perpetrated on the art world. Then you will invite him and everyone else in the art and antiquities field to the first public exhibition of rare amber artifacts from the vaults of Amber Inc. Said exhibition to be held at the Halifax Gallery."

"Good grief." Lyra could not believe her ears. "It's brilliant."

"Are you serious?" Nancy's eyes widened. "You'd really let me do an exhibition of objects from the Sweetwater family's personal collection?"

"Hell, I'll pay you to clean out that vault." Cruz opened a drawer and found a whisk. "It's about time we got rid of some of the junk and took a decent inventory."

Lyra laughed. "In the antiquities world, one man's junk is another man's priceless artifact."

Cruz began to beat the eggs. "There is one small favor I'd like to ask in return, Nancy."

Lyra stopped laughing. "Here it comes. I told you, Nancy. Doing a deal with a Sweetwater is like dining with the devil. You want to bring a really, really long spoon."

"Are you kidding?" Nancy rubbed her palms briskly together. "For a chance to clean out the Sweetwater vault, I'll gladly sit down to dinner with old Lucifer, himself." She looked at Cruz. "What's the catch?"

"The catch is that I think that you should attend my grandfather's birthday party on Saturday evening. You'll go as Jeff's date, since I've already got one of my own."

Nancy stared at him, dumbfounded. "Well, sure. No problem. But, uh, why?"

"Because the news that you were invited to attend the event will be leaked to the media which, in turn, will ripple through the art world and start an early buzz for the exhibition," Cruz explained.

Lyra blinked. "Talk about strategic thinking."

"Thanks." Cruz put the whisk aside. "I can't help it. Goes with the talent."

Nancy looked at Lyra. "We've got to go shopping. We need dresses. The most fabulous dresses we can find."

"I thought you were afraid of being recognized on the street," Lyra said.

Nancy waved that off. "Cruz is going to make that problem go away, aren't you, Cruz?"

"That's what I do." Cruz opened a package of coffee. "Make problems go away."

"See?" Nancy said. "We've got Sweetwater muscle now. It's safe to go shopping."

Cruz spooned ground coffee into the pot. "But you've got time to eat breakfast first."

Chapter 39

ON SATURDAY NIGHT LYRA STOOD ON THE SWIMMING pool terrace of the Big House on Amber Island, looking out over a moonlit sea. One of the two boats that was running a shuttle service for the Sweetwater guests had just left the dock and was headed back toward the mainland. Its lights bobbed as the vessel caught the waves. The churning wake phosphoresced a brilliant white.

Cruz lounged beside her, one foot propped on the low railing, his forearm resting on his thigh. Nancy and Jeff were to her right. She and Nancy had champagne glasses in their hands. The men were drinking beer.

The night was warm. The scents of the garden perfumed the air. Music from a live band spilled out of the great room of the Big House and across the shadowed terrace. The voices and laughter of nearly two hundred guests fluttered and buzzed in the night. It was a perfect evening.

Lyra was fuming.

"I swear," she muttered, "if just one more person comes up to me and says, 'Oh, so you're the woman who broke Cruz Sweetwater's heart,' I'm not going to be responsible for my actions."

She had been introduced to innumerable wealthy, powerful people, including the bosses of the Crystal City and Aurora Springs Guilds and their wives. She had also met some "friends of the family" who were not particularly wealthy or powerful but who seemed to have ties to the Sweetwaters. One of them was a private investigator named Davis Oakes. His wife, Celinda, proved to be the author of *Ten Steps to a Covenant Marriage: Secrets of a Professional Matchmaker.* Lyra had nobly refrained from informing her that she had hurled the book off her balcony after Cruz had left.

Another interesting couple, Emmett and Lydia London, who appeared to have mysterious connections to the head of the Cadence Guild, were also present. In addition she had met a variety of movers and shakers, including the mayor of Frequency and her husband and the governor of the city-state.

But it was the members of the Sweetwater family that had gradually elevated her temper. Time after time the first words out of every Sweetwater mouth after introductions had been made were, "So you're the woman who broke Cruz's heart." Granted, Cruz's two brothers had looked amused when they said it, but *still*. She could tell they were serious.

Nancy giggled. "Well, it has been sort of funny, you have to admit. First his mother, then his grandmother, a couple of nephews, both of his brothers—"

"There is nothing funny about it." Lyra gulped some of her champagne and glowered at Cruz. "As for you, you're not helping one bit."

He shrugged. "What am I supposed to say? It's the truth."

Jeff grinned. "And everyone in the family knows it. The boss couldn't deny it, even if he tried."

"Well, I think it's very romantic," Nancy declared.

"That's because you're not the target of the joke," Lyra said.

"It's no joke," Jeff said. "We Sweetwaters take these things seriously."

Lyra gritted her teeth. "I knew it would be a mistake to come here tonight. I should never have let you talk me into it, Cruz."

"I didn't talk you into, it," he said mildly. "We had a deal. You agreed to come here with me in exchange for my keeping quiet about those three pyramids that you concealed."

Lyra gave Nancy a bright little smile. "You see? There's nothing romantic about it. It's just business."

"And also because we're involved in a very hot affair," Cruz added. "I like to think that's part of the reason you agreed to come with me."

The heat of embarrassment sizzled through her. "For heaven's sake," she muttered. "Don't say things like that in public."

Nancy laughed. "Come on, Lyra. Lighten up. This is a night we're both going to remember for a long, long time. Just think about it. You and I are attending one of the ritziest social events of the year. We're on the Sweetwaters' private island, for crying out loud. It doesn't get any more posh."

"Hey," Jeff said, contriving to look deeply hurt. "At least let me entertain the illusion that you wanted to be my date for the evening."

"Absolutely," Nancy said. She patted his arm. "That, too. You know how I feel about FBPI agents. They are so incredibly sexy."

"Whew, thanks," Jeff said. He wiped his brow with the back of his hand. "For a while there I was a little worried that this was all about Cruz."

Lyra looked at him. "How's that new career plan of yours going?"

"Going good," Jeff said. "My application to the academy goes in on Monday."

"How did Big Jake take the news?" Lyra asked.

"Well, after we peeled him off the ceiling, Cruz here pointed out how useful it would be to have someone from the family working inside the FBPI. That calmed him down somewhat. But I should warn you that he blames you for being a bad influence on me."

"I'm a Dore. I do bad influence."

Jeff grinned. "This family needs shaking up."

Before anyone could respond to that remark, a woman emerged from one of the clusters of guests gathered on the terrace. She looked to be in her late fifties, well-preserved and stylishly dressed in a long, blue gown. Her hair was a discreet shade of silver blonde. An amber and diamond necklace framed her throat. More amber and diamonds dangled from her ears.

She circled the pool, walking briskly toward Lyra and the others.

"Here we go again," Lyra muttered. "Just remember I warned everyone."

"There you are, Cruz," the woman said. "Hello, Jeff, dear. Sorry I'm late. My flight out of Cadence was delayed."

"Better late than never, Aunt Teresa," Cruz said. He took his foot down off the railing and gave her an affectionate kiss on the cheek.

"Hi, Aunt Teresa," Jeff said. "I wondered where you were. Thought maybe you'd actually worked up the nerve to duck this gig."

Teresa uttered a warm, throaty laugh. "Not a chance. No one gets out of this event. You know that. By the way, Big Jake tells me that you've decided to apply to the FBPI academy."

Jeff smiled. "Gotta say, Big Jake is taking the news fairly well, all things considered."

"That's because he's decided that it will be useful to have a Sweetwater on the inside of regular law enforcement," Teresa said. She winked at Cruz. "Can't imagine where he got that idea."

"I'd like you to meet Lyra Dore and Nancy Halifax," Cruz said. "Lyra, Nancy, this is Teresa Sweetwater. She's married to one of my uncles on my father's side."

"How do you do, Mrs. Sweetwater," Nancy said politely.

"Call me Teresa."

"Nice to meet you, Teresa," Lyra said. She took another swallow of champagne and braced herself.

"What a pleasure it is to meet you," Teresa said, smiling. "I've heard so much about you. I understand that you're the woman—"

"Please don't say it," Lyra whispered.

". . . who broke Cruz's heart," Teresa concluded.

The night turned red, at least on the paranormal plane. A fierce, hot energy welled up inside of Lyra.

"That does it," she said. "I've had it. This has gone far enough."

She was aware, in a remote way, of the sudden hush that had come over the crowd arrayed around the pool; aware that people were turning their heads to look. She knew that her voice was rising. That was not a good thing. A small warning sounded somewhere in her head, urging her to shut up right now and not say another word. But she was powerless to stop.

Nancy cleared her throat. "Uh, Lyra?"

"I told you," Lyra said, her throat tightening. "I warned you that I would not let one more person accuse me of breaking Cruz Sweetwater's heart."

"It's okay," Nancy said. "Really. Why don't we take a little trip to the powder room. You can calm down there."

Lyra ignored her. She turned toward the audience on the terrace and threw her arms out wide.

"Once and for all, I did not break his heart," she shouted. "*Cruz broke mine.* What's more, he never even said he was sorry. Never apologized. He just let everyone think I had hurt him."

"Lyra," Nancy said urgently. "You may not want to do this."

"*I'm* the one who cried every night for days after I found out how he had deceived me," Lyra said at the top of her voice. "*I'm* the one who nearly went bankrupt trying to sue Amber Inc. just to get a little revenge. And then he walks back into my life as if nothing ever happened. As if we should just pick up where we left off and, oh, by the way, would I do him a favor and rescue five people from the ruin that he stole from me."

"Oh, Lyra," Nancy groaned. "This is not good."

"Damn, arrogant Sweetwaters," Lyra said. She was on a roll now. Her aura was so hot she was amazed that she did not set herself on fire. *"Who do you think you are?"*

A shocked, fascinated silence gripped the terrace. Everyone was staring at her. Without warning, tears flooded her eyes. She went from rage to despair in an instant. She was suddenly sobbing as she had on only two other occasions in her life: the day her grandfather had died and on the night she had discovered that Cruz had deceived her.

She was crying a river in front of an audience of Sweetwaters and their guests. It was unbearable, intolerable. She whirled and ran down the terrace steps. When she reached the beach, her stiletto heels stabbed into the sand and stayed there. She floundered, tipped forward, lost her balance utterly, and toppled out of her shoes. In that terrible moment she knew she was going to fall flat on her face, humiliating herself even more than she already had in front of the entire Sweetwater family and their wealthy, powerful friends.

Damn Dore luck, she thought. *You can always count on it to fail when you need it most.*

But just before she flopped ignominiously into the sand, a strong arm caught her around her waist. She was suddenly standing upright and barefoot on the beach.

"Lord, I do love you so," Cruz said. "You're magnificent."

He swept her up in his arms and carried her across the beach toward the water's edge. She heard a cheer go up on the terrace. It was followed by a round of applause.

She clutched her evening bag with both hands. "This is so embarrassing."

"No, it's just a little over the top," Cruz said. "But that's okay. I've told you before, when it comes to love, we Sweetwaters do over the top."

"I don't know what to say. Something came over me. I just lost it back there on the terrace."

"You were wonderful."

When he reached the wet sand, he turned and carried her along the edge of the beach until they rounded the rocky outcropping. When they were out of sight of the terrace, he set her back on her feet and enfolded her in his arms.

"Did I really break your heart?" he asked gently.

She wiped her eyes with the back of her hand. "Yes, you did."

"I'm sorry. I never meant to do that."

"Uh-huh."

"Broken hearts are serious business in my family."

"Got news for you, Sweetwater. Your family isn't the only one that takes that kind of stuff seriously. We Dores care about broken hearts, too."

He touched her damp cheek with his fingertip, swiping away a teardrop. "You really did fall in love with me three months ago?"

"Of course, I did. You think I would have wasted all that money trying to sue you and your company if you hadn't broken my heart?"

"I told myself it was a good sign," he admitted. "But it did complicate things."

"I had to do something. I couldn't just let it stand."

"I know. You needed some revenge."

"But I was moving on," she whispered. "I was putting my life back together. And then those orchids started arriving, and I told myself they were from you. The next thing I know, you're walking back into my life. Then you inform me that the only reason you're back is because you needed me to open that damned gate."

"I screwed things up. I realize that. But you've got to trust me when I tell you that I fell in love with you the first time I saw you, and I've never stopped loving you."

She managed a shaky smile. "I believe you."

"You do?"

"Yes. I loved you, too. But I'm a Dore and you're a

Sweetwater, and you took my amber ruin, and then people were trying to kill you, and Quinn was stalking me, and . . ."

"And things got complicated again," Cruz said. "But from now on we can handle any and all complications because we know we love each other."

She put her arms around his neck. "I do love you so, Cruz. I will always love you."

He kissed her there in the moonlight, and she felt the energy of the bond between them blaze in the night. When he finally lifted his head, she smiled.

"What?" he asked.

"I think my luck just changed."

"Well, sure. You're about to become a Sweetwater. What did you expect?"

She laughed, joy effervescing through her. And then he was kissing her again, and the night glowed invisibly around them with the power of their love. She knew that radiant energy would be with them all of their lives.

The charms on her bracelet clashed musically in the night. Green fire burned in the heart of obsidian amber.

ON THE SECOND FLOOR OF THE BIG HOUSE, VINCENT hopped down from the windowsill where he had been keeping watch. The energy of the night felt right now. Time to party.

He tumbled across the vast library to join the cluster of dust bunnies gathered there. The others had accompanied their persons to the island, just as he had. They all possessed human names—Fuzz, Rose, Max, Araminta, Elvis—but they knew and recognized each other in a different way.

He bounced up onto the big table at the end of the room where someone had very thoughtfully left a large box of rez-brush paints. There was an easel with a half-finished canvas next to the table, but he ignored both.

He used his two front paws to push the box of paint-brushes over the edge. It landed on the floor with a thud. The lid flew off, and the brushes, each with their tubes of paint neatly attached, scattered across the carpet.

He fluttered down to the floor, grabbed a psi green brush, and dashed out into the hall, chortling for the others to follow. Delighted with the prospect of a new game, each dust bunny selected a brush and scampered after him.

Out in the hall, Vincent pulled the cap off the green rez-brush paint tube. After watching him, it took the others only a moment to figure out how to remove the caps from their brushes.

Vincent surveyed the long, empty corridor. There was a vast expanse of white stone on the floors. The walls were covered with panels of pale, bleached wood.

The perfect canvas.

TURN THE PAGE FOR A LOOK AT

FIRED UP

Book One of The Dreamlight Trilogy
by Jayne Ann Krentz

Coming soon from G. P. Putnam's Sons.

The Dreamlight Trilogy

Dear Reader:

The Arcane Society was founded on secrets. Few of those secrets are more dangerous than those kept by the descendants of the alchemist Nicholas Winters, a fierce rival of Sylvester Jones.

The legend of the Burning Lamp goes back to the earliest days of the Society. Nicholas Winters and Sylvester Jones started out as friends and eventually became deadly adversaries. Each sought the same goal: a way to enhance psychic talents. Sylvester chose the path of chemistry and plunged into illicit experiments with strange herbs and plants. Ultimately he concocted the flawed formula that bedevils the Society to this day.

Nicholas took the engineering approach and forged the Burning Lamp, a device with unknown powers. The radiation from the lamp produced a twist in his DNA, creating a psychic genetic "curse" destined to be passed down through the males of his bloodline.

The Winters Curse strikes very rarely, but when it does, the Arcane Society has good reason for grave concern. It is said that the Winters man who inherits

Nicholas's genetically altered talent is destined to become a Cerberus—Arcane slang for an insane psychic who possesses multiple lethal abilities. Jones & Jones and the Governing Council are convinced that such human monsters must be hunted down and terminated as swiftly as possible.

There is only one hope for the men of the Burning Lamp. Each must find the artifact and a woman who can work the dreamlight energy that the device produces in order to reverse the changes brought on by the curse.

In the Dreamlight Trilogy you will meet the three men of the Burning Lamp, past, present, and future. These are the passionate descendants of Nicholas Winters. Each will discover some of the deadly secrets of the lamp. Each will encounter the woman with the power to shape his destiny.

And ultimately, far in the future, on a world called Harmony, one of them will unravel the lamp's final and most dangerous mystery, the secret of the midnight crystal.

I hope you will enjoy the trilogy.

Sincerely,
Jayne

Prologue

CAPITOL HILL NEIGHBORHOOD, SEATTLE

THE TWO-BLOCK WALK FROM THE BUS STOP ON BROADway to her apartment was a terrifying ordeal late at night. Reluctantly she left the small island of light cast by the streetlamp and started the treacherous journey into the darkness. At least it had stopped raining. She clamped her purse tightly to her side and clutched her keys the way she had been taught in the two-hour self-defense class the hospital had offered to its staff. The small jagged bits of metal protruded between her fingers like claws.

Should never have agreed to take the night shift, she thought. But the extra pay had been too tantalizing to resist. Six months from now she would have enough saved up enough to buy a used car. No more lonely, late-night rides on the bus.

She was a block and a half from her apartment when she heard the footsteps behind her. She thought her heart would stop. She fought her instincts and forced herself to turn around and look. A man emerged from a nearly empty parking lot. For a few seconds the streetlight gleamed on his shaved head. He had the bulky form of a bodybuilder on steroids. She relaxed a little. She did not know him but she knew where he was going.

The big man disappeared through the glass doors of the gym. The small neon sign in the window announced that it was open twenty-four hours a day. It was the only establishment on the street that was still illuminated. The bookstore with its window full of occult books and Goth jewelry, the pawn shop, the tiny hair salon, and the payday loan operation had been closed for hours.

The gym was not one of the upscale fitness clubs that catered to the spandex-and-yoga crowd. It was the kind of facility frequented by dedicated bodybuilders. The beefy men who came and left the premises did not know it but she sometimes thought of them as her guardian angels. If anything ever happened to her on the long walk home, her only hope was that someone inside the gym would hear her scream and come to help.

She was almost at the intersection when she caught the shift of shadows in a doorway across the street. A man waited there. Was he watching her? Something about the way he moved told her that he was not one of the men from the gym. He wasn't pumped up on steroids and weights. There was instead a lean, sleek, almost predatory air about him.

Her pulse, already beating much too quickly, started to pound as the fight-or-flight response kicked in. There was a terrible prickling on the nape of her neck. The urge to run was almost overwhelming but she could hardly breathe now. In any event she had no hope of outrunning a man. The only refuge was the gym but the dark silhouette on the other side of the street stood between her and the entrance. Maybe she should scream. But what if her imagination had gotten the better of her? The man across the street did not seem to be paying any attention to her. He was intent on the entrance of the gym.

She froze, unable to make a decision. She watched the figure on the other side of the street the way a baby rabbit watches a snake.

She never heard the killer come out of the shadows behind her. A sweaty, masculine hand clamped across her mouth. A sharp blade pricked her throat. She heard a clatter of metal on the sidewalk and realized that she had just dropped her only weapon, the keys.

"Quiet or you die now," a hoarse voice muttered in her ear. "Be a shame if we didn't have time to play."

She was going to die, anyway, she thought. She had nothing to lose. She dropped her purse and tried to struggle but it was useless. The man had an arm around her throat. He dragged her into the alley, choking her. She reached up and managed to rake her fingernails across the back of his hand. She would not survive the night but she could damn well collect some of the bastard's DNA for the cops.

"I warned you, bitch. I'm really going to take my time with you. I want to hear you beg."

She could not breathe and the hand across her mouth made it impossible to scream. To think that her fallback had always been the plan to yell for help from the gym.

The alley was drenched in night but there was another kind of darkness enveloping her. With luck she would suffocate from the pressure of his arm on her throat before he could use the knife, she thought. She'd worked in the trauma center at Harborview. She knew what knives could do.

A figure loomed at the entrance of the alley, silhouetted by the weak streetlight behind him. She knew it was the man she had seen in the doorway across the street. Two killers working as a team? She had sunk so far into panic and despair that she wondered if she was hallucinating.

"Let her go," the newcomer said, coming down the alley. His voice promised death as clearly as the knife at her throat.

Her captor stopped. "Get out of here or I'll slit her throat. I swear I will."

"Too late." The stranger walked forward. He was not rushing in, but there was something lethal and relentless about his approach; a predator who knows the prey is trapped. "You're already dead."

She felt something then, something she could not explain. It was as if she was caught in the center of an electrical storm. Currents of energy flooded her senses.

"No," her captor shouted. "She's mine."

And then he was screaming, horror and shock mingling in a nerve-shattering shriek.

"Get away from me," he shouted.

Suddenly she was free; falling. She landed with a jolt on the damp pavement. The man with the knife reeled back and fetched up against the alley wall.

The unnerving energy evaporated as swiftly and mysteriously as it had appeared.

The killer came away from the wall as though he had been released from a cage.

"No," he hissed, madness and rage vibrating in the single word.

He lurched toward the other man. Light glinted on the knife he still clutched.

More energy shivered in a heavy wave through the alley.

The killer screamed again, a shrill, sharp screech that ended with stunning abruptness. He dropped the knife, clutched at his chest, and dropped to the pavement.

The dark figure loomed over the killer for a moment. She saw him lean down and realized that he was checking for a pulse. She knew that he would not find one. She recognized death when she saw it.

The man straightened and turned toward her. Fear held her immobile. There was something wrong with his face. It was too dark to make out his features but she thought she could see a smoldering energy in the dark spheres where his eyes should have been.

Another wave of panic slammed through her, bringing with it a fresh dose of adrenaline. She scrambled to her feet and fled toward the street, knowing, even as she ran, that it was hopeless. The creature with the burning eyes would cut her down as easily as he had the killer with the knife.

But the monster did not pursue her. A block away she finally stopped to catch her breath. When she looked back she saw nothing. The street was empty.

She had always hoped that if the worst happened on the way home she might get some help from the men in the gym. But in the end it was a demon that had saved her.

Chapter 1

DREAMLIGHT GLOWED FAINTLY ON THE SMALL STATUE of the Egyptian queen. The prints were murky and thickly layered. A lot of people had handled the object over the decades but none of the prints went back any further than the late eighteen hundreds, Chloe Harper concluded. Certainly none dated from the Eighteenth Dynasty.

"I'm afraid it's a fake." She lowered her senses, turned away from the small statue, and looked at Bernard Paddon. "A very fine fake, but a fake nonetheless."

"Damn it, are you absolutely certain?" Paddon's bushy silver brows scrunched together. His face reddened in annoyance and disbelief. "I bought it from Crofton. He's always been reliable."

The Paddon collection of antiquities put a lot of big city museums to shame but it was not open to the public. Paddon was a secretive, obsessive collector who hoarded his treasures in a vault like some cranky troll guarding his gold. He dealt almost exclusively in the notoriously gray world of the underground antiquities market, preferring to avoid the troublesome paperwork, customs requirements, and other assorted legal authorizations required to buy and sell in the aboveground, more legitimate end of the trade.

He was, in fact, just the sort of client that Harper Investigations liked to cultivate, the kind that paid the bills. She did not relish having to tell him that his statue was a fake. On the other hand, the client she was representing in this deal would no doubt be suitably grateful.

Paddon had inherited a large number of the Egyptian, Roman, and Greek artifacts in the vault from his father, a wealthy industrialist who had built the family fortune in a very different era. Bernard was now in his seventies. Sadly, while he had continued the family traditions of collecting, he had not done such a great job when it came to investing. The result was that these days he was reduced to selling items from his collection in order to finance new acquisitions. He had been counting on the sale of the statue to pay for some other relic he craved.

Chloe was very careful never to get involved with the actual financial end of the transactions. That was an excellent way to draw the attention not only of the police and Interpol but, in her case, the extremely irritating self-appointed psychic cops from Jones & Jones.

Her job, as she saw it, was to track down items of interest and then put buyers and sellers in touch with each other. She collected a fee for her service and then she got the heck out of Dodge, as Aunt Phyllis put it.

She glanced over her shoulder at the statue. "Nineteenth century, I'd say. Victorian era. It was a period of remarkably brilliant fakes."

"Stop calling it a fake," Paddon sputtered. "I know fakes when I see them."

"Don't feel bad, sir. A lot of major institutions like the British Museum and the Met, not to mention a host of serious collectors such as yourself, have been deceived by fakes and forgeries from that era."

"*Don't feel bad*? I paid a fortune for that statue. The provenance is pristine."

"I'm sure Crofton will refund your money. As you say, he has a very good reputation. He was no doubt taken in, as well. It's safe to say that piece has been floating around undetected since the eighteen-eighties." Actually, she was sure of it. "But under the circumstances, I really can't advise my client to buy it."

Paddon's expression would have been better suited to a bulldog. "Just look at those exquisite hieroglyphs."

"Yes, they are very well done."

"Because they were done in the Eighteenth Dynasty," Paddon gritted. "I'm going to get a second opinion."

"Of course. If you'll excuse me, I'll be on my way." She picked up her black leather satchel. "No need to show me out."

She went briskly toward the door.

"Hold on, here." Paddon rushed after her. "Are you going to tell your client about this?"

"Well, he is paying me for my expert opinion."

"I can come up with any number of experts who will give him a different opinion, including Crofton."

"I'm sure you can." She did not doubt that. The little statue had passed for the real thing since it had been created. Along the way any number of experts had probably declared it to be an original.

"This is your way of negotiating for an additional fee from me, isn't it, Miss Harper?" Paddon snorted. "I have no problem with that. What number did you have in mind? If it's reasonable I'm sure we can come to some agreement."

"I'm sorry, Mr. Paddon. I don't work that way. That sort of arrangement would be very damaging to my professional reputation."

"You call yourself a professional? You're nothing but a two-bit private investigator who happens to dabble in the antiquities market. If I'd known that you were so unknowledgeable I would never have agreed to let you examine the piece. Furthermore, you can bet I'll never hire you to consult for me."

"I'm sorry you feel that way, of course, but maybe you should consider one thing."

"What's that?" he called after her.

She paused in the doorway and looked back at him. "If you ever did hire me you could rest assured that you would be getting an honest appraisal. You would know for certain that I could not be bought."

She did not wait for a response. She walked out of the

gallery and went down the hall to the foyer of the large house. A woman in a housekeeper's uniform handed her the still-damp trench coat and floppy brimmed hat.

Chloe put on the coat. The trench was a gift from her aunt Phyllis. Phyllis had spent her working years in Hollywood. She claimed she knew how private investigators were supposed to dress because she'd known so many stars who played those kinds of roles. Chloe wasn't so sure about the style statement but she liked the convenience of the numerous pockets in the coat.

Outside on the front steps she paused to pull the hat down low over her eyes. It was raining again and although it was only a quarter to five, it was almost full dark. This was the Pacific Northwest and it was early December. Darkness and rain came with the territory at this time of year. Some people considered it atmospheric. They didn't mind the short days because they knew that a kind of karmic balance would kick in come summer when there would be daylight until nearly ten o'clock at night.

Those who weren't into the yin-yang thing went out and bought special light boxes designed to treat the depressive condition known as SAD, seasonal affective disorder.

She was okay with darkness and rain. But maybe that was because of her talent for reading dreamlight. Dreams and darkness went together.

She went down the steps and crossed the vast, circular drive to where her small, nondescript car was parked. The dog sitting patiently in the passenger seat watched her intently as she came toward him. She knew that he had been fixated on the front door of the house, waiting for her to reappear, since she had vanished inside forty minutes ago. The dog's name was Hector and he had abandonment issues.

When she opened the car door he got excited, just as if she had been gone for a week. She rubbed his ears and let him lick her hand.

"Mr. Paddon is not a happy man, Hector." The greeting ritual finished, she got behind the wheel. "I don't think we'll be seeing him as a client of Harper Investigations anytime soon."

Hector was not interested in clients. Satisfied that she was back, he resumed his customary position, riding shotgun in the passenger seat.

She fired up the engine. She had told Paddon the truth about the little Egyptian queen. It was a fake and it had been floating around in the private market since the Victorian period. She was certain of that for three reasons, none of which she could explain to Paddon. The first reason was that her talent allowed her to date objects quite accurately. Reason number two was that she came from a long line of art and antiquities experts. She had been raised in the business.

Reason number three was also straightforward. She had recognized the workmanship and the telltale dreamlight the moment she saw the statue.

"You can't rat out your own several times great-grandfather, Hector, even if he has been dead since the first quarter of the twentieth century. Family is family."

Norwood Harper had been a master. His work was on display in some of the finest museums in the Western world, albeit not under his own name. And now one of his most charmingly brilliant fakes was sitting in Paddon's private collection.

It wasn't the first time she had stumbled onto a Harper fake. Her extensive family tree boasted a number of branches that specialized in fakes, forgeries and assorted art frauds. Other limbs featured individuals with a remarkable talent for deception, illusion and sleight of hand. Her relatives all had what could only be described as a true talent for less-than-legal activities.

Her own paranormal ability had taken a different and far less marketable form. She had inherited the ability to read dreamlight from Aunt Phyllis's side of the tree. There were few practical applications—although Phyllis had managed to make it pay very well—and one really huge downside. Because of that downside, the odds were overwhelming that she would never marry.

Sex wasn't the problem. But over the course of the past year or two she had begun to lose interest in it. Perhaps that was because she had finally accepted that she would never have a relationship that lasted longer than a few months. Somehow, that realization had removed what little pleasure was left in short-term affairs. In the wake of the fiasco with Fletcher Monroe a few months ago, she had settled into celibacy with a sense of enormous relief.

"There is a kind of freedom in the celibate lifestyle," she explained to Hector.

Hector twitched his ears but otherwise showed no interest in the subject.

She left the street of elegant homes on Queen Anne Hill and drove back downtown through the rain, heading toward her office and apartment in Pioneer Square.